Praise for

A Killer Plot

"Ellery Adams's debut novel, *A Killer Plot,* is not only a great read, but a visceral experience. Olivia Limoges's investigation into a friend's murder will have you hearing the waves crash on the North Carolina shore. You might even feel the ocean winds stinging your cheeks. Visit Oyster Bay and you'll long to return again and again."

—Lorna Barrett, *New York Times* bestselling author of the Booktown Mysteries

"Adams's plot is indeed killer, her writing would make her the star of any support group, and her characters—especially Olivia and her standard poodle, Captain Haviland—are a diverse, intelligent bunch. *A Killer Plot* is a perfect excuse to go coastal."

—*Richmond Times-Dispatch*

"A fantastic start to a new series . . . With new friendships, possible romance(s), and promises of great things to come, *A Killer Plot* is one book you don't want to be caught dead missing." —*The Best Reviews*

"[An] exciting new killer of a series . . . It's one of those 'don't bug me, I'm reading' books you're going to savor from the first page to the last."

—*Feathered Quill Book Reviews*

A BOOKS
BY THE BAY
MYSTERY

The Last Word

ELLERY ADAMS

BERKLEY PRIME CRIME, NEW YORK

THE BERKLEY PUBLISHING GROUP
Published by the Penguin Group
Penguin Group (USA) Inc.
375 Hudson Street, New York, New York 10014, USA

Penguin Group (Canada), 90 Eglinton Avenue East, Suite 700, Toronto, Ontario M4P 2Y3, Canada
(a division of Pearson Penguin Canada Inc.)
Penguin Books Ltd., 80 Strand, London WC2R 0RL, England
Penguin Group Ireland, 25 St. Stephen's Green, Dublin 2, Ireland (a division of Penguin Books Ltd.)
Penguin Group (Australia), 250 Camberwell Road, Camberwell, Victoria 3124, Australia
(a division of Pearson Australia Group Pty. Ltd.)
Penguin Books India Pvt. Ltd., 11 Community Centre, Panchsheel Park, New Delhi—110 017, India
Penguin Group (NZ), 67 Apollo Drive, Rosedale, Auckland 0632, New Zealand
(a division of Pearson New Zealand Ltd.)
Penguin Books (South Africa) (Pty.) Ltd., 24 Sturdee Avenue, Rosebank, Johannesburg 2196,
South Africa

Penguin Books Ltd., Registered Offices: 80 Strand, London WC2R 0RL, England

This is a work of fiction. Names, characters, places, and incidents either are the product of the author's imagination or are used fictitiously, and any resemblance to actual persons, living or dead, business establishments, events, or locales is entirely coincidental. The publisher does not have any control over and does not assume any responsibility for author or third-party websites or their content.

THE LAST WORD

A Berkley Prime Crime Book / published by arrangement with the author

PRINTING HISTORY
Berkley Prime Crime mass-market edition / December 2011

Copyright © 2011 by Ellery Adams.
Excerpt from *Written in Stone* by Ellery Adams copyright © by Ellery Adams.
Cover illustration by Kimberly Schamber.
Cover design by Rita Frangie.
Interior text design by Tiffany Estreicher.

ISBN: 978-0-425-24500-2

BERKLEY® PRIME CRIME
Berkley Prime Crime Books are published by The Berkley Publishing Group,
a division of Penguin Group (USA) Inc.,
375 Hudson Street, New York, New York 10014.
BERKLEY® PRIME CRIME and the PRIME CRIME logo are trademarks of Penguin Group (USA) Inc.

PRINTED IN THE UNITED STATES OF AMERICA

10 9 8 7 6 5 4 3 2 1

*This book is dedicated to teachers everywhere,
but especially to John Bowden, Gilbert Tippy, Jonathan
Stapleton, Jan Chock, Frank Brogan, and Roger Erickson.*

*These men inspired and challenged me from an early age.
I wouldn't have had the courage to become an author
without their guidance. Thank you.*

Chapter 1

"All houses have secrets."

Olivia Limoges was surprised to hear such an enigmatic statement from her contractor, but there wasn't a hint of humor on Clyde Butler's weathered face. Perhaps the seasoned builder was merely trying to make a point to the eager first-time homebuyer who stood nearby, one arm wrapped possessively around the porch post.

Harris Williams gazed toward the front door of the aged bungalow with a look of pure devotion, and Olivia could tell he was already visualizing himself living there.

"Regardless of what you've discovered, Clyde, I don't think you can talk Harris out of purchasing this place," Olivia stated with amusement. "He's clearly fallen in love."

Captain Haviland, Olivia's standard poodle, sniffed around the foundation of the 1930s home and then trotted around the corner, conducting a canine version of a house inspection.

Wearing a hopeful grin, Harris watched the poodle until Haviland disappeared from view, and then picked at a flake of peeling paint with his fingernail. "Everyone thinks I'm crazy, but I can feel that this place has history. That's important to me. There's more character in this rusty nail than in all the other places I've seen put together."

Olivia surveyed the facade of the two-bedroom bungalow. It had whitewashed brick walls and rows of large windows with black shutters. Olivia's favorite feature was the wide and welcoming front porch. Leaves had gathered in between the railings and there were rents and holes in the screen door, but the slate steps felt solid under her feet. She'd been inside with Harris a few days ago and had liked the house. Harris was right. The place had a warm personality. Its modest design spoke of simpler times, of family traditions, hard work, and perseverance. She believed Harris was making a good choice.

Harris continued to defend the bungalow even though no one had argued with him. "I've seen a dozen new houses in my price range and, yeah, sure, they all had pristine white walls and stainless steel appliances and shiny light fixtures to go along with the flat lawns and four little bushes and a pair of ornamental trees, but they had *zero* personality." He puffed up his cheeks. "They were all like the straw house from the *Three Little Pigs*, but the wolf doesn't stand a chance against this place. It's a rock."

Clyde nodded. On this, he and Harris agreed. He gestured toward the front door. "If you want strong bones and a solid foundation, you'll find them here. Houses are like women. The new ones might seem attractive because no one's touched them and you feel like they'll treat you well without giving you an ounce of trouble." A snort. "But they're built out of cheap materials and will start falling down the second you move in. This old girl is sagging in places and, yes, she's a bit wrinkled, but she can be made over until she looks like a June bride. She'll be faithful to the end, but it'll take lots of labor and expense on your part, my boy."

Harris's grin expanded. "Did you know that all the houses on this street were moved during the late sixties to make way for the highway's expansion? Twelve houses were trucked right down Main Street and brought back to this stretch of empty land like horses being set free on an open pasture."

Olivia rolled her eyes. "This is one of those times I'm thankful you write science fiction, Harris. If you had put a metaphor like that in your recent chapter, I would have sliced it out with a box cutter."

Harris pushed a strand of unruly, ginger-colored hair away from his eyes. His looks were often compared to those of Peter Pan, and Harris was constantly striving to prove that he was a man, not a boy. Olivia knew her friend believed that being a homeowner would make him appear more of a bona fide adult, and he certainly behaved like he wanted to acquire this house without delay.

As though sensing her thoughts, Harris eased back the sleeves of his shirt and flexed his left bicep. "This property has half an acre bordering on three more acres of woodland. Think of all the manly man activities I can do here. I can chop wood, refinish furniture, spackle walls, grout tile!" He held out his arms, encompassing the house. "I'll be like Ty Pennington. A bachelor handyman with mad computer skills to boot! Before you know it, I'll have my own reality show."

Clyde shook his head. "Before you start rewiring ceiling fans and installing A/C units, we'd better go over my inspection list."

The two men moved into the house, which Harris's real estate agent had unlocked a few minutes earlier before retreating to the comfort of her Cadillac. Her daughter, who happened to be nine months pregnant, had phoned shortly after the Realtor had turned the key in the front door. Gesturing for the threesome to enter without her, she'd hurriedly rushed off to take the call in the privacy of her car.

Inside the bungalow, Harris listened carefully as Clyde pointed out flaw after flaw, from the presence of mold behind the wallpaper to wood rot on the stair treads. Pulling back a corner of the stained and faded blue carpet running down the stairs and into the living room, Clyde showed Harris a series of water stains and areas of damage permeating the subfloor. From there, the contractor reviewed every item in his report, explaining how to address each problem and offering an estimate as to what it would cost to fix.

When they were finished, Olivia joined them on the back patio. Haviland reappeared from a copse of trees and settled on his haunches, his warm caramel-colored eyes darting from one face to another, his mouth hanging open in a toothy smile.

Harris rubbed the black curls on the poodle's neck and then walked over to the brick retaining wall and sat down. He gazed first at the house and then toward the woods, which bordered the scraggly patch of lawn.

Winter's chill had abated for good and the sun lit the pines, dappling the soft needles on the forest floor with a ruddy light. Squirrels raced up and down the rough bark, and birds twittered from the branches.

Olivia sat beside Harris on the wall, relishing the peacefulness of the moment. Her life had had little quiet of late, and this patio of cracked flagstones surrounded by a garden of weeds was an oasis of blissful calm.

Clyde's focus remained on the house. He glanced from his notes to the structure and back at Harris. "I know I took some of the wind out of your sails, boy, but I don't want you to think this is going to be easy. She's going to make demands of you, but all houses do. In the end, she'll be worth the work you're going to have to put in."

Harris smiled, his cheeks dimpling with pleasure. "And you'll help me find the right guys to do the jobs I can't figure out how to do?"

After a solemn nod, Clyde jerked his thumb at Olivia. "I'd get in here with my own toolbox if my taskmaster would let up on me for just a day or two, but she's hell-bent on opening her Bayside Crab House by Memorial Day weekend."

"So *that's* why you've been so interested in real estate lately," Harris said. "You must be scoping out houses for your brother and his family."

"*Half* brother," Olivia corrected tersely. "And it's not for me to decide where they're going to live. I just thought I'd rule out the duds to save time. I need Hudson to review the final kitchen layout for the restaurant, and if he's running all over Oyster Bay comparing three-bedroom properties, we're sure to fall behind deadline."

Clyde gave Harris a meaningful look. "See what I mean? We should send her to Washington. She'd have the deficit licked and both our jobs and our soldiers back from overseas before the lawmakers knew what hit 'em."

Olivia grimaced. "I have no interest in politics. Let's go, gentlemen. I believe Harris has an offer to submit before this day is done."

Olivia shot a glance at Millicent Banks, Harris's real estate agent, who was parked alongside the curb in front of the picturesque bungalow. She'd been chatting on her cell phone since they'd arrived, and Olivia had hoped the conversation would be a long one. In fact, she had been pleased to have been left alone with Harris and Clyde. Millicent was a shrewd saleswoman, and Olivia hadn't wanted the Realtor to talk their ears off the whole time. One could glean the true sense of a house only in absolute silence. It was a feeling really. A hunch.

Having stood side by side with Harris inside the sturdy bungalow, Olivia saw no reason to dissuade her friend from submitting a bid, and as the amicable young software designer waved good-bye to Clyde and approached Millicent's Caddy, the look on his face made it clear that he was smitten with the house.

Olivia smiled as Millicent hastily completed her phone call and sat back against the supple leather of her seat with a nearly imperceptible smirk of satisfaction. Millicent was also the listing agent on this house and stood to make a tidy commission on the property, and while Olivia admired the older woman's drive, she didn't want her friend to pay a single cent over what she deemed to be a fair price for the house.

"Can we go back to your office and draw up the papers?" Harris asked as he jumped in the car.

Millicent was about to answer when Olivia leaned against the open passenger door. She gestured for Harris to come close and then whispered a figure into his ear.

"In this market, that's a solid offer," she said firmly and then acknowledged Millicent's presence with a polite nod. "Fixing this place up will put a strain on his savings account as it is." She fixed her sea blue gaze on Millicent. "The Bayside Book Writers need him to have enough money left over to buy coffee and printer paper, so I've given him my recommendation on what I consider to be a fair price. I'm sure there's wiggle room to be had, seeing as you represent the sellers as well. Am I right?"

"Of course!" Millicent readily agreed and plastered on her best saleswoman grin. "Any friend of yours is a friend of mine."

"That's good to know." Olivia tapped on the Caddy's hood as though giving Millicent permission to drive away. She then whistled for her poodle and strode to her Range Rover, casting one last glance at the house Harris longed to call his own.

Inside her SUV, she noted the time on the dashboard clock and cursed. She was supposed to meet April Howard for a business lunch at Grumpy's Diner to go over paint and carpet colors for The Bayside Crab House and was now sure to be late. Olivia hated tardiness. She preferred to arrive for any prearranged meeting at least ten minutes ahead of schedule. Now, she'd have to rush downtown, search for a parking spot along Main Street, and hope that April had secured Olivia's favorite window booth before anyone else could.

With the onset of spring, tourists had begun streaming back to Oyster Bay. The coastal North Carolina town was already thirty degrees warmer than many northern locales, and the pale-faced, sun-starved vacationers had been counting down the days until their children's schools let out for spring break. Bypassing long flights to Cancun, Caribbean cruises, and the chaos of Disneyworld, the residents of a dozen snow-covered states opted for the quiet beauty of Oyster Bay instead.

Ditching heavy parkas in favor of T-shirts and sunglasses the moment they arrived, the vacationers hopped aboard rental bicycles and pedaled merrily through town, passing yards filled with blooming dogwood trees, pink and purple azalea bushes, and oceans of daffodils. The lawns were Ireland green, and the buzzing of industrious bees and hummingbirds blended with the tourists' contented sighs.

The locals were equally relieved to see the last of what had been a particularly long and damp winter. Oyster Bay's economy depended heavily on tourism, and a dry and sunny spring meant the replenishment of the town's depleted coffers.

Olivia Limoges was landlady to many downtown merchants, but she spent most of her time overseeing the management of her five-star restaurant, The Boot Top Bistro. Today, she drove right by the entrance, searching for a parking spot closer to Grumpy's Diner, but decided on a space in a loading zone.

A middle-aged dwarf wearing roller skates and

pigtail braids met her at the diner's door. "As I live and breathe!" Dixie Weaver declared, waving at her flushed face with her order pad. "Miss Punctuality is *late!*"

Frowning at her child-sized friend, Olivia stepped aside as Haviland entered the diner. He placed his black nose under Dixie's palm and gazed up at her in adoration.

"You sure know how to turn on the charm, Captain." Dixie ruffled the poodle's ears and then accepted one of his gentlemanly kisses on the back of her hand. "I know you're just anglin' for a juicy steak or some turkey bacon, but I'm the closest thing you've got to a godmother, so I might as well spoil you silly!"

It was unlikely that Haviland had heard anything beyond the word "bacon," as he'd turned tail and made for Olivia's customary window booth before Dixie could finish speaking, but the diner proprietor gave him an indulgent smile nonetheless.

"You're certainly in a good mood," Olivia said, still holding the door. An elderly couple shuffled in and headed for the *Evita* booth.

Dixie had a strange fascination with Andrew Lloyd Webber's musicals. As a result, she'd plastered Broadway paraphernalia on every inch of available wall space. Each booth had its own unique theme, and while most patrons found the décor charming, Olivia did not share in her friend's Webber worship.

Her eyes gleaming with excitement, Dixie looked over her shoulder and then whispered, "You too would be as happy as a cat in a tuna factory if you knew whose lovely, rich buns were planted on the leather in the *Starlight Express* booth."

Olivia stole a glance at the middle-aged man dining

on a chicken salad sandwich and a mountain of fries. He looked vaguely familiar, but she couldn't place him. "He's handsome in a bookish sort of way. An older version of Brad Pitt in spectacles. I suppose he's a celebrity, since you're this flustered. Let me guess. He played the lead in *Jesus Christ Superstar*?"

Placing a hand over her heart, Dixie released a dramatic sigh. "You've got the wrong field, but he does work in the arts. Keep guessin'. He's good-lookin', smart, is in great shape for a man in his fifties, has the Midas touch. And I just read in *People* that he sold the film rights to his famous novel for a figure with lots and lots of zeros."

Now Olivia knew the identity of the diner. "Ah, it's Nick Plumley, Booker Prize–winning author of the international bestseller *The Barbed Wire Flower*. I wonder if he's here conducting research. The Internet's been rife with rumors regarding a sequel, and his groundbreaking novel was set down the road in New Bern."

"You'll have plenty of chances to ask him," Dixie replied enigmatically. When Olivia didn't rise to the bait by asking her how, the diner proprietor gave an irritated tug to her sequin-covered lavender top. "You're about as fun as a preacher at a strip joint, but I'll tell you anyhow. Mr. Plumley's rented a house down the beach from your place. You two can bump into one another on a lonely stretch of sand." Her eyes were shining with mischief. "There'll be an instant spark between you. Passion will ignite! You'll tear off your clothes and have wild, steamy—"

"Dixie! You'd better go. The lady in the *Evita* booth is waving her menu at you. I promise to ogle Mr. Plumley during my meeting with April, but we both have far too much work to do for me to stand here staring at him any longer." Olivia turned away.

"First you dump Oyster Bay's most eligible bachelor, and now you don't give a fig that a gorgeous, unattached, and gifted *writer* is sittin' ten feet away, ripe and ready for the pluckin'," Dixie muttered loudly enough for Olivia to hear. "Maybe what folks say is true: You *do* have ice runnin' through your veins."

"A large cup of your excellent coffee should clear that ailment right up. You can decide what I want for lunch too. You always seem to know what's best," Olivia said over her shoulder and then greeted April Howard, the woman in charge of interior design for The Bayside Crab House.

Olivia and April spread swatches of fabric, paint palettes, and carpet samples across the booth, barely leaving room for their lunch plates. April had chosen Grumpy's famous country fried steak, and Olivia was envious of the lightly battered meat smothered in gravy until Dixie appeared with her lunch—a generous wedge of cheese, shrimp, and mushroom quiche. Olivia had to taste only one bite of the golden crust to know that she'd been given the superior dish.

After serving the two women, Dixie lingered at their booth. She gave Haviland a platter of ground sirloin mixed with rice and vegetables and then asked after April's kids. She voiced her opinion on the array of fabric samples, picking the gaudiest one of the lot and chiding Olivia for being too conservative.

"This place should be lively! Red, white, and blue, with a few disco balls here and there!" Dixie exclaimed. "Where's your sense of adventure? Folks are gonna be crackin' crab claws with little mallets and tearin' at the meat with their front teeth. This isn't fine dinin', you know."

"We'll have checkered tablecloths," April said with a conciliatory smile. "But we need to keep the wall color relatively neutral because we plan to hang dozens of nautical flags in place of framed photographs or posters. Trust me, it'll be bright and busy."

"Bright and busy, huh? Just how I like my men," Dixie joked and skated away to clear dishes from the countertop.

Olivia concluded her business with April, insisted on paying for lunch, and then remained behind while her employee left to make phone calls to suppliers before meeting her kids' school bus.

Watching April jog across the street, Olivia recalled how she'd first met the talented designer. Last September, April's husband had been murdered and Olivia had been involved in the investigation. She'd appeared at the Howard's home in search of a clue and had found one that helped break the case wide open.

Slowly, April was healing from the devastating loss. She often called in sick, and on those days, Olivia guessed the mother of three had been assaulted by a wave of grief too potent to overcome. Olivia knew plenty about the grieving process and was fully aware that time wasn't the consummate healer people claimed it to be. There were stretches of time in which the pain surfaced with such a raw and unexpected power that it crippled the grief-stricken until it required an immense feat of strength just to get out of bed.

"You did a good thing, takin' her on." Dixie had appeared bearing a fresh carafe of coffee.

Olivia waved off the suggestion. "I needed an interior

designer and she needed a job. Nothing more to it than that."

Dixie snorted. "You're as transparent as a ghost, 'Livia. I know you're payin' for her kids to be on that special soccer team. Fixed it up to look like some kind of sports scholarship, but you can't fool *this* dwarf."

Olivia put her fingers to her lips. "Don't tell anyone about that. April isn't looking for handouts."

The bells above the diner door tinkled and a man wearing a pale blue blazer strolled in. Both women recognized the logo on the nametag pinned to his lapel. Engraved with a beach house, a lone wave, and the words "Bayside Realty," the tag indicated that Randall McGraw had come to Grumpy's to meet with a prospective client. He headed straight for Nick Plumley's booth and, after shaking the author's hand, pulled a sheet of paper from a yellow folder bearing the realty's name and placed it reverently on the table.

Dixie and Olivia exchanged curious glances.

"What are you waiting for?" Olivia hissed. "Get those wheels spinning! I'm dying to know which property he's looking at."

With a toss of her bleach blond pigtail braids, Dixie zipped over to Nick's table, held out the order pad she only pretended to use, as she'd never forgotten an order in her life, and beamed at the real estate agent. She then took her time clearing Nick's plate and finally skated into the kitchen.

Before Dixie had the chance to report back to Olivia, Nick was pulling bills from his wallet. He collected the sheaf of paper from the Realtor, folded it in half, and left the booth. Instead of exiting the diner, however, he walked right up to Haviland and stopped.

"Your companion is beautiful. Male or female?" he asked Olivia, his eyes on the poodle.

"His name is Captain Haviland," Olivia answered. "No need to be shy. He's extremely friendly."

The author extended his hand, palm up, and Haviland immediately offered him his right paw in return.

"I miss having a dog," Nick said wistfully. "But I travel so much and it wouldn't be fair to leave a pet in someone else's care all the time."

Olivia grinned, for Nick had given her just the opening she needed to satisfy her curiosity. She gestured at the man in the blazer who was pouring sugar into a glass of iced tea. "It looks like you might be thinking about staying in one place for a while."

The writer adjusted his glasses and cleared his throat. "I'm renting a place at the moment, but I'd like to put down roots here. I have ties to Oyster Bay, and I believe I can achieve a level of anonymity in this town that I've yet to find in other places."

Playing dumb, Olivia cocked her head. "Should I recognize you?"

Nick laughed, and attractive crinkles formed at the corners of his mouth and eyes. "That'll bring me down a peg." He extended his hand. "I'm Nick Plumley, author and dog lover at your service."

Olivia was pleased that his handshake was firm and that his eyes held a smile as he asked for her name.

"I knew who you were," Olivia confessed after introducing herself. "Still, I couldn't resist giving you a hard time. Consider it one of our new-resident initiation rites."

"As long as you don't shave my eyebrows while I

sleep," Nick replied smoothly and took a seat across from Olivia. "It's taken me years to perfect this arch."

The pair began exchanging ideas for other pranks when one of the public school librarians entered the diner. She stopped just inside the door and scanned the room. When she saw Nick, her eyes widened and she scurried over to the window booth, clutching a hardcover against her chest.

"I am *so* sorry to interrupt, Mr. Plumley." Her voice was an animated whisper. "But when I heard you were here, *in our little diner*, I had to rush right over. I am *such* a big fan. This book—" She gently eased the novel away from her body and touched the cover with reverence. "I thought of those German soldiers as my own brothers. Now *that* is skillful character development, to make *me* empathize with Nazis when I lost *two* uncles to that war."

My, but Dixie got the word out fast. What's she doing? Sending out tweets about the diner's guest? Olivia wondered, watching the author's reaction over having failed to avoid his celebrity status.

Nick Plumley opened his mouth to thank the elderly librarian, but she didn't give him the opportunity. "And the *murder scene*! Utterly chilling. I researched the actual events, of course. We even had the son of one of the Nazi prison camp guards speak at the school's annual fund-raiser." She glanced behind her as though the rest of the diners were hanging on her every word. "If you're working on the sequel, you should interview him. He says he remembers all kinds of stories from those days. I could introduce you."

Something altered in Nick's expression. The change

was subtle. The laugh lines became shallower, and a shadow darkened his eyes until he blinked it away. His smile, which had been sincere when the librarian first approached the booth, became stiff.

He recovered quickly, however, and offered to sign the woman's book. She prattled on about area book clubs, wringing her hands in delight as she spelled her last name with deliberate slowness.

"I have *quite* a collection of signed books," she informed Nick. "And this one will be given a place of pride among the John Updikes and the Dan Browns."

Olivia was growing bored with the librarian's fawning and wondered how the man seated opposite her had survived hundreds of events in which he was subjected to an endless horde of such sycophants.

Without regard for the librarian's feelings, Olivia cleared her throat and made a show of examining her watch. Luckily, the older woman took the hint and scuttled off, the book once again pressed against her chest.

"Sorry about that," Nick said, looking strangely weary from the encounter. He sat back, withdrawing into himself, and all traces of the amiable camaraderie that had begun to bloom between them evaporated.

Her curiosity aroused, Olivia tried to draw Nick into revealing more about his personal life, but he politely deflected all of her questions and began to shift in his seat. In a moment, she knew, he'd be gone.

"At least let me see the house listing you've got there. I know the best contractor in town, should you need an inspection or repairs." She gave Nick her warmest smile, opening her deep sea blue eyes wide.

It worked. "Showing you where I hope to live doesn't say much for my ability to guard my privacy, but for some reason I trust you." He slid the paper across the table to her.

Olivia unfolded the sheet and drew in a sharp breath. Of all the houses in Oyster Bay, the wealthy writer wanted to purchase the one Harris was dead set on buying.

As Olivia stared at the familiar bungalow, Nick excused himself and headed toward the restroom. Within seconds, Dixie was leaning over Olivia's shoulder, studying the black-and-white photo.

"I'd have thought he'd go for somethin' fancier." Dixie frowned. "What's the point of bein' loaded if you don't toss your money around. It's not like you can take it with you."

Olivia jabbed at the paper with her index finger. "Never fear, Dixie. Nick Plumley won't be living here. He'll have to choose something more suitable."

Dixie shook her head. "I don't think so. I heard him tell the real estate broker that he *had* to have this house, so I reckon it's as good as sold."

Handing Dixie some cash, Olivia stood up and signaled to Haviland to follow suit. "You tell Nick Plumley that this house is unavailable. Tell him it has ghosts or asbestos or that it's been condemned. Tell him it's built on sacred Indian burial ground. I don't care what you say, but tell him it's off the market."

Dixie put her hands on her hips. "What on earth has gotten into you, 'Livia? Whether you like it or not, Oyster Bay's newest celebrity is gonna leave that gorgeous place he's renting and set out a welcome mat at this little house by Memorial Day. You just mark my words."

Olivia snatched the paper from the table and opened the front door. As soon as Haviland had trotted outside,

Olivia turned to Dixie and calmly declared, "The only way he gets this house is over my dead body."

Without waiting for a response, she left, shutting the door so firmly that the bells were still ringing when Nick Plumley returned from the restroom to find that the woman, the poodle, and his house listing were gone.

Chapter 2

*I don't believe the accident of birth makes
people sisters or brothers. It makes them
siblings.*

—MAYA ANGELOU

Ten minutes after leaving the diner, Olivia was rapping on Millicent Banks's office door.

"Oh, Ms. Limoges!" The real estate agent opened the door while dabbing at the corner of her mouth with a napkin. "I'm afraid you've found me eating on the job. Do come in." Peering around Olivia's shoulder, she caught sight of Haviland and retreated a step. "How can I be of assistance?"

"Actually, I'm here to thank you." Olivia gave the older woman a grateful smile. "Harris was fortunate to have had such an experienced agent on his side to guide him through the biggest purchase of his life. To show you my appreciation, I've brought you a gift certificate to The Boot Top. I'd like to treat you and Mr. Banks to a memorable dinner."

Millicent accepted the gift with obvious pleasure. "How lovely! But this is quite unnecessary. I was merely doing my job."

"I know. Still, men don't always know how to express themselves, and Harris would approve of me doing so on his behalf." Olivia noticed a folder on Millicent's desk bearing Harris's name. "Was his offer accepted?"

Hesitating, Millicent walked around her desk and examined her computer screen. "The sellers have agreed to the price via e-mail, but they haven't signed any papers yet. The husband plans to swing by after work. I'm certain everything will work out just fine."

Olivia didn't share the agent's optimism. She had to act fast to ensure that the sellers signed the necessary documents before Nick could present an offer that would make their heads spin.

"Mrs. Banks, I know I'm behaving like an overprotective sibling, but I just want to see that everything's in order before I head in to the restaurant. Can I persuade you to drive the paperwork to the sellers *now* instead of waiting until later this afternoon?" Without giving Millicent a chance to protest, Olivia continued. "In short, I'd like to offer you an incentive. You see, I've noticed your fondness for Chanel bags and I have a contact in New York City who can send me the grand shopper tote from the upcoming line. I'd be more than glad to acquire one for you if you'd only do me the favor of getting those papers signed directly. I can guarantee that you'll be the first woman in the county to possess Chanel's newest gem."

Millicent had a dreamy look in her eyes. "I've seen photos of that bag in *Vogue*. It's magnificent." She shook the image away. "But I can't accept, Ms. Limoges. It's too expensive and there's really no need to offer me gifts. The seller is a man of honor. If he's given me a verbal agreement, then he'll stand by it. By five thirty, the offer will be accepted."

Not if Nick Plumley offers twice the amount, Olivia thought anxiously. She needed to get Millicent out of the office with that paperwork.

"You can accept a gift knowing that I can afford a crate of Chanel bags," Olivia remarked flatly, reaching down to stroke Haviland's black curls. "But money can't buy friends. Not a true friend like Harris in any case. Because this house is important to him, it's important to me. Please. Make this deal official."

Collecting her black-and-white Chanel hobo from her chair, Millicent shrugged. "Well, this old thing *is* a bit past its prime. I've got an appointment at three, but I can see the sellers before then."

"Thank you!" Olivia exhaled in relief. However, she remained where she was until the real estate agent had her paperwork and car keys in hand before following her out of the office.

Olivia waited on the sidewalk as the older woman eased her Cadillac away from the curb. Millicent gave the tall, headstrong woman and her poodle a little wave before pulling onto Main Street.

"Ma'am, is that your vehicle?" a man's voice asked from behind Olivia. "The Range Rover? If so, you are currently obstructing the fire hydrant and I'm going to have to write you a citation."

Olivia fought back a guilty smile. "I'm sorry, Officer, but that's not my car. I would never drive such a gas-hungry, environmentally unfriendly road hog."

"So you're all about going green, huh? Word has it you don't even recycle—that you toss empty whiskey bottles off the lighthouse landing right into the ocean."

Olivia feigned offense. "I most certainly do not! What a vicious rumor. Isn't the chief of police above listening to idle gossip?"

"Not when it concerns you." Chief Rawlings had been grinning, but now his mouth drew into a tight line. "I have to rely on hearsay, seeing as how you seem to be avoiding me at every turn."

It was true. Ever since Olivia had gone to Okracoke Island to bear witness to the death of her father, she'd become even more aloof than usual.

She hated that a man who'd disappeared thirty years earlier, letting his only child believe he'd been lost at sea, still had so much power over her. He'd begun a new life on Okracoke while Olivia had struggled to live hers as an orphan. Her father found a literal port in a storm, gained employment, and had even remarried and sired a son. She'd drifted around the globe, unable to form a genuine relationship with a single human being.

For the past thirty years, Olivia's father had been a ghost, haunting her sleep with unwanted memories until the day a woman from Okracoke mailed her an anonymous letter. The letter declared that the man she'd known as Willie Wade was alive. Alive and unwell and only fifty nautical miles away from his abandoned daughter.

Olivia was still coming to grips with having rediscovered her father only to reach him hours before he passed away. To say she had mixed feelings about her half brother, Hudson, was a gross understatement. The siblings had grown up in different worlds. Olivia had been exposed to the finer things in life while Hudson had worked hard since boyhood to please his father and, later, to support his family. He was taciturn and guarded, but Olivia also believed he was loyal, determined, and a hell of a cook.

Now Hudson, his pregnant wife, and their six-year-old daughter were all Olivia had by way of family. In hopes of becoming closer to these strangers, Olivia had invited Hudson to move his family to Oyster Bay and take over the management of her newest restaurant, The Bayside Crab House.

The siblings had barely spoken since Olivia had left Okracoke. Hudson preferred to let his wife, Kim, handle all communication, and Olivia wondered if she'd ever develop even a tenuous bond with her gruff half brother.

After her father's death, Olivia had spent the winter moody and withdrawn. She'd attended all the Bayside Book Writers meetings and worked hard to provide thoughtful critiques, but had avoided any other social engagements.

"I didn't expect to return to my hermitlike ways," she now confessed to Rawlings. "But after Okracoke, my defenses were raised and now I can't seem to take off the armor. It's too familiar. Too comforting."

Rawlings studied her, his hazel eyes dark beneath the shadow of the building's awning. "You moved back to Oyster Bay to reconnect with the people of this town, to claim the sense of belonging you felt as a kid. You're one of us, Olivia, and that means you can't hole up in your oceanfront home and shut us out. It's too late for that."

Olivia smiled. The chief's words were a balm to her injured heart. "I'm back to patronizing Grumpy's. That's a step in the right direction."

"And what of Through the Wardrobe?" Rawlings

asked nonchalantly, but a twinge at the corner of his mouth betrayed his mistrust. "Bought any books lately?"

"Flynn McNulty and I are just friends. Actually, that term isn't quite accurate. I'm merely another customer." Olivia disliked having to defend herself. "Flynn is dating Haviland's veterinarian, and I'm indebted to her. Without Diane entering the picture, I couldn't have disentangled myself with such ease."

Rawlings didn't look convinced. "When you and Flynn parted ways, I thought it was because of me. I know I wanted you, but you slammed the door on us." He took a step closer, his face coming out from beneath the shelter of the awning. The sun lit his eyes a feline gold. "I'd kick that damned door right off its hinges if you'd give me the slightest sign—"

"Chief!" A police cruiser paused in the middle of the road and a young officer waved out the open passenger window. "We're all done with that funeral detail. Want a ride back to the station?"

Without answering, Rawlings turned his gaze back to Olivia.

"Go on," she whispered. Part of her wanted to escape the heat of the chief's stare while the rest wanted to be engulfed in the intensity of his desire. Over the winter, she'd denied her hunger for this man, burying it beneath to-do lists and memories of her father's betrayal.

Resigned, Rawlings gave her a polite nod, scratched Haviland's neck, and got into the sedan.

"Crap," Olivia muttered. Haviland whined, sniffing the air where Rawlings had stood. "I know you like him, but it's not a good time for me to get involved. My life has become too complicated as of late. Case in point, Hudson and company will be showing up at The Boot Top any moment. Let's not keep them waiting."

As always, Haviland was thrilled to enter the restaurant's kitchen, his nose raised high in the air in search of the source of a dozen mouth-watering smells. He was an obedient dog, however, and knew he was not supposed to linger in the room in which so many tantalizing dishes were prepared. Reluctantly, he trotted to Olivia's office and sat on his haunches in the center of the doorway, eyes hopeful and mouth open in anticipation.

Michel, The Boot Top's master chef, was too busy inspecting a baking sheet piled with rows of fresh beef tenderloin to notice the poodle's beseeching looks.

"A wine reduction for tonight's beef. We'll serve it with a medley of spring vegetables. Jeremy?" he called to one of the sous-chefs. "You're in charge of the asparagus."

After collecting a bowl of peeled garlic cloves from the walk-in, Michel began sharpening the long blade of a chopping knife, humming merrily all the while.

"You're quite chipper," Olivia observed. "The DAR's monthly social usually has you bent out of shape. You always complain about having to prepare entrees before six o'clock."

Without glancing away from the cutting board, Michel began to mince garlic. Olivia loved to watch him work. The knife blade became an extension of his hand, flashing as it moved with lighting quickness from left to right, then top to bottom, leaving a mound of perfectly diced garlic on the striated wood of the cutting board.

"It's my new muse," Michel stated with a wiggle of his brows. "She inspires me to overlook those blue-blooded hags who force me to begin my workday too early."

Olivia watched as the pile of garlic grew higher. "A *new* muse? That's good. For a while there I was genuinely concerned that you'd fallen for Laurel."

Michel turned his face away. "She is *très magnifique*, your friend, but she is devoted to that miserable husband of hers. If she only knew . . ."

He abruptly scooped the garlic into a metal bowl and walked over to the sous-chef's station to collect bunches of fresh parsley. He avoided meeting Olivia's sharp gaze.

"Michel?" Olivia felt a tightening in her muscles. She felt protective of Laurel, even though the young mother of twin boys had begun to exhibit a refreshing amount of grit and determination. Laurel fought a daily battle with her family over the right to continue her work as a writer for the *Oyster Bay Gazette*, and Olivia hated the thought of anyone bringing her friend down. "What were you going to say?"

"That Lovely Laurel doesn't know what she's missing," Michel answered airily. "A man of my skills and my passion comes along once in a lifetime, am I right?"

Olivia laughed, relaxing. "And modest as well."

The Boot Top's bartender entered the kitchen. "There's a Hudson Salter here to see you," Gabe announced over the din.

Issuing a resigned sigh over having to hold a conversation with her moody and tight-lipped sibling, Olivia followed Gabe through the swinging door and out to the bar area. Hudson was standing with his arms crossed over his lean chest, shifting uncomfortably. Dressed in denim overalls over a faded blue T-shirt, he looked out of place in the sleek, sophisticated room with its polished wood, leather seats, and ochre walls. His wife, Kim, was also ill at ease but disguised it better. She had one hand resting on her swollen belly and the other on the crown of her daughter's head. Caitlyn hid her face in her mother's cotton dress and peeked out at Olivia with a mixture of curiosity and apprehension.

Of the three Salters, the little girl interested Olivia the most. As a general rule, she didn't find children very fascinating, but here before her was a pint-sized human being who shared her DNA.

"Hi," she said quietly, directing a small smile at the child. "I know someone who will be very pleased to see you again. Do you remember Haviland?"

Caitlyn nodded once.

"Would you like to feed him dinner? He's waiting very patiently in my office, which is back through that door leading into the kitchen."

Kim nudged the little girl forward. "Go on, honey. We'll be right out here."

Shaking her head, Caitlyn refused to leave her mother's side.

Unasked, Gabe moved forward and extended his hand. "Maybe I could show you how I make a very special drink for very special kids. It's called a Shirley Temple. Have you ever had one?"

"No, sir." Caitlyn's voice was a whisper.

"I always put an orange slice and *two* cherries in mine. Do you want to help me? I might give you an extra cherry as payment, and you can still see your folks from behind the bar."

Caitlyn ignored Gabe's hand, but she did detach herself from Kim and follow the bartender. Olivia felt a rush of pride and affection for Gabe. For a man in his midtwenties, he was skilled at reading people of all ages. With his all-American, surfer-boy good looks and gentle, earnest manner, he charmed everyone he met.

"Can I get you anything?" Olivia asked the Salters, though she knew her offer would be refused. Hudson's body language proclaimed his desire to escape the upscale atmosphere of the restaurant as soon as possible.

Olivia sympathized with Hudson. He'd spent his entire life on the small island of Okracoke where he and Kim had run a small inn and café. He was a simple man and showed incredible talent in the kitchen, but he hadn't been exposed to many cultural experiences, and Olivia suspected he often felt inferior to his older half sister.

But Hudson and Olivia had bonded over one thing: the lack of affection shown to them by their late father. Luckily for Hudson, he had a sweet and patient wife and a lovely daughter to keep his heart from hardening, and Olivia hoped that by working together with her brother, she and he would come to truly care for each other.

"We think we found a house today," Kim said brightly and smiled at her husband. "It's real cute, but it'll be strange to not be able to see the sea out the window."

Olivia nodded. "I remember feeling that way when I lived in my grandmother's house. It had dozens of rooms and beautiful gardens, but I had a hard time going to sleep because I couldn't hear the ocean. There was no rhythm without the waves." She paused. "Do you want to keep looking? I could get you a rental until you find the right place."

"We can't afford an ocean view. Ever," Hudson said grimly. "They've all been taken by folks that only live here a few months a year."

Kim put a placating hand on her husband's arm. "The view's not important. Really. What's important is that there are a bunch of kids in the neighborhood. Caitlyn needs to make friends her own age. She's been playing with make-believe ones long enough." Worry creased her brow. "Caitlyn believes she can tell when folks are up to no good." She put both palms on her belly and rubbed tenderly, as though trying to assure the child she carried that all was well. "Other kids think she's weird and—"

"Kim, we're here on business." Hudson's dark eyes reminded Olivia so much of her father's that she nearly flinched. There was a constant spark of wariness deep in both men's pupils. Apparently, Caitlyn's odd behavior had touched a nerve in Hudson.

Olivia touched the starfish pendant that had once belonged to her mother and calmly asked her brother if he'd had a chance to work on the menu for The Bayside Crab House.

Food was a topic that brought out the best in Hudson Salter. He was a gifted cook and was as particular and creative as Michel when it came to presentation, the use of fresh ingredients, and unique flavor combinations.

Hudson pulled a sheet of paper from the center pocket of his overalls and shyly handed it to Olivia. For an instant, she longed to grab his hand, to tell him that she understood how difficult it must have been to have spent a lifetime desperate to earn his father's approval, and that she believed in him, but the moment passed.

She leaned over and studied his menu suggestions.

"I've got local suppliers for clam, shrimp, and every fish in the sea, but I don't have anyone I trust to supply oysters or mussels." She pointed to the section on the paper listing Hudson's ideas for raw bar items.

"I'm gonna need to meet your guys," Hudson said. "No one from the island will cross the channel to bring me so much as a stick of butter. They all think I'm turning my back on my home."

Olivia dropped her eyes to the menu. "Change is hard on those who leave and on those who are left behind. But you're going to be a part of a landmark eatery. Both of you. And with these entrees, The Bayside Crab House is going to be packed every night. I love your idea to blend the crab with avocado and pico de gallo. Also, this seafood platter combo that includes scallop scampi, coconut shrimp, snow crab, and a petite lobster tail is sure to be a crowd pleaser."

Hudson's expression didn't change, but Olivia knew the compliment had registered by the way her half brother's shoulders relaxed a fraction.

"Overall, I think this is an excellent menu. We'll have to add another fishless vegetarian item and a few additional topping options for the burger platters. If we get a patron who doesn't care for seafood, then at least we can smother that customer's burger with grilled onions and bacon." She made a note on Hudson's paper. "Otherwise, I think we're ready to print our first menus. Do you want to be involved in the graphic design decisions?"

Hudson shook his head, but Kim raised her hand as though she were in school. "I'd like to help with that. I know our place on Okracoke was nothing fancy and

I just ran off our menus on the computer, but I was a pretty good artist once. Since I'm not much use in the kitchen . . ."

"You got that right," Hudson teased.

Olivia gave her brother a playful shake of her index finger and then looked at Kim. "I'd love to have your assistance. As a matter of fact, I thought I'd leave Hudson in the capable hands of my contractor. He'll be down at the site. You and Caitlyn can hang out in my office and we'll go through catalogues, come up with a layout, and then call the printers."

Kim beamed.

When Olivia and Kim arrived in Olivia's office, Caitlyn was sipping her drink happily on the floor. Haviland was stretched out alongside the little girl, his head resting on her skinny leg.

"She wants a pet real bad," Kim whispered to Olivia. "But Hudson's always said she wasn't old enough to handle the responsibility. Maybe once we get settled and he has the restaurant to run, he'll give in." She reached out and grabbed Olivia's arm. "He may not speak the words, but we're grateful to you. We were barely staying afloat, and our house felt strange after Willie died. Now we can have a fresh start." She glanced at Caitlyn, and worry tugged at the corners of her mouth. "All of us."

Embarrassed by the compliment, Olivia suggested they get to work. Kim had a talent for drawing and quickly sketched several designs for the menu's cover. Olivia liked the one featuring Oyster Bay's lighthouse and harbor in the background with a plump, mischievous-looking crab in the foreground.

"How about a sunset?" Kim asked, tapping her lips

with a pencil. "It would make you feel like night's coming on and there isn't a better place to be come suppertime than at The Bayside Crab House. Sit out on the deck, listen to live music, and eat the best seafood in town while the sun goes down."

Buoyed by Kim's enthusiasm, Olivia agreed to the final design and then searched the computer for additional images and fonts.

While they worked, the noise in the kitchen escalated. Haviland had obviously been fed, as he was no longer gazing at Michel in worship, and Caitlyn was amusing herself by slowly consuming every piece of ice in her glass. Everyone was busy. Olivia felt a sense of deep satisfaction. She loved the sound of people at work.

After scanning Kim's sketch, Olivia asked her to type up Hudson's menu items. Once that was done, Olivia would e-mail the document to the printer along with their font choice. Kim readily agreed and began to peck at the keys one finger at a time. Not wanting to hover as Kim worked, Olivia left Haviland with the Salters and walked back out to the bar area.

"Gabe, I believe you've added another name to your long list of female admirers. Thank you for being kind to Caitlyn."

Gabe acknowledged the praise with a smile and pointed at the brass clock in the shape of a ship's wheel. He then set a tumbler filled with irregular-shaped ice cubes and two fingers' worth of Chivas Regal Reserve on a napkin. "She's a neat kid. Doesn't say much, but you can tell she's smart." He poured a blend of tropical juices over ice in a highball glass and then added a splash of lemon-lime soda. "That's for the other lady. Is she your . . . ?"

"Sister-in-law," Olivia replied. "Hudson is my half brother. I didn't even know he existed until this fall."

Gabe paused in the act of polishing the spotless bar. "Whoa. And he's going to move here?"

Olivia nodded and took a large sip of her drink.

Obviously sensing his employer's reticence to elaborate on her newfound family, Gabe continued with his prep work. But after she'd collected Kim's drink and turned toward the kitchen, he looked up from the dish he was filling with green olives and said, "It's probably going to be weird for a while, but I'm glad you found each other. Family keeps you anchored, you know? Like the boats out that window. Even in a strong wind, they won't be set adrift."

Olivia was tempted to give Gabe a snide retort about bartender wisdom but knew that he meant well. She acknowledged his statement with a dip of her chin and returned to the kitchen.

Michel had just left the office, and Caitlyn was once again buried in the folds of her mother's sundress.

"Why are you acting like this, honey?" Olivia heard Kim ask.

"I don't like that man," Caitlyn murmured, her voice trembling.

Kim stroked her daughter's hair, but she didn't look concerned. "Sweetie, he just looked scary using those big, sharp knives. But Daddy has the same ones at home. It doesn't mean they're going to hurt anyone. It's just a tool, like how a barber uses scissors."

Caitlyn scooted away, her eyes flashing. "I'm *not* scared of knives. I just don't like him."

Clearing her throat, Olivia entered the office and

handed Kim her drink. She looked at Caitlyn. "Why does he scare you?" she asked very gently.

Perhaps because an adult was taking her seriously, Caitlyn answered right away. "He's got a secret. I can tell."

Olivia nodded. "He probably does. Most people have secrets, I think."

Caitlyn was silent for so long that Olivia doubted she'd answer, but the little girl finally murmured, "Like Betty did. I knew she wrote you that letter. The one she sent when Grandpa got too sick to come downstairs anymore. Mom told me. She said that's why we met you."

Taking an involuntary step backward, Olivia recalled the mixture of anger and anguish she'd felt after reading the anonymous letter. The claim that her father was still alive coupled with the demand for one thousand dollars in cash for more information had filled her with fury. Even now, a fresh wave of hostility toward her father's longtime friend and nurse swept over her at the memory.

Kim looked down at the floor, discomfited by the topic, but Caitlyn moved forward and took hold of Olivia's hand. "But I'm glad she wrote it, because my daddy found a sister," she whispered and then immediately retreated to the floor and buried her small fingers in Haviland's fur.

After the Salters left, Olivia stood in the doorway of her office, studying Michel's face as he shoved a live lobster deep into a pot of boiling water.

Nothing struck her as being amiss.

But I've been wrong before, Olivia thought and returned to the bar for a refill.

Chapter 3

As for my next book, I am going to hold myself from writing it till I have it impending in me: grown heavy in my mind like a ripe pear; pendant, gravid, asking to be cut or it will fall.

—VIRGINIA WOOLF

Olivia came home from an exhilarating inspection of the refurbished harborside warehouse that would soon become The Bayside Crab House and brewed a pot of strong coffee. Carrying the coffee and a white chocolate chip biscotti to her desk overlooking the ocean, she printed out Laurel's chapter, uncapped the green pen Harris had given each of the writers to use for critiques, and began to read.

No one ever explained what was meant by happily ever after.

I asked. Through a champagne haze, I voiced the question during my bachelorette party. My married friends exchanged lopsided, knowing smiles and murmured vague replies about the rewards of serving my husband wholesome meals, creating a home of my own, and giving birth to children.

But there was something in their eyes that betrayed their words. It was an indistinct flash, a hesitation brought on by self-doubt. I didn't recognize what their looks meant at the time. I believed my friends were just searching for thoughtful answers.

In reality, of course, they were simply considering how much to lie to me the eve before my wedding, before I would walk down the aisle, white rose petals scattered at my feet.

They kept their secrets close. The wives.

It was my first lesson.

Later, after I became one of them, I checked off the list of the requirements they'd deemed necessary for me to live happily ever after. I cooked my husband meals that could outshine any restaurant's, I decorated our home until it resembled a magazine spread, and I gave birth to three healthy children.

When nothing magical happened to my marriage after our third child entered the world, I began to work harder at my job. I gardened, ran for miles to turn my body into a toned work of art, and coordinated the social events sponsored by my husband's company. I even got us accepted to the finest country club in town. My husband finally got to play golf on the course of his dreams.

And still, not a speck of glimmering fairy dust rained down onto our marital bed. There were no sparks of enchantment in my husband's eyes when he looked at me across a candlelit table. He didn't reach for my hand in the dark movie theater or whisper his hopes and fears across my pillow before we drifted off to sleep. We made love like it was a chore on Saturday's to-do list. My husband never murmured my name.

Somehow, I had failed.

Olivia put down her pen, too stunned to make a single mark on Laurel's paper.

"What is this?" she asked, flipping to the next page and skimming over the lines. "What happened to the duchess? She was falling for the highwayman. He was on his way to collect the ransom from the duke. Laurel had set up an ambush. This is supposed to be the ambush scene!"

Reaching for her computer mouse, she clicked on Laurel's e-mail. Olivia hadn't bothered to read her friend's note. Too interested in seeing what would befall the rakish highwayman, she'd just opened the file and printed out the chapter. Now she carefully read Laurel's note.

Dear Bayside Book Writers:

I am not sending any more chapters about the duchess. I'm shelving that project for now. I just didn't feel that it was working. Instead, I've attached the first chapter of my new manuscript, which I'm calling Lessons for Ever After.

It is a contemporary romance but won't feel very romantic at first. The upside is that this story feels much more genuine. I can barely sleep because I want to work on it all the time. The characters are so alive in my head! Sorry to do this without warning, but I hope you understand.

See you Saturday,
LH

Olivia sat back in her chair and took a bite of biscotti. Laurel had written over one hundred pages in her historical romance and now she was just going to stick it in a drawer and begin a new project? The decision took courage, Olivia knew, but she wondered if something else hadn't prompted the change. Was the passage she'd read an autobiographical account of Laurel's marriage to Steve? Olivia truly hoped not.

"I can't read into it like that," she admonished herself out loud and handed Haviland an organic dog treat from the jar on her desk. "That's not my job as a critique partner."

It didn't take long for Olivia to finish a run-through of the chapter. She was surprised to find that it was much stronger than Laurel's previous work. She made a note below the last line that she'd never sensed the presence of voice in the historical romance, but that this woman's voice, whom Laurel refers to only as "The Wife," was both vibrant and authentic. The duchess was self serving and often shallow, but Laurel's new protagonist was an interesting blend of self-doubt and pluck. She was sympathetic and multidimensional, and Laurel's switch to first-person succeeded in drawing in the reader.

"I can't wait to see what the rest of the group makes of this new chapter," Olivia said to Haviland and drained her coffee cup.

Unfortunately, it was two weeks before the Bayside Book Writers were able to meet again. The sellers had officially accepted Harris's offer, and the closing went through without a hitch. Clearly Millicent Banks had gotten the job done. It had been decided to postpone the next meeting until moving day. They'd all promised to help Harris cart boxes and small pieces of furniture from his old apartment to his new house on Oleander Drive.

Whether Nick Plumley had made any attempt to contact the sellers, Olivia didn't know, but she'd seen Millicent at the grocery store, showing off her new Chanel purse to a group of admirers gathered around the deli counter.

Despite overcast skies and the fact that the day would be spent hauling things from one residence to another, Harris couldn't stop smiling. Upon seeing Olivia standing in his living room, he greeted her with an exuberant embrace and then shook Haviland's paw. The poodle quickly disengaged and jogged off to explore the apartment. With the knickknacks boxed and the furniture piled in the center of each room, there was an array of exposed scents waiting to be investigated.

Harris had secured the aid of two coworkers by bribing them with promises of pizza and beer in exchange for helping him move the bed, sofa, and kitchen table. The congenial software developers made several trips in a commercial-sized pickup, sparing the Bayside Book Writers from having to manhandle the massive leather sectional or the heavy oak coffee table.

However, they were all sore, sweaty, and tired by the time the last box had been carried across the bungalow's threshold. Olivia sank down on the sofa while Millay perched on the coffee table, surveying the haphazard arrangement of furniture and accessories.

"Where's Little Administrative Assistant?" she asked Harris. "Isn't it the girlfriend's job to help haul her lover boy's crap when he moves? This is, like, a *major* Kodak moment. A freaking milestone. How can she miss it?"

Harris blushed and turned away from Millay's sharp

stare. "Estelle volunteers at a senior center on Saturdays. She would have been here if she didn't have another commitment."

"How sweet of her!" Laurel quickly exclaimed. "And I'm sorry I arrived so late to the moving party. The twins are going through this biting phase, and I'm afraid Dermot sank his teeth into my father-in-law's thigh and hung on like a little bulldog."

Rawlings and Harris hooted with laughter.

Millay nodded her head with approval. "A pint-sized vampire. Way to go, Dermot."

"The in-laws don't think he's so cute at the moment," Laurel answered with a giggle. "And Steve tried to make it seem like Dermot's bad behavior was *my* fault for not being by his side every second of the day. I told them Maddie Jackson is still biting people and she's old enough to wear a training bra!"

Harris's house was filled with the sounds of mirth.

Later, over six-packs of cold beer and several large ham and pineapple pies from Pizza Bay, Harris's friends toasted his new home.

The coworkers took off with the leftover food, but only after pausing at the doorway to haze Harris about spending Saturday night with his book club.

Millay was on her feet in a flash. "It's not a book club, nerds. We're a *writers'* group. We *write* books. Book clubs discuss someone else's published works. You just wait." She pointed a finger at their chests while slinging her free arm around Harris. "One day, this übergeek is going to be signing his book for packs of hormone-crazed hotties. And what'll you clowns be doing? Playing online video games with some twelve-year-old in Albuquerque?"

Instead of being offended, the young men were delighted by Millay's sauciness. "Now we see the benefits of this group. You've got sweet Millay on Saturday and Estelle Sunday through Friday. We didn't know you were such a player, dude!" They took turns exchanging high-fives with a dumbstruck Harris.

Harris pushed them onto the porch just as Millay lunged forward, her eyes flashing. Amused, Rawlings mollified the lovely bartender by handing her a fresh beer. He raised his own bottle in salute.

"If you ever consider a job in law enforcement, come talk to me. You could scare the good back into half the town's criminals."

Millay grinned, her face relaxing as she took a sip of beer. Twirling a strand of her glossy black hair, which was dyed fuchsia at the tips, she walked back to her spot on the coffee table, giving Laurel a squeeze on the arm in passing. "Let's get down to it. Mama's got a brand-new bag."

Harris dug around in a nearby box until he found a file folder from which he pulled out Laurel's chapter. "Is it okay to ask why you ditched the duchess?"

Laurel had clearly been anticipating this question. "The more I worked on that book, the less sincere it felt. With every paragraph, I was struggling to place myself in her shoes. The scenes felt forced and then, one day, I realized I didn't even like her."

"You could have gone back and edited her," Rawlings pointed out.

"Sure," Laurel agreed. "But it was too late. She is who she is. I just got to this point where I didn't care what happened to her and so how could I expect a reader to care?" She pointed at the pages in Harris's hands.

"But *this* woman! She leapt from my mind like, um, who was the Greek goddess who was born fully matured?"

Millay tapped her forehead. "Athena, goddess of wisdom. She busted right out of Zeus's head wearing a full suit of armor. Talk about some serious labor pains . . ."

"Imagine if he'd had twins!" Laurel chuckled. "Anyway, that's how The Wife came about. She literally forced every other character out of my mind and started whispering her story to me. I literally cannot stop writing. It's like being high on drugs."

Rawlings arched a brow. "Oh? Is that something you've personally experienced?"

"No!" Laurel cried in horror and then realized the chief was joking. "I know I just dropped this on all of you with no warning, but I wanted this chapter to be read without any preconceptions. So I'm ready now. Fire away!"

Millay volunteered to go first. "I totally thought this woman was going to be some whiny Stepford wife, and I guess, on the surface, she is. She's got the tan and the toned bod and the French manicure, but I felt sorry for her when I read about all the things she did to make herself more attractive to her husband. I was, to my own surprise, rooting for her."

"You did an incredible job describing the scene where she gets Botox." Harris gave a little shiver. "I hate needles. And the way she just sits there—thinking about how good she'll look without those lines on her forehead and around her mouth while the doc sticks her again and again—I kind of wanted to shake her and tell her she didn't have to go through that."

The group of writers began to argue vociferously over whether The Wife had been wasting time and money trying to improve her physical appearance, since her husband didn't seem to notice anything she did.

"You're forgetting that she also attempts to become a better person on the inside," Olivia said. "She begins volunteering at the hospital. She bakes meals for the employees at her husband's company that have had babies or fallen ill. She reads dozens of biographies about strong and powerful women. *That's* what saved her as a character in my eyes. She wants to be the whole package. She is deeper than she appears."

Rawlings threw up his hands. "But she wants to be Wonder Woman and that's ridiculous. Impossible."

Everyone began talking at once. This was unusual, as the writers were careful never to interrupt one another. Olivia wondered if the afternoon's physical labor coupled with several beers had produced this chaotic atmosphere. She glanced over at Laurel and saw her friend smiling with happiness.

Eventually, the rest of the group noticed her expression and fell silent, gazing at her inquisitively.

"It doesn't bother you that we want to push this woman off a bridge half the time?" Millay asked.

"Not at all," Laurel replied. "She's evoked emotion in you in a way the duchess never did. I'm thrilled."

Rawlings reviewed the notes on his paper. "An excellent point, but I think you need to revamp your title. *Lessons for Ever After* doesn't seem to reflect the complexity of The Wife's character."

Olivia agreed. She'd made a note about the title as well. "You may need to wait until your story develops further before deciding what to call this book. We already know from reading one chapter that The Wife must figure out what makes *her* fulfilled, with or without the husband, and that she needs to redefine her definition of happily ever after." She scanned over the pages in her hand. "Don't get too caught up in the fairy-tale theme," Olivia cautioned. "I sense this romance is going to have more depth than your previous project. It might turn into more of a Chicklit romance if you use too many Cinderella elements."

Laurel nodded in agreement and then Harris pointed out bits of unclear dialogue. Millay finished the critique by voicing reservations about Laurel's word choice in the final paragraph, but overall, it was clear that the Bayside Book Writers were impressed by her new project.

"You're on the chopping block next week," Millay informed Olivia after examining her day planner. "It'll be nice to be back in the lighthouse keeper's cottage. I like your choice of booze better."

Olivia gestured at the pair of empty bottles at Millay's feet. "You didn't seem to suffer. Besides, you've never been much of a wine drinker."

"And what about you, Chief?" Millay's eyes sparkled with mischief. "You going to wash down that Coors with a chocolate milk chaser?"

Rawlings, who was known to have a penchant for chocolate milk, gave Millay a wink. "You should get in at least three servings of dairy per day. It's never too late to protect yourself against bone loss."

Millay threw one of the sofa cushions at him.

Harris rose, banged his pen on the neck of his beer bottle, and cleared his throat. "I have a strange and wonderful announcement."

"Estelle is knocked up and you're eloping to Vegas?" Millay interrupted. Rawlings returned fire with the pillow and gestured for Harris to continue.

"Thanks, Sawyer." Even after months of having the

chief as a critique partner, Harris always looked pleased to be able to address the policeman by his first name. "You'll never believe it, but I met Nick Plumley yesterday. *The* Nick Plumley. Right in front of my house." He beamed. "Man, that feels so good to say. My house."

Olivia frowned. The bestselling author had failed to buy the bungalow, but he was clearly still interested in it. "What was he doing here?"

"Said he'd been doing research for the sequel to *The Barbed Wire Flower* and came across a newspaper article describing how all the houses on Oleander Drive had been relocated. I told you guys about that earlier, but what I didn't know was that one of the trucks broke down in the middle of Main Street on a Sunday. A local minister with initiative blessed the house and held an impromptu service inside." Harris smiled. "It wasn't my house though. Plumley came inside and looked around but said the floor plan didn't match the description in the newspaper. He's lucky he caught me. I was only here because I'd come over to meet the cable guys."

Nick Plumley's motive to see the inside of Harris's house sounded plausible, but something in Olivia's gut told her that there was more to it than research. For some reason she could not fathom, the writer had a connection to this house. It was important to him. Because it could enable him to pen another excellent novel? Perhaps. But would he decide to purchase the property just to be able to study the interior? Olivia didn't think so. Nick might be wealthy, but he didn't seem like a compulsive spender. When she'd met him at the diner, he'd been dressed in khaki trousers and a white buttondown. His shoes and watch were of good quality, but neither was especially costly.

Even his soft briefcase was modest and similar to the one Rawlings carried. It had the worn suppleness of those toted around by professors, not millionaires. Yet Nick had wanted to buy this house instead of continuing the lease on the spectacular beachfront property near Olivia's place. She wondered if he was still a mile down the road or if he'd bought another home. Dixie hadn't seen him at the diner for the last two weeks, and Olivia's feisty friend had pretended to be extremely offended that Oyster Bay's newest celebrity had eschewed Grumpy's in favor of other eateries.

"Are you certain he's defected?" Olivia had asked, amused.

Dixie didn't even crack a smile. "He's been at Bagels 'n' Beans every single day. Even if he doesn't like eggs or pancakes, there's still Grumpy's lunch menu! I can't stand the thought that he didn't like our club sandwich. Who makes a better one, I'd like to know!"

Olivia had tried to assure her flustered friend that there wasn't a restaurant within two hundred miles that could top Grumpy's "mile-high club sandwich," but Dixie was not to be consoled.

Except for the fact that Flynn McNulty had created an entire window display at Through the Wardrobe featuring signed copies of Nick's book, no one in Oyster Bay had called attention to the writer's presence. This in itself was an oddity. Normally, a rich, handsome, and unattached celebrity would have had the gossip chain on red alert, but even though he'd been in town for several weeks already, Nick had kept such a low profile that Olivia had nearly forgotten about him.

After all, she was a busy woman. Between preparing for the grand opening of The Bayside Crab House, outlining the next chapter in her novel, and adjusting to the existence of her new family, Olivia hadn't had time to dwell on Nick Plumley.

"Wait, there's more to this story!" Harris declared exuberantly. "When Plumley heard I was an aspiring writer, he actually offered to read my work in progress. He said that he loves science fiction and has always admired authors of the genre. He's going to swing by on Tuesday to pick up my manuscript." Glancing around at the scores of unpacked boxes, Harris's eyes took on a frantic look. "I totally have to get my computer and printer hooked up."

Laurel's mouth had formed a perfect *O* of surprise. "Harris, this is *wonderful*! I'd heard that Mr. Plumley was in town, but I still haven't laid eyes on him. Do you think he'll give you feedback?"

Harris tried to look modest. "Yeah, I do. In fact, he said he'd love to attend one of our meetings if we were willing to have him."

"Seriously?" Millay asked. "Why would he want to do that? He's already made it."

"Maybe he wants to share his knowledge of the publishing process with us," Laurel suggested. "Maybe he wants to pay it forward."

Rawlings crossed his arms over his chest, as though pondering what it would be like to receive constructive criticism from the famous author. "I wouldn't say no to an offer of assistance from Mr. Plumley. I truly admire his work and would enjoy hearing the story of his success."

"That's three votes for him," Harris stated, raising the fingers of his right hand in front of Millay's face. "Your book is closest to being ready for publication.

I bet Plumley could tell you a thing or two about finding a literary agent."

Millay gazed dreamily at her writing journal. "I do have a *ton* of questions about the querying process, so it's fine with me if Oyster Bay's own Dan Brown wants to hang out. Let's see what he can do for us." She turned to Olivia. "Does this mean you'll be breaking out caviar and the top-shelf liquor?"

Olivia wasn't pleased. "We're not changing a thing for Nick Plumley's visit. Personally, I don't care for the idea of him being there for the critique of my chapter, but I guess I'll deal with it, as everyone else wants to extend him an invitation."

Having come to a decision, the group broke up. Millay left for her shift at Fish Nets, Rawlings needed to swing by the station to sign paperwork, and Laurel had to be home in time to bathe the twins and put them to bed.

Even after taking Haviland outside for a brisk walk down Oleander Drive, Olivia felt restless. She could go home, change clothes, and get to The Boot Top in time for the evening rush, but she was reluctant to leave Harris's house. She wanted to know why Nick Plumley found the modest bungalow so intriguing.

"I need to do a little snooping," she told Haviland. "You'll have to wait another hour for dinner. I'm going to offer to help Harris unpack some boxes and see if the house wants to whisper a clue in my ear."

Harris was delighted to accept her offer. "Could you set up the kitchen? Not to sound old-fashioned, but women have a better sense of where stuff should go in that room."

"I doubt Michel would agree with that statement," Olivia remarked with a laugh and got busy putting away dishes, pots, and pans, and Harris's odd collection of flatware and cooking utensils.

The kitchen, like the rest of the house, was dated. It desperately needed new flooring and a fresh coat of paint, but the cabinets were solid, and Harris had done his best to clean them. The entire room was redolent with the smell of bleach.

When she was done setting up the room, she began to make a mental list of all the changes that would have to be made to freshen up the space. She hadn't bought Harris a house-warming gift but decided on the spot to splurge and hire one of the men from Clyde's team to rip up the worn and discolored linoleum and replace it with tile.

She wandered around the rest of the downstairs but found nothing unusual in the coat or broom closets and didn't feel she had cause to be poking around upstairs. Harris, who was putting clothes in the chest of drawers in his bedroom, might find it odd to discover her jumping up and down on the floorboards in the attic. After scrutinizing the paneling in the living room for a final time, she gave up. Haviland hadn't picked up any alarming scents either, and the house felt as it had each time she'd visited: solid and dependable.

Thoroughly tired now, Olivia wished Harris good night and stepped out into the warm evening. Casting a backward glance at the illuminated bungalow, Olivia decided she was going to have to investigate any and all public documents pertaining to its history. As Clyde had said, all houses had secrets.

"Yours might be well hidden," Olivia addressed the timeworn facade. "But I will discover it."

Chapter 4

At a dinner party one should eat wisely
but not too well, and talk well but not too
wisely.

—WILLIAM SOMERSET MAUGHAM

The following Monday Olivia began her search into the history of Harris's house at the offices of the *Oyster Bay Gazette*. She could have just asked Laurel to look into the matter, as her friend wrote for the paper, but Laurel had enough to juggle as it was.

The receptionist at the *Gazette* listened politely to Olivia's request to root through the paper's archives but was quick to offer her an alternative to spending hours going through decades' worth of dusty tomes. "You should just talk to Mrs. Fairchild over at the library. She's lived here forever and has a larger memory capacity than my computer. If your research has anything to do with this town or its residents, she's the person to see." She shook her head. "Wow, I'm having a major case of déjà vu. I made the same suggestion to that good-looking author, Nick Plumley, last month."

Olivia did her best to appear disinterested in this bit of gossip. Thanking the woman, she got back in the

Range Rover and drove to the public library. She didn't park in the lot, opting for a space in front of the historical society instead.

She opened Haviland's door, and the pair strolled along the sidewalk. Olivia slowed to a halt as they arrived at the tree-lined parking lot.

"I haven't been inside that building since I was six years old," she told Haviland. "Nearly seven. I'd just finished reading *Misty of Chincoteague*, and the librarian, her name was Miss Leona, gave me a horse sticker as a prize." Olivia smiled at the memory. "I didn't need any incentive, of course. Even then, I knew the stories were their own reward, but Miss Leona used to put all my favorites on hold. She made me the prettiest bookmarks out of felt. I cherished every one."

Haviland veered off to the left, his attention diverted by a squirrel chattering in one of the high branches of an oak tree. Olivia followed the poodle's gaze, her eyes traveling over the sun-dappled foliage and the aged bark, and then she reached out and touched the trunk.

It was here, a few feet away, that Olivia's mother had died. She'd worked as a librarian in the building at the end of the lot. There were three full-time librarians back then. Miss Leona, Mrs. Dubney, and Olivia's mother. The women were a tight-knit group. Olivia knew this from the tenderness that would enter her mother's voice whenever she spoke of her coworkers. At a time when most careers were dominated by males, this triumvirate of women ruled the Oyster Bay library with wisdom and kindness.

They also looked after one another outside of work. When Miss Leona was diagnosed with breast cancer, the other women covered her shifts and cooked her meals. When Mrs. Dubney's husband died, they offered her food and company. Olivia remembered tagging along to the older woman's house weekend after weekend.

She'd weed the vegetable garden or sweep the front path while her mother whispered words of comfort. Mrs. Dubney would take out photo albums or sit on the porch swing and tell rose-colored stories about her husband. Her entire body would shake with sobs, and the tears would stream down her cheeks until there were no more left. Olivia's mother would hold her friend's hand and listen, long after the stories began to repeat and the widow was able to smile during her reminiscences.

Eventually, the weekend visits to Mrs. Dubney became less frequent, yet there was always another townsperson who required compassion or cookies or a ride to work, and Olivia's mother never failed a neighbor in need. Olivia did not resent the time or affection bestowed on these people because her mother always set out on each visit by saying, "They're not lucky like I am, Livie. From the moment you were born and I held you in my arms, I knew I could never be unhappy again."

Naturally, Olivia's doting mother wanted her only child's seventh birthday to be truly memorable and refused to allow the onset of a category two hurricane to stop her from picking up Olivia's special gift. The big surprise, a Labrador puppy who'd been dropped off at the library by the breeder, was being cared for by Miss Leona until Olivia's mother could collect the dog from the library staff room.

Because Olivia's mother had been preoccupied decorating the house and baking her daughter a butterscotch cake, it was evening by the time she left the lighthouse keeper's cottage and headed into town for the puppy. Wary of the storm, Miss Leona had closed the library early and had headed home, guiltily leaving the young dog in his crate in the staff room. The pup whined and yelped in fear as the rain smacked against the roof and the wind shook the trees around the building.

Hearing his cries, Olivia's mother rushed into the library, leaving sodden boot prints on the carpet in her wake. She touched the puppy's silken ears and stroked him tenderly. But he wouldn't be consoled, so she grabbed the crate and tried to comfort the shivering pup after she'd settled him onto the passenger seat. Seconds later, a rotten telephone pole crashed through the windshield, killing the young wife and mother instantly.

The dog was unharmed.

Olivia never laid eyes on the puppy. And she planned to never go near the library again. Yet here she was.

"I guess we'll find out if the current librarians like dogs," she told Haviland and resolutely made her way toward the double doors.

The building had been given a facelift while Olivia was away at school. The facade was a mass of sparkling glass windows through which metal sculptures of flying gulls hung from vaulted ceilings. Their steel wings caught the light and threw reflections onto the lobby's tiled floor.

"Lovely," Olivia remarked as Haviland sniffed a rolling cart containing hardcovers for sale at a dollar apiece. "Anything good?" she asked him and then noticed a copy of *The Barbed Wire Flower* on the top shelf. Thinking the book might serve as a useful prop when she tried to glean information on Nick Plumley's current research, Olivia took it from the cart along with a copy of Jodi Picoult's latest release.

"I should shop here more often," she murmured,

recalling how awkward it had felt the last time she'd patronized her former lover's bookstore.

She hesitated at the automatic door leading to a spacious carpeted area where the most popular fiction releases were displayed on shelves of blond wood. Olivia knew that while most local businesses welcomed Haviland and knew that he had impeccable manners, there were merchants who preferred him to remain in the Range Rover while Olivia did her shopping.

Olivia tended to judge people based on their reaction to her constant companion. As she approached the circulation desk, she steeled herself against possible disapproval and kept her gaze deliberately fixed upon the woman behind the counter. Olivia didn't dare glance in the direction of the reference desk. That had been her mother's desk, her mother's blue swivel chair, her mother's perfume clinging to the flyers and bookmarks and summer reading lists. If Olivia turned, she might be haunted by the sound of a tender whisper or a sweet smile.

"Livie?" A woman's voice inquired softly. "My gracious, after all this time!"

Olivia knew her instantly. "Miss Leona. I can't believe it's you!"

The older woman chuckled, hiding her mirth behind her hand. "Well now, I haven't been a 'miss' for decades, dear. I'm Mrs. Fairchild, but since I've known you since you were in diapers, you can just call me Leona."

Olivia was amazed that Leona was still working at the same library after all these years. She'd been younger than Olivia's mother and had aged gracefully. Now in her midfifties, Leona's bright blond hair had become a darker, more muted shade, like the beach at twilight.

She had laugh lines radiating from the corners of her gull gray eyes, and her figure was fuller, but she carried her extra weight well on her tall frame. Unruffled by Olivia's scrutiny, she gazed at the daughter of her old friend with a frank gentleness unchanged by the passage of time.

To Olivia's extreme annoyance, she suddenly felt shy and uncertain in the librarian's presence. Not only was Leona one of the few townsfolk who'd known her as a child, but she'd also been privy to the intimate thoughts and secret longings of Olivia's mother.

"Is it okay for Haviland to be here?" Olivia whispered.

Grinning, Leona reached out and stroked the poodle. "As long as he doesn't lift his leg on the periodicals, it's fine by me." Her smile disappeared. "I know it wasn't easy for you to come in, but I believe your sweet mama would have expected you to be a regular patron. There wasn't a day that went by when she didn't try to find you a special book or ask the other librarians for advice on how to instill in you a lifelong love of reading."

"She succeeded in that goal," Olivia said and noticed a look of satisfaction settle on the librarian's face. "I'd like to sign up for a library card, but I'm also here on a research mission. Do you have a few minutes to spare?"

Leona took Olivia's hand and gave it a squeeze. "For you? I have nothing but time."

After listening to a single sentence, the librarian cut Olivia's request short. "How strange! Mr. Plumley wanted information on the same house." She lowered her voice until it was barely audible. "Tell me. Is it haunted? I don't recall a single episode of violence occurring in that house, and there are no records documenting anything unusual about the people who lived there, but *something* must set that house apart. Within one month, a bestselling author and the long-absent daughter of my dear friend and colleague are seeking information on the same property." She put her hands on her hips. "I suggest we trade information. You show me your cards and I'll show you mine."

Olivia hadn't expected the librarian to be so plucky, but she liked her all the more for it. She raised her hands in surrender. "I'll come clean, but what I'm about to say is for your ears alone."

Leona led Olivia and Haviland into the staff room. She poured two cups of coffee, set them on the table, and offered the poodle a bowl of cool water. "Nick Plumley said he was conducting research for his sequel to *The Barbed Wire Flower*. You're read it, haven't you?"

Brandishing the hardcovers she had tucked under her arm, Olivia said, "Yes. I thought it was a compelling story."

"Me too." The librarian poured a generous splash of milk into her coffee and, seeing no spoon handy, stirred it with a plastic straw. "As you know, the novel is based on a prison camp set up in New Bern. It was a large camp and employed many families from the surrounding counties. Men who were too old or had a physical disability that prevented them from enlisting became the prison's guards. Some of the German POWs spent four years in that camp. Plumley's descriptions of the guards educating their captives about democracy and capitalism are accurate. He was also correct in his depiction of how well the prisoners were treated. It was, for most of the war, a community of men exhibiting mutual respect and even friendship."

Though this recap was interesting, Olivia didn't see

that it had much to do with Harris's house. "Yes, I remember that. The Germans were also encouraged to make items out of scrap materials for their own use or to sell. They were allowed to keep every cent of the profits they earned. The prisoners were so content that they never tried to escape—at least not until the pivotal scene in which a disgruntled Nazi captured and transported here toward the end of the war plans a rebellion. One of his confederates kills a guard, and together the escapees hop a freight train for the Midwest and are never seen again."

"What many people don't know is that the event Plumley depicts so graphically actually happened," the librarian stated solemnly. "The murdered guard was from Oyster Bay. His name was James Hatcher. Plumley gave both him and the Germans fictional names, of course, but I've met Hatcher's son, and he believes Plumley described that night in perfect detail."

Olivia tried to rein in her impatience. "Did James Hatcher live in the house Plumley's researching?"

"No. I thought one of his descendants might have and that's why Mr. Plumley was fixated on it, but that turned out to be a dead end." Leona took a sip of coffee and stared at Haviland, her eyes glazing as she traveled into the past. Olivia began to shake her foot under the table. She was not accustomed to sitting still.

Finally, the librarian blinked twice and, surfacing from the past, returned her attention to Olivia. "I wrote down the names of three families who've lived in the house. During the war, it was the Whites, but they moved out of town before the armistice. The next family, the Carters, were there the longest. They raised two boys in that house before moving to Florida in the early nineties. After that, it belonged to the Robinsons, the couple that sold it to your friend last month. They're childless, and if the gossip chain is accurate, the wife is an agoraphobic."

That explains the dated interior, Olivia thought.

"And there was nothing extraordinary about the Whites or the Carters?" she asked.

Leona shook her head. "Not on paper. I pulled every bit of microfiche that had any bearing on those families and shared them with Mr. Plumley. Like you, I wondered why he was so interested in these rather unremarkable folks."

"If Plumley's working on a sequel, there might be a connection between someone who lived in the house and the prison camp," Olivia insisted.

"That was my theory as well, but those families were made up of fathers who went to the office five days a week, mothers who tended house, and children who did their best in school and stayed out of trouble. They were churchgoers and sailors, gardeners and Masons. They played baseball and went to proms. I don't see them as book material."

Olivia didn't either, but asked Leona for printouts of the same material Plumley had collected.

"That'll be quite a bit of work on my part," Leona said with a playful wink. "I'm perfectly willing to do it and I understand that you feel protective of your young friend, but I doubt he faces any danger from the house or from Mr. Plumley. He seems like a good man and he *is* an author.

High praise from a librarian, Olivia thought and decided she would have to find an alternate means of snooping or run the risk of offending her mother's friend by confessing that she suspected Plumley's interest in Harris's house wasn't as innocent as it seemed.

"You're right," she conceded. "I'm sure the real source of my anxiety stems from the fact that Mr. Plumley will be a guest at our book writer's group next week and my chapter is up for review."

"You're writing a book?" Leona clasped her hands together in delight. "My dear girl, your mother would be *so* proud!"

To Olivia's dismay, a lump formed in her throat and her eyes grew moist. Abruptly, she pushed back her chair, stood, and carried her empty mug to the sink. The librarian's words had caught her by surprise and moved her deeply, but she didn't want it to show. Gesturing for Haviland to follow, she moved toward the staff room door. "Thank you for your help."

Leona didn't rise but studied Olivia fondly. "She's still with you, child. We carry those we love in our hearts. It's where heaven truly exists."

Olivia paused at the threshold. "If you believe in heaven," she murmured to herself as she walked away.

Thwarted in her detective work, Olivia turned her attention back to the grand opening of The Bayside Crab House. She arrived at the restaurant in a sour mood that neither the smell of fresh paint nor the sight of the banners announcing opening day could dispel. The visit to the library had raised too many old memories, and Olivia disliked how vulnerable she felt whenever the past collided with the present. Failing to discover what Nick Plumley was after was extremely frustrating, but since April Howard was waiting, eager to show off the restaurant's interior, Olivia did her best to adopt an amicable expression.

The Bayside Crab House was a formidable structure. The entrance, with its heavy wood entry doors flanked by rows of porthole windows, faced Water Street. Customers would enter under a cheerful red awning, pass by oversized planters brimming with coleus, red geranium, and marigolds, and finally step up onto a gentle ramp built to feel like a dock. Ship's anchors partially submerged in a sea of blue gravel surrounded both sides of the makeshift wharf.

Olivia had decided to maintain the original appearance of the warehouse by keeping the clapboard the same dolphin gray hue. Most of the wall space to the right of the entrance now featured an electrified sign bearing the restaurant's name and the image of a smiling neon red crab.

Inside, the tables, chairs, and floor were of pine, but the uniform appearance of yellowish wood complemented the bright, checkered tablecloths, red napkins, and multicolored nautical flags pinned to the walls.

A large bar area occupied the length of the left-hand wall and featured five television screens and a small stage where local musicians would perform on weekend nights. Nautical pennants dangled a few feet above a mirror reflecting an impressive pyramid of liquor bottles. Old barrels, sawed in half and turned on their sides, served as storage vessels for the restaurant's wine selection.

"It's perfect," Olivia told April, allowing a sigh of satisfaction to escape from between her lips. "You've done an amazing job."

April smiled. "I'll probably never pour so much of myself into a project again, but it was worth it. This building helped me put myself together. The least I could do was return the favor."

"And I hear Clyde's taken you on as a full-time

employee. You'll be working for the best contractor in town. Congratulations."

"Yep. I'm the first woman on his team," April replied proudly.

Olivia shook her head. "About time he came to his senses. Come on, Haviland, let's check out the outdoor seating area."

April moved ahead of the pair and opened a set of double doors leading to the deck with a triumphant flourish. Immediately, the jovial sound of fiddle music burst into the air.

"What's going on?" Olivia stepped out onto the expansive deck and immediately smelled jasmine. Pots of the vine bearing heady yellow flowers flanked the doors and had grown halfway up the lattice trellis that covered the deck. Thousands of tiny white electric lights shone down from the trellis's frame and would compete with the stars on clear summer nights.

At one end, a fiddler was swaying on the balls of his feet while a young woman bobbed her head in time with the music. The fiddler dipped his chin her way, and she lifted a pennywhistle and effortlessly fell into harmony with his jaunty tune.

The Bayside Book Writers, seated at a large picnic table in the center of the deck, began to clap, and the musicians responded to their encouragement by putting even more energy into the song.

"Welcome aboard!" Millay shouted. She rose to her feet and saluted Olivia with a glass of beer. Haviland darted toward the table, clearly hoping to escape the high pitch of the pennywhistle. The lucky poodle was greeted warmly by Laurel, who slipped him something under the table and stroked his black fur.

"I kind of feel like we're embarking on an ocean voyage," Laurel said. "A feast before we set off to raid and pillage."

Harris gestured at Rawlings with a king crab claw. "Sounds like your book, Chief."

"Congratulations, Olivia." Rawlings also stood and gave her a warm smile. "This place is going to be a hit."

At that moment, Hudson walked onto the deck carrying a pair of oval platters filled with crab cakes, lobster tail, and fried shrimp. Kim followed behind bearing a bowl of cheese grits and a basket of hushpuppies.

"Caitlyn's eating in the kitchen," Kim whispered in Olivia's ear. "Too many people for her liking."

"I'll bring Haviland back to keep her company," Olivia replied and then indicated the food-laden table. "I take it this impromptu party is your idea."

Kim shrugged, her face pink with happiness. "What better way to test the kitchen before the big day?"

Rawlings pulled out the chair placed at the end of the table and bowed gallantly at Olivia. Their eyes met, and as always, Olivia found it difficult to look away. "Thank you," she said as he laid a napkin on her lap and then let his fingertips linger on the nape of her neck long enough to send a shiver down her spine.

Millay handed her a glass of beer. "A toast to vats of melted butter and food you can hit with a hammer!"

The company shouted a hearty, "Here! Here!" and then eagerly began to pass dishes around the table.

Olivia waited until she'd had her fill of scallops tossed in a Parmesan cream sauce, Creole-style crab cakes, and Hudson's homemade slaw before taking Haviland into the kitchen. "Someone wanted to see you," she told

Caitlyn. "Do you think there are any leftovers for a hungry poodle?"

Caitlyn nodded shyly. "I could fix him something."

"That would be splendid. No shrimp though. Too many of those aren't good for his tummy." Olivia walked around the kitchen, newly christened with dirty pots, remnants of steam, and a blend of scents, the most notable being crabmeat and cayenne.

Hudson had made the entire meal himself, and Olivia was impressed by his versatility. She was also relieved that she'd trusted her instincts in offering him the manager's job, but he told her that he was meant to wear an apron, not a jacket and tie. He'd hired several assistant cooks but told her that he planned to be in the kitchen as much as possible.

"I can run the place a helluva lot better from behind a stove," he'd said. "If the food isn't right, folks won't come back. Kim'll do the books. She can't boil an egg, but she's got a good head for numbers."

"Can she handle that responsibility with a newborn at home?" Olivia had asked.

"She's juggled more than that before. We'll make this place our second home, you'll see." Hudson had put a hand on her shoulder to reinforce his point, and for once, Olivia backed down. She could tell that her brother and his wife were completely dedicated to seeing that The Bayside Crab House was a success.

So far, Kim had managed the preopening pressure without difficulty, but her due date was only days away, and tonight she was looking worn to a nub. When she came into the kitchen to fetch extra bowls of melted butter, she leaned heavily on the counter near Caitlyn. Her eyes were bloodshot from lack of sleep and the skin on her face had a sallow tinge. When Olivia looked down at her sister-in-law's ankles, she gasped.

"Kim, look how swollen you are!" Olivia pushed a stack of empty crates across the floor and gestured at them. "Sit down on this stool and put your feet up this instant. I'll bring the damn butter out." She locked eyes with Caitlyn. "You watch your mother. Do not let her get up. Your shift is over, Kim!" Olivia was angry with Hudson, not Kim, and forced herself to speak more gently. "Thank you for arranging this for me. I'm really thrilled by all you and Hudson have accomplished, but you need to go home. I don't want my niece or nephew being born on my new floor."

Outside, Olivia dumped the butter unceremoniously on the table and glared at Hudson. "Your wife needs to lie down. Her legs look like tree trunks, and she's so exhausted she can barely hold her head up."

Hudson didn't respond. Instead, he shrugged and took a long pull from his beer bottle. As Olivia felt her indignation mounting, Rawlings put a hand on Hudson's shoulder. "We'll take care of the dishes. It's the least we can do after you've served us a feast fit for Poseidon himself." He gave Hudson a coaxing smile. "Go on, man. You deserve to spend the rest of this fine evening watching a ball game on TV."

Laurel and Millay hugged the gruff cook, and he was clearly startled to be the recipient of their affection. He didn't return the embraces, but there was a smile in his eyes and he gave Olivia a nearly imperceptible nod as he passed.

Olivia turned to Rawlings, wanting to demonstrate her gratitude with a look, but his eyes were focused on the remnants of food on his plate. For a moment, she wished they were alone together. No friends, no musicians, no family members, just the two of them sharing a meal beneath the open sky and the glimmer of tiny white lights.

Yet she'd decided to push him away, closing herself off to possible heartbreak. Her life was too complicated for anything other than a one-night stand, and she knew that Rawlings would never enter into a shallow relationship. He wanted to know her, body and soul, and she'd placed her privacy above his feelings.

As she watched Rawlings now, however, she felt her flesh humming with desire for him. She imagined being pressed against his bearlike chest, exposing deeply concealed feelings to the man, but fantasy was as far as she was willing to go.

I belong only to myself. If the trade-off for independence is loneliness, then I'll be lonely.

The mention of Nick Plumley's name brought an end to Olivia's ruminations.

"What did you say?" she asked Harris.

"Nick's coming over to pick up my manuscript on Tuesday. He's going to read the whole thing! Isn't that awesome?"

Olivia raised her brows. "He's coming to the office or to your house?"

"The house. He's going to hang out and read while I paint the living room. I told him I'd taken a personal day from work and that things were going to be chaotic because the floor guys will be laying tile in the kitchen and removing the nasty carpet from the stairs." Harris winked at her. "All thanks to a friend who gave me a grade-A, killer housewarming present."

"How sweet of Mr. Plumley," Laurel stated, stacking dirty dishes into a tall pile. "We all think of him as this rich and famous novelist, but he's only human, and it sounds like he's looking to make some new friends." She grabbed the stack of dishes and headed inside, signaling the end of the party.

After making sure she and the Bayside Book Writers had left the restaurant kitchen spotlessly clean, Olivia and Haviland headed home. Instead of going inside, the pair strolled along the beach. Olivia removed her shoes and stepped into the cold water, staring at the distant lights of the boats in the harbor and the illuminated windows of town buildings.

Olivia considered Laurel's words about the celebrity writer. Was Plumley lonely? Had she completely misjudged him? Being a writer could be a lonely existence, and not everyone cherished solitude like she did. Perhaps he was looking for a little companionship.

By the time Haviland was ready to call it a night, Olivia had grown bored of brooding.

"I'm a hypocrite," she told the poodle. "Just because Plumley's rich and acts a bit eccentric doesn't mean he's full of character flaws. People have judged me by the same standards and I've resented them for it. Starting tomorrow, I will try to get to know Nick Plumley. Maybe then, he'll willingly share his secrets."

After kissing Haviland on the nose, Olivia collected her shoes and turned toward home, where she planned to slip between her cool, clean sheets and allow the whisper of the surf to ease her into a dreamless sleep.

It would be the last restful night she would have for a long time to come.

Chapter 5

It is the spectator, and not life, that art really mirrors.

—OSCAR WILDE

By Tuesday, Olivia hadn't even looked at the chapter she was supposed to e-mail to her critique group by Friday morning. The Bayside Crab House was set to have its grand opening on Friday night, and a million tiny details had to be seen to before the mayor cut the yellow ribbon and eager diners were treated to a half-price menu and a free pint of beer.

From the beginning, Olivia decided that the crab house would not accept reservations. The new hostess was trained to create a wait list and encourage hungry patrons to linger in the bar until their names were called. It was a time-honored trick in the restaurant business to funnel customers into the bar, as the sale of alcohol was more profitable than that of the food. Of course Olivia planned to sell a great deal of both and hoped to create a loyal customer base like The Boot Top Bistro enjoyed.

After a brisk walk on the beach, Olivia drove into town and headed to Grumpy's for breakfast, which she planned to follow by a marathon writing session. She dined on a short stack of fluffy whole-wheat pancakes bursting with tart raspberries, blackberries, and blueberries. Haviland filled his belly with scrambled eggs and beef and then stretched out on the floor to take a nap. Olivia smiled indulgently as the poodle got comfortably settled, and then booted up her laptop. She read the last couple of paragraphs she'd written and the diner quickly faded away as the world of her Egyptian courtesan drew her in.

In Olivia's previous chapter, the mighty and powerful pharaoh, Ramses the Great, had decided to include Kamila in the small entourage accompanying him on a trip to Thebes. The king planned to inspect the progress of his tomb and to make certain that the priests he'd hired to care for the tomb of his father, Seti I, were being diligent in their duties.

Kamila traveled with the other high-ranking servants and did not see the king. She wasn't called to Pharaoh's tent until the third night of their stay in Thebes, and only then was she washed, oiled, perfumed, and dressed in a nearly transparent white shift. A wig was placed on her shaved head, and her eyes were rimmed with kohl and painted with a powder of green malachite. Lastly, a ring of lotus blossoms encircled her neck. The king was particularly fond of the flower's heady scent.

Olivia was so lost in the scene that the sounds of clinking silverware and conversation fell away. Raising her hands, she began to type.

The tent of Ramses II was richly decorated. Lush carpets covered the ground, and chairs, tables, and a bed made of ebony and gold stood against the rear wall. Servants had laid out bowls of honeyed dates and pitchers of water and wine. Incense burned in every corner, and Kamila felt a little dizzy as she fell to her knees and prostrated before the Living God.

"Come," he told her in his rich voice. He gestured at a rug made of leopard pelts. "Sit."

Kamila did as Pharaoh commanded, keeping her shift drawn demurely over her legs. She was a concubine and belonged to the king, but since he had never claimed his right, she felt like a shy child in his presence. It was true that Ramses called her to his bedchamber more than any of the other girls, but he never touched her. Instead, she sang to him, told him the palace gossip, or was defeated by him in games of senet.

The concubines knew the king was besotted with his beautiful wife, yet it was also his duty to sire as many heirs as possible to strengthen his legacy and the greatness of Egypt. Kamila had watched with ill-disguised envy while the bellies of other girls swelled with the king's child and had tasted a bitterness she'd never known before when confronted with these fortunate concubines. They'd languish in the women's quarters of the palace wearing smug, contented smiles, knowing their futures were secured.

"Your thoughts are as distant as Ra's chariot," the king said, drawing Kamila's attention to his desert-tanned face, his dark eyes, and strong jaw. "Will you sing for me?"

Kamila nodded and did her best to conceal her disappointment, for the request meant that the king was ready to retire for the evening and that, once again, she'd return to her own sleeping pallet without having known his touch.

Deciding to take matters into her own hands, Kamila opened her mouth and began to sing a love song. As she sang, she swayed her body enticingly, her honey-colored eyes never leaving the king's face. She loosened her shift, and by the end of the song, she was again kneeling before her king, only this time, her clothes were a pool of linen at her feet.

The king's eyes revealed his desire as they traveled down the smooth skin of her elegant neck to her supple breasts, flat belly, and finally, to the soft curve of her hips. Then, at long last, he reached out and pulled her down onto the bed.

Olivia's cell phone rang. Startled out of her narrative, she cursed. She'd been fully prepared to write a sex scene between Kamila and Ramses and had been thinking about how to proceed for days. In fact, ever since Rawlings had touched her at The Bayside Crab House, she'd been focused on little else.

As she frowned at the numbers identifying the caller, Dixie appeared to refresh her coffee. Instead of skating away when she was done, she set the coffeepot down and waited to see if Olivia would answer her phone.

"I'll go outside," Olivia said and stood up. "I don't want to be rude."

"Oh, sit on down, Emily Post," Dixie commanded. "If that's your brother I wanna know if their new baby's made his way into the world."

Olivia gently rolled her friend backward. "It's Harris," she said while simultaneously answering the phone and stepping out the front door into the May sunshine.

"This had better be good," she growled before Harris had the chance to speak. "I was working on my chapter and was completely in the groove."

"Sorry, but I didn't know who else to call." Harris sounded excited, but not alarmed. "Remember I told you that Nick Plumley was coming over today and that the floor guys would be here, too?"

"Yes."

"Well, right after Nick left—he stayed a long time and even helped me paint—the guys took out some of the rotten treads on the staircase. Apparently the wood was so deteriorated that it was only a matter of time before I put my whole foot through the steps."

Shifting impatiently, Olivia frowned. "Can we skip the Bob Vila details, please?"

"I'm trying to give you a bit of backstory here, okay? Build up the dramatic tension," Harris stated good-naturedly. "Anyway, about fifteen minutes ago, one of the workmen removed a tread near the landing and guess what?"

Olivia didn't enjoy guessing games. "He got a splinter?"

"He found a secret compartment carved *in* the step. The preexisting hollow space had been enlarged, and inside, there was a metal thermos. An old one, from the forties or fifties. You could tell just by looking at it that it had some serious age to it."

Harris had managed to capture Olivia's attention. Kamila and Ramses were forgotten in the face of such interesting news. "Was there anything inside the thermos?"

"Yep. I unscrewed the top half thinking I'd discover some sixty-year-old petri dish of mold and gunk, but I found an unbelievably well-preserved painting instead! A beautiful landscape of a snowy forest was rolled up and tucked into that metal thermos. There are some words on the back too, but they're pretty faint and I need to look at them more closely." Harris's words were tumbling out. "That's why I called you. What should I do about the painting? What if it's valuable?"

Glancing at her watch, Olivia decided she had plenty of time to write later that afternoon. "I'm coming over."

The two workmen from Clyde's crew were taking an early lunch break when Olivia pulled up in front of the bungalow. Recognizing Haviland, the men offered him a few slices of turkey and ham, which the poodle wolfed down as though he hadn't already eaten a full breakfast at Grumpy's.

"Don't be a glutton," Olivia scolded fondly and then told him he was free to explore the woods surrounding the bungalow. Despite her desire to rush inside the house, she paused to exchange small talk with the workmen. Acquaintances in Oyster Bay never passed one another by without demonstrating this courtesy. Often the cause of slow-moving shop lines, traffic jams, and other such delays, it was simply the way things were in the small southern town.

Finally, Olivia used the pretense that she was eager to check out their handiwork in Harris's kitchen to get away.

"Your money's been well spent, Ms. Olivia," one of the men called after her. "Looks like a whole new room now."

Olivia thanked him and hastened into the house, where she found Harris at his desk in the living room, the painting spread out on the clean wood surface. He'd used some heavy books as paperweights, but Olivia could still see the creases in the painting as a result of being rolled up for so many years.

Harris moved to the side to give Olivia room. Instead of bending over the painting, which reminded her of an ancient Japanese scroll in its dimensions—it was at least two feet long but no more than a foot wide—she sat down in the desk chair and slowly absorbed the scene.

At first, it didn't seem very remarkable. Olivia wouldn't normally find a snowy forest, a frozen stream, and a small cabin in the distance compelling, but the painting was multilayered.

The artist had made the left-hand side feel hostile and cold. Glacial blues blended into desolate gray, and the stark tree branches were sharp and brittle. Shards of ice poked at sinister angles from the rock-strewn stream, but as the viewer's eye traveled to the right, the forest grew more inviting. The pine trees were enveloped in cloaks of feathery white snow, and the frozen water was glassy and calm. Then, on a slight rise toward the upper right, was the cabin itself. Smoke curled from the chimney and light poured from the single window. There was also a sliver of yellow beneath the door, casting a welcoming beam onto the packed snow.

Olivia could imagine a weary traveler raising his eyes to the sight of home. She could almost feel the heat of a wood-burning stove and the scents of bread baking or a stew bubbling over an open flame. A loved one waited within. Sanctuary could be had there, in the cabin on that gentle slope.

The painting could have been set anytime within the century, and though Olivia was no expert, even her untrained eye could see that it was clearly not the work of an amateur.

She noticed a symbol in the bottom right-hand corner but couldn't make sense of it. "Did you try to look this up on the computer?"

Harris nodded. "Couldn't find a thing, but I'll try again later. Check out the back."

Carefully removing the books from the painting's corners, Olivia turned the paper over. She accepted a flashlight from Harris and swept the beam across its surface. Along the top, someone had lightly written a few words in pencil. The cursive looked masculine to Olivia, but the sentiment could have been expressed by either gender.

My darling, soon we will have togetherness. I will make us a life.

"Interesting syntax," Olivia remarked. She gently turned the paper over again. "The painting is both captivating and well executed." She turned to Harris. "Listen, I'm going to Raleigh in the morning to meet with the PR firm I hired to publicize The Bayside Crab House. If you'd like, I could make it a point to stop by the North Carolina Museum of Art. I'm certain someone on staff could tell us more about this painting. If it's worthless, then you can hang it on your wall and enjoy your discovery. If it's valuable, you need to know everything you can about its provenance before you decide what to do with it."

Harris looked relieved. "I knew you'd have the answer. Do you want to see where it was hidden?"

Olivia grinned. "Of course."

The two friends peered inside the empty space hollowed out in the step below the second-story landing.

Whoever had created the extended niche had little skill with carpentry. The edges of the hole were uneven and the interior was covered by tool marks.

"Not very neat, were they?" Harris's eyes gleamed. "I imagine this person sneaking out in the middle of the night or when the house was empty and chipping away at the space bit by bit." He pointed at the landing. "The carpet has a seam here, so it would have been easy to peel back, do a little novice woodworking, and replace. This little fantasy only holds water if the stairs were carpeted back then."

Olivia smiled at his vision. "I like the picture you've created. Perhaps the novice woodworker was a woman. I see her in a flannel nightgown, hiding a small hand saw in the fold of her robe." She touched the scarred wood. "But why hide this painting? And whose handwriting is on the back?"

"I don't know, but it sounds like a love story to me," Harris murmured, his cheeks tinged with pink.

Observing her friend's wistful expression, Olivia patted him on the shoulder. "With a little luck, we'll discover what part this painting plays in your narrative."

Olivia tarried a little while longer to view the handsome tile in the kitchen and to praise Harris on the paint color he'd chosen for the room. The calm tones of the heron blue walls combined with the white cabinets and slate floor looked clean and contemporary.

Whistling for Haviland, she was about to take leave of the proud homeowner when she was struck by a thought. "I forgot to ask. What did Nick Plumley say about your manuscript?"

"Oh, he took it with him. He read a page or two while he was here, but then he stopped and offered to help me paint. He said it would be good for him to do some physical labor and that I could use the time to question him about the publishing industry."

Olivia hid her skepticism. "How generous. And he was gone before the thermos was found?"

"Yep. Poor guy missed all the excitement. He could probably have dreamed up a whole book about it too." Harris brightened. "But he took my manuscript and said he'd have something for me when the Bayside Book Writers meet this weekend."

"It certainly promises to be one of our most interesting sessions," Olivia remarked with a wry grin. "And we've had our share of interesting, haven't we?"

The next morning, Olivia and Haviland embarked on the two-and-a-half-hour trek to the capital city. Olivia disliked driving to the PR firm because the office was located off the inner beltway, requiring several complex maneuvers on more than one highway to reach.

Despite the inconvenience, Olivia was very satisfied with the firm's work. They'd gotten the word out on The Boot Top Bistro, helping it become a required stop for those with a taste for haute cuisine traveling to the coast.

The firm had drawn up a plan to target a wider audience for The Bayside Crab House, and Olivia examined with approval the ads that would appear in national magazines and on billboards lining Interstate 95. The advertisements were vibrant and appealing and created the same effect as Kim's menu design. They made the viewer feel like an amazing dining experience was waiting to be had at The Bayside Crab House restaurant and that to pass up a chance to visit would be to miss out not only on fabulous food, but also on an evening of unadulterated fun.

"These are good," Olivia stated, studying the images once more. "You've captured the freshness of the seafood, the beauty of the waterfront view, and the lively ambience." She set the folder containing the proposed magazine ads back on the conference table and rose. "Thank you. I'll be in touch regarding the autumn campaign."

One of the junior executives walked her to the Range Rover, keeping a safe distance from Haviland, because no matter how many times Olivia had made assurances that the poodle didn't shed, the dapper young man was fearful of getting black fur on his tan business suit. He did open Haviland's door, however, and handed Olivia a package of dog treats. As soon as he'd said good-bye and disappeared into the office building, she strolled a few feet up the sidewalk and dumped them into a trash can.

Inside the car, Haviland shot Olivia a dirty look. "I won't let you eat that chemical crap. *Your* treats are made from all-natural ingredients." She cupped his snout in her palm. "Don't worry, Captain. I have some lovely dried lamb for you to snack on while I'm meeting with the curator."

Appeased, Haviland stuck his head out the open window and enjoyed the blast of warm air as Olivia headed toward Blue Ridge Road and the vast campus of the North Carolina Museum of Art.

The museum was relatively new. Its buildings and outdoor sculptures sparkled in the sunshine. Olivia had attended the opening gala and had also donated a generous sum of money when plans were first being laid to build the finest art museum in the state.

Right from the start, Olivia had admired the renderings of the aluminum structure that would house millions of dollars of paintings, sculptures, photography, prints, and textiles. With floor-to-ceiling windows and a roof punctuated by hundreds of skylights, the exhibit halls were roomy and had enough natural light to allow the true essence of each piece of art to show through.

Haviland was not permitted inside the museum, and though Olivia was reluctant to leave him in the car, she knew that a few minutes alone with a water bowl and a pile of lamb treats wouldn't kill him. She parked in the shade, put the windows down halfway, told the poodle she wouldn't be long, and collected Harris's painting.

The moment she stepped into the cool building, she was immediately tempted by the posters announcing a pair of current special exhibits. One gallery boasted a collection of Audubon's works while another featured a modern collection of video art. Silently vowing to return another time, Olivia informed a volunteer that she had an appointment with Shala Knowles. The volunteer made a quick call and then asked Olivia to follow her to the back of the museum where the offices were located.

Olivia had expected the curator's space to be stuffed full of books and paintings, for the desk to be covered with artsy knickknacks and strewn with disheveled piles of paperwork. She'd pictured Shala Knowles as a female version of Professor Indiana Jones—bespectacled, disorganized, and surrounded by unusual objects. She couldn't have been more mistaken.

The office was meticulously neat. There was a sleek chrome desk, a pair of black leather side chairs, and a drafting table. One wall was occupied by a bookcase containing art reference tomes of all shapes and sizes while the space above the drafting table displayed a series of black-and-white engravings of geisha girls.

Shala herself looked like she'd stepped from the pages of *Vogue*. Tall and voluptuous, she flaunted her curves in a belted shirtdress of off-white cotton. A leopard-print pashmina was draped across one shoulder and tucked beneath the belt. As she came forward to shake hands with Olivia, the light streaming through the office windows illuminated bright strands of copper in her layered hair.

As Olivia took Shala's hand, she caught a delicate hint of camellia-scented perfume.

So much for my absentminded professor image, Olivia thought with amusement.

"I've been looking forward to your arrival since I woke up this morning," Shala told Olivia, her eyes glimmering with anticipation.

"I was surprised to have gotten an appointment so easily," Olivia confessed and laid the painting, protected between parchment paper and two pieces of clean cardboard, on the drafting table. "What did I say on the phone to capture your interest?"

Shala slipped on a pair of glasses with chic red frames and reached for a journal on her bookshelf.

"It's the signature mark you described." She opened the journal and pointed to an enlarged image of the same symbol Olivia and Harris had seen on the bottom corner of the found watercolor.

"That's what it looks like!" Olivia felt a growing excitement but didn't want to hear anything else in case the painting turned out to be a fake. She gestured at the cardboard. "Please, feel free to examine it."

The curator put on a pair of white gloves and then unwrapped the package with infinite care. She used felt-lined paperweights to anchor the watercolor's four corners and then backed away, staring down on the scene. She stood like this for several minutes, and Olivia sensed that the rest of the world had ceased to exist for Shala Knowles. Olivia felt the same way when she was writing about Kamila.

Finally, the curator leaned in closer to the painting. Using a large magnifying sheet, she examined the work section by section, spending the longest amount of time on the signature symbol on the bottom right-hand corner.

When she straightened, she was smiling. "I am quite confident that this painting is the work of Heinrich Kamler. His subject matter, technique, and signature are unmistakable. If you look closely, you can see that the symbol is made of two intertwining letters, an *H* and a *K*. This is a *very exciting* discovery!" Her face was glowing. "And you say this was hidden in a thermos beneath a stair tread?"

Olivia nodded. "The house is a 1930s bungalow. When my friend moved in, he had the carpet over the stairs taken out. Quite a bit of the wood covered up by the carpet had rotted, and when one of those damaged treads was removed, the thermos was revealed." She gestured at the journal. "Who is this Heinrich Kamler?"

Shala indicated Olivia should make herself comfortable in one of the black leather chairs. "Would you care for some coffee?"

"No, thank you. I've left my dog out in the car, so I can't stay much longer."

The curator seemed troubled by this fact. "Oh, dear.

I was hoping to take measurements and photographs. I'd also like to get a second opinion from a colleague before you leave." She grew thoughtful. "What if we had lunch outside? I could tell you all about Heinrich Kamler and your dog could stretch his legs. If you're willing, my colleague could examine the painting while we eat."

"That would be fine."

Smiling, Shala presented Olivia with a menu from the museum's eatery, Iris. She then phoned her fellow curator and made arrangements for him to view the watercolor. Olivia was impressed by the quality of food offered by the café and had a hard time choosing between two tempting dishes. In the end, she selected a sandwich made of balsamic roasted portabella, thyme, spring leeks, and Gruyère served on ciabatta flatbread.

Haviland, delighted to be sprung from the Range Rover so quickly, showed his gratitude by being especially obedient. Olivia knew the poodle longed to explore the museum's extensive grounds, but he contented himself with the picnic area and was very careful to keep his distance from other museums visitors.

Once Shala had eaten a few bites of her artichoke and grilled shrimp salad, she laid down her fork and took a sip of iced tea. "Heinrich Kamler was a German prisoner of war. He was captured when his U-boat sank off the North Carolina coast in the early days of World War II."

Olivia nearly choked on her sandwich. She took a large swallow of San Pellegrino and managed to say, "Was he interred at the New Bern Camp?"

It was Shala's turn to be surprised. "Why, yes. As it sounds like you're familiar with the camp, you may also know that both the guards and the local population treated the prisoners quite well. They were encouraged to learn Americanisms such as democracy and capitalism by creating goods and selling them. I'm not sure which products Heinrich and his friends first crafted, but he eventually earned enough to purchase painting supplies. His most famous works were of the camp itself, but he also created stunning landscapes of his home in Germany. His village bordered the Black Forest, and I believe that's the scene your friend's painting depicts."

Olivia's thoughts were racing. Had Nick Plumley known about the painting? Was it the reason he repeatedly sought access to Harris's home? But how could he know of its existence when it had remained hidden for so many years?

"Are Kamler's paintings valuable?" Olivia asked the curator.

"Indeed. Your friend's is worth at least twenty thousand dollars. If placed in auction, it could bring double that amount. Maybe triple." Shala speared a shrimp on her fork. "It will certainly generate a buzz. A fresh Kamler work after all this time? I'm certain our director will try to acquire the painting for the museum, and he won't be alone. The wolves of the art world will gather the moment the news gets out."

Olivia wondered how Harris would respond when she informed him that he had discovered a genuine treasure. "What happened to Kamler?"

Shala's attractive face clouded. "For some reason, he and another prisoner decided to escape. He killed one of the guards—a knife with his initials carved into the handle was found protruding from the victim's back.

Kamler just disappeared afterward." She pushed pieces of lettuce around in her bowl. "Who knows? He could still be alive today. A very old man, yes, but it's possible. He was only twenty-one when he escaped. Seventeen in 1941. That's when the U-boat sank."

"Fascinating," Olivia said and meant it. After all, Shala had just described the pivotal scene of Nick Plumley's novel, *The Barbed Wire Flower*. "How many of his paintings exist?"

"Fifty-two." Shala grinned. "Unless there are more in your friend's staircase."

Olivia returned the smile while simultaneously thinking, *Harris needs to comb every inch of that house*.

Their lunch finished, Olivia returned Haviland to the Range Rover and accompanied Shala inside to collect the painting. Several museum employees were gathered in the curator's office when they returned. The air was electric.

"It's genuine!" a man stated gleefully. "And I'm intrigued by the note on the back." His eyes met Olivia's. "Did Heinrich Kamler have a romantic attachment to someone who lived in the house where this was discovered?"

Shala edged forward to examine the script. "I was so caught up in examining the front that I never turned it over. Jeez, you'd think I was still in grad school."

"I don't know much about the people who lived there, but believe me, I plan to conduct some research as soon as possible," Olivia answered the man's question.

"Please keep us in the loop," he pleaded and began to package the painting. After placing it between sheets of acid-free paper, he then secured it on both sides with white cardstock and slid the bundle into a zippered canvas bag. "Consider the bag a gift. Perhaps the owner would loan us this piece for our Arts of the Coast exhibit next winter in return."

"I'll pass on the request," Olivia promised and took her leave. She was eager to return to the quiet of her car and to spend two hours ruminating over the connection between Nick Plumley and Heinrich Kamler.

As she roared west down I-40, she couldn't stop thinking about the note on the back of the painting. It made sense that the syntax seemed a little off. After all, if the author of the brief lines was Kamler, then his primary language wasn't English. It was German.

"A bestselling novelist paying house calls on a young and naive aspiring writer, a valuable painting hidden under a stair tread, and a mysterious romance. Perhaps even a forbidden one? Local girl falls for German prisoner?" Olivia glanced at Haviland, who was sniffing at the salt-tinged air with eagerness. They were almost home.

Olivia reached over and placed a hand on the back of the poodle's neck. "Captain, why do the most interesting things happen just when I am about to open a new restaurant?"

She was in the middle of an internal debate over whether to start digging through town records when her phone rang. The dashboard display, which included GPS and a hands-free phone, flashed Hudson's number in electric blue digits.

"Hello?" Olivia shouted over the rush of air streaming in through Haviland's open window.

"It's Hudson. Kim's in labor." Olivia heard fear in his rough voice, and it was not the kind experienced by all nervous fathers-to-be. It was far more acute. "She's asking for you. There's something wrong with the baby and she wants you here. Please, Olivia. Hurry."

"I'm coming," Olivia replied. "Hang in there, Hudson. I'm coming."

Chapter 6

Faith is an oasis in the heart which will never be reached by the caravan of thinking.

—KAHLIL GIBRAN

For the first time in her life, Olivia didn't know what to do with Haviland. She couldn't bring him into the hospital and she couldn't leave him sitting in the Range Rover for the second time in one day. Desperate, she pulled in front of The Canine Cottage and raced inside with the befuddled poodle.

One of the groomers smiled at her over the sudsy back of a Great Dane. "Hi, Ms. Limoges. We didn't expect to see you today."

Olivia hesitated. She hated begging for favors and it was plain to see that the groomers were very busy. "I'm in a tight spot. My sister-in-law is having a baby and I can't waltz Haviland through the labor and delivery unit. He's been in the car all day and he's hot and tired." She paused. "I never expected my sister-in-law to ask for me. I think something's wrong . . ." She took a deep breath and finished the thought. "When my brother called, I could tell he was terrified. Can you help?"

The young woman touched the Dane on the flank and walked around the tub. "Don't you worry about a thing. Haviland can stay here until we close. We'll pamper him so much that he won't even notice you're gone."

"Thank you *so* much. I won't forget this." Olivia kissed Haviland on the snout and rushed out to her car.

When she reached the hospital, she found Hudson prowling around the labor and delivery waiting room like a caged leopard. Caitlyn was there as well. Clutching a picture book in one hand and a ragged Barbie in the other, she seemed to be trying to shrink into her chair. Her knees were drawn up to her chest in a protective gesture, and she watched her father through dark, worried eyes.

Olivia grabbed her brother's hand. "How's Kim?"

He squeezed hers in return, the desperate pressure of his conveying his distress. "It's not her. It's the baby. Something's not right with his heart."

"Why aren't you back there?" Olivia asked without judgment.

Hudson shook his head. "They took Kim into an operating room for a C-section. I couldn't leave Caitlyn out here all alone." Hudson swallowed hard. "A doctor stopped by a few minutes ago to explain our 'options.' There's some kind of surgery that could fix the baby's heart, but they can't do it here. I gotta tell you—I didn't understand what the hell the man was talking about. It was like he was talking in another language." Still holding on to Olivia's hand, he nearly crushed her bones with the force of his grip. "Help us. Please."

A lump formed in Olivia's throat, but now was not the time to get emotional. "It'll be okay, Hudson." She reclaimed her throbbing hand. "Go comfort your daughter. She knows something's wrong. I'll go back there and find out exactly what's going on and what needs to be done."

Olivia paused only long enough to put her hand on Caitlyn's shoulder. "Hey. Long day, huh?"

Caitlyn nodded.

"Sit tight for a little while longer and then you and I will hunt down some ice cream. I hear this hospital has a pretty cool cafeteria." Olivia did her best to sound calm and in control. "First, I want to check on your mom. Be back soon."

The little girl didn't say anything, but her body relaxed a fraction. She unfolded her legs and opened her book. Hudson took the seat next to his daughter and pretended to be interested in the illustration of a princess choosing which accessories to wear with her gold and ivory ball gown. Caitlyn leaned toward her father and whispered "Once upon a time . . ."

Olivia pressed a button on the wall and announced herself to the nurse on duty. A buzzer sounded and the door leading into the ward was unlocked. Olivia squared her shoulders and stepped through. She walked briskly up a hallway lined with dozens of photographs of smiling babies, but she kept her gaze locked straight ahead. At the moment, it was disconcerting to see the apple-cheeked faces of those healthy infants.

"I'm here to see Kim Hudson," she informed the nurse seated behind a low counter, and then quickly added, "She's been asking for me."

The nurse made a quick phone call and then suggested Olivia take a seat, but Olivia shook off the suggestion and remained where she was. When the nurse looked up from her paperwork, she must have realized that Olivia wasn't going to sit and wait quietly.

"I'd like to know if my sister-in-law is out of surgery," Olivia said, looming over the counter.

Another nurse approached the desk. She smiled at Olivia and said, "Mrs. Hudson is doing just fine. She's in her room. I was heading in that direction anyway, so you can come on back with me."

Olivia felt a slight loosening of the knot that had formed in the pit of her stomach. "And the baby?"

The nurse walked briskly down a silent corridor, her rubber-soled shoes making no noise on the white laminate flooring. "They're going to take him to Pitt Memorial, but I'll let the pediatric nurse explain everything."

Him? Olivia slowed her pace. A boy. Before she had time to take this in, the nurse knocked lightly on a door marked with the name Salter and entered. "Mrs. Hudson? Your sister-in-law's here!" she announced brightly.

Seeing Olivia, Kim's face immediately crumpled. Tears ran in rivulets from her eyes onto the stiff white pillow. "Oh, thank God. I don't understand what's wrong with my baby! Why can't I see him?"

Olivia had little skill when it came to bedside manner. Trusting her instinct, she laid a hand on Kim's arm and promised to do anything she could to help. As she spoke, she spied an African American woman wearing a scrub top covered with pink and purple hearts. She was standing quietly near the window, the afternoon light casting a white corona around her head, giving her an angelic appearance. She walked around the bed and introduced herself to Olivia as Dru Ann Love. Her name and the heart design on her shirt were certainly comforting, but it was the woman's sense of calm that inspired confidence.

"Mrs. Hudson asked for me to explain things after you arrived. I don't have much time, but I'll explain as quickly and succinctly as I can," Nurse Love stated plainly and looked at Kim. "Your son was born with a congenital heart defect. It's called atrial septal defect. In layman's terms, it basically means that there's a hole in his heart."

Kim made a whimpering sound, and Olivia stroked her arm, her gaze never leaving Nurse Love's warm brown eyes.

"In a normal heart," the nurse continued, "blood that is low in oxygen passes through the right ventricle and into the lungs where it receives oxygen. These two chambers of the heart are separated by a thin wall called the atrial septum. Because your nephew has a hole in his atrial septum, the oxygen-rich blood is mixing with the oxygen-poor blood, and the lungs are receiving an increased amount of blood. Basically, they're getting too much blood."

"And this doesn't show up in utero?" Olivia asked.

Nurse Love shook her head. "Not always. Sometimes pediatricians discover the condition when they hear a heart murmur and sometimes the stress of labor makes it obvious, but the bottom line is that your nephew requires a pediatric cardiologist and we don't have one at this hospital. As we speak, he's being prepped for transport to Pitt Memorial in Greenville. They have an excellent pediatric cardiology department there."

Kim tried to sit up in bed. Wincing in pain, she cried, "I have to be with him!"

Olivia didn't need a medical degree to know that

her sister-in-law wasn't going anywhere. The last thing she wanted to do was volunteer to take her place. To sit in an ambulance with a newborn infant stuck full of wires and tubes and requiring emergency surgery was Olivia's idea of hell. The truth was that Olivia Limoges was afraid of babies. She'd never held one in her life. Children were disconcerting enough, but a baby was the epitome of helpless fragility. Still, she couldn't ignore the agony on Kim's face, and she'd promised her brother that she'd do anything to help.

"There, there," Nurse Love tried to soothe Kim. "I'll be with him every second of the drive and for the surgery too. We've already made a connection. I just came from his room. He's quite a handsome little man."

Kim collapsed against the pillow. "But he needs one of his parents. I'm stuck here and Hudson has to look after Caitlyn." She shot Olivia an apologetic look. "She likes you, but I've never left her with anyone before. I don't think she'd handle it too good."

The nurse came forward with a clipboard and a pen. The family's arrangements were secondary to the health of her tiny patient. "I need you to sign some consent forms, Mrs. Salter. Or would you prefer I let your husband handle this so you can rest? We need to be on our way now."

Kim glanced at the pile of forms and blanched. "I don't even know if our insurance will cover the surgery."

"Trust me, you're covered." Olivia took the clipboard from Nurse Love's hands. "I'll take these to Hudson, explain what's happening, and then drive to Greenville."

There, she'd spoken the words and there was no rescinding the offer now, no matter how uncomfortable it made her.

When Kim's eyes filled with fresh tears, Olivia knew that she'd done the right thing. This woman was her sister by marriage, and her half brother waited in silent anguish on the other side of the hospital. Her young niece was confused and frightened and they had no one else to turn to. They needed her.

Olivia felt a warmth spread through her chest. These people *needed* her. They were her family. In that moment, she believed she'd have gone to any length for them but knew there was no time to express how this realization made her feel. Instead, she told Kim that she'd be in touch and then gave her a quick kiss on the cheek.

"Wait." Nurse Love reclaimed her clipboard and handed it to Kim. "There's one form you *do* need to complete to get a birth certificate. Have you chosen a name for your son?"

Kim accepted the pen. "Before I went into labor, Hudson and still I couldn't agree on one . . ."

"Pick the name you liked," Olivia ordered. "You're the one with staples in your belly. Hudson will accept your choice."

"Kyle, after my father." Kim wrote swiftly. "And then Anders, my maiden name. Kyle Anders Salter. And I do believe I'll call him Anders. He's got to grow into Kyle." She handed the clipboard back to the nurse, her lips trembling. "Please give Anders a kiss for me. Tell him that his mommy loves him. That I'll be there as soon as I can. Tell him I'll be praying that I can hold him soon . . ." The rest of her words turned into sobs.

Olivia escaped from the mother's heart-rending grief. She knew that Kim desperately wanted to be with her baby, but necessity required her to settle for Olivia's presence instead.

With the weight of her obligation lying heavily on her shoulders, Olivia strode out to the waiting room and explained to Hudson why his son was being transferred to another hospital. Before he could ask a single question, she assured him that she planned to drive to Greenville as soon as she made arrangements for Haviland.

"Your wife is terrified," she whispered to Hudson before leaving. "Go to her. I'll call you the minute your son comes out of surgery. Don't worry." She gave him a brave smile. "It's amazing what doctors can fix these days."

Relieved to see Hudson take Caitlyn gently by the hand and turn toward the labor and delivery ward, Olivia pulled out her phone and began to make the first of many important calls.

It was nearly midnight by the time Olivia returned to the quiet and comfort of her own home.

Under any other circumstances, Olivia would have deemed it downright rude to call Diane, Haviland's vet and Flynn McNulty's girlfriend, at eleven forty at night in order to pick up her dog, but after the day she'd had, she didn't feel a single twinge of regret. She needed Haviland.

"At least *you* had a nice dinner," Olivia told the poodle, who was giving her the canine version of a cold shoulder by averting his gaze. "I feasted on mystery meat from the hospital cafeteria."

Haviland groaned and trotted away.

Ignoring the blinking light on her answering machine, Olivia wearily climbed the stairs, changed into her nightgown, and fell into bed. She expected sleep to come immediately, but her mind was still pacing the halls of Pitt Memorial Hospital.

Nurse Love had been a gem. True to her word, she'd scrubbed in and stayed with Anders throughout his surgery. Olivia wiled away the hours watching CNN, flipping through insipid women's magazines, and drinking cup after cup of watery coffee, but the dedicated pediatric nurse left the operating room only to let Olivia know that the surgery was complete and that her nephew was doing fine.

"How long will the recovery take?" Olivia had asked.

"It varies. Some children go home after two weeks, some three. There's really no science to this sort of thing." She removed the blue cloth cap she'd worn for the past four hours and ran a hand over her short, black hair. "Do you want to see him?"

Olivia shook her head. "Not with all those tubes and things," she admitted. "I just want to be able to call his parents, say that he's doing well and that they needn't worry, and go home."

Nurse Love smiled knowingly. "His mother's going to ask if you saw him. Trust me." She put a hand on Olivia's shoulder. "You've been sitting here for hours wondering about your nephew. Now come meet him face-to-face."

Incredibly nervous, Olivia had waited until the baby was admitted to the NICU and, after being given instructions on how to wash her hands and forearms and dress herself in a sterile gown, she'd entered a room populated by nurses and miniscule babies in incubators.

Olivia had never been so frightened in her life. Her navy eyes grew round as they took in the sight of the tiny arms and legs of the diapered forms. Even the crying sounded undeveloped. They were more like bird cries than the lusty howls she'd heard from full-sized babies in the grocery store. These were pitiful, like the mews of a kitten. Olivia wondered if these miniscule infants would all make it, and the thought redoubled her fear and discomfort.

"Jesus," Olivia breathed.

Nurse Love put a hand on her shoulder. "Yes, I do believe our Lord and Savior pays special attention to these little ones. Come on, you're not the only person who's been scared to death by the NICU. Look at it this way. Most of these babies just decided to move up their arrival dates. They're not fat and pink like the full-term ones, but they will be soon enough." She stopped in front of an incubator bearing a paper sign that read, "Salter, K."

Olivia had exhaled slowly. Here he was, the child that had been taken from her sister-in-law's womb mere hours ago and had spent the first day of his life in an operating room instead of cradled in his mother's arms. Olivia reached her fingers toward the letters of the baby's name, and then hastily withdrew them.

"My daughter tells people that babies are brought here to finish cooking," Nurse Love had said with a quiet chuckle. "Look at Anders. He weighs over seven pounds. In here, that makes him a giant. He's going to do great."

Olivia had forced her gaze down to the still form of her nephew. He slept on his back, arms splayed wide, eyes closed. Like most of the babies in the room, his body was connected to a network of tubes and wires, and Olivia's heart ached at the sight.

"You can put your hand in that hole if you want to touch him." Nurse Love had pointed at the side of the incubator.

Olivia had been astounded that she really did want to reach out, to make a physical connection with the little being in his nest of white cotton. Timidly, she'd stretched her fingers forward, touching the blanket lining the incubator and then, the skin of her nephew's arm. She stared at his small fingers, noticing the long and nearly transparent fingernails. They reminded her of dragonfly wings.

"Oh, my God," she murmured, her eyes filling with tears.

Nurse Love had sighed at the scene. "I never get tired of watching people do that for the first time."

The women fell silent, wordlessly observing the rapid rise and fall of Anders' chest.

"I'm ready to go now," Olivia had whispered. "I can't *do* anything for him."

"You already did," the nurse had assured her. "You were here. On some level, through some wonderful and mysterious means, he knows it too."

Brushing the moisture from her cheeks, Olivia had cast one more glance at her sleeping nephew and hurriedly left the ward.

After calling Kim with the news that Anders' surgery had been a success and that he was resting peacefully in the care of a team of skilled doctors and nurses, Olivia had driven over to the closest hotel offering suites with kitchens and paid in advance for a two-week stay. "I need a list of area restaurants that make deliveries," she told the manager. She then drove to the nearest grocery store, where she bought a cartload of food and sundries, including several coloring books and Barbie dolls, and put everything away in the suite. Lastly, she placed a few hundred dollars in cash in the room's safe.

It was her intention to bring Kim the room key when she was released from the hospital in two days' time. Kim had already informed her that Hudson refused to shirk his duties at The Bayside Crab House during its first weekend in operation, so she and Caitlyn would stay in Greenville until Anders could go home.

Olivia had pointed out that the assistant chefs could handle the grand opening but was honestly relieved to know that Hudson would be in the kitchen later that weekend.

Now, in her dark bedroom, Olivia tried to relax, but failed.

"If I don't get some sleep tonight," she spoke to Haviland, "it won't matter how many chefs are in the kitchen. I've got to bring my A game to tomorrow's staff meeting." Olivia thumped the space on the bed beside her. "Come here, Captain. Chase those hospital images away, would you?"

Haviland jumped onto the bed, licked her cheek, and snuggled against her, sighing contentedly. As Olivia listened to him breathe, the sights and sounds of the tiny babies in the NICU finally released their hold on her.

The next morning, she stood with coffee cup in hand and listened to her messages. There were half a dozen calls pertaining to Friday's grand opening, one from Harris asking what she'd discovered at the art museum, and a surprise call from Nick Plumley. Apparently, he was still renting the house down the beach from hers and said to stop by anytime she wanted.

Olivia copied down his number from her caller ID and then dialed.

When Plumley answered, she immediately apologized for phoning so early in the day. "It's just that I have a historical object here that you might be interested in seeing," she explained.

"Don't tease me," he complained good-naturedly. "I haven't even had my coffee yet."

Olivia hesitated. She wanted to see Nick's face when he first looked at the painting, but something prompted her to show more of her hand right now. "Harris found a watercolor hidden inside one of his stair treads. Turns out, the artist was Heinrich Kamler. Does that name ring a bell?"

She heard a sharp intake of breath over the line. The name definitely meant something to Plumley. "Is there a connection between this artist and your sequel? Didn't you already write about how he murdered a prison guard in order to make his escape?"

There was a long moment of silence. "May I see the painting today? How about now?" The eagerness in Plumley's voice was transparent.

"Sure," Olivia replied brightly. "I'll be there in fifteen minutes, but I expect an answer to my question first."

"Kamler's story might not be finished," Nick murmured cryptically, and Olivia could sense that a measure of anxiety, perhaps even a little desperation, tinged the writer's mumbled words. Soon, she would discover why Heinrich Kamler was so important to him. Was it possible Kamler was still alive?

Olivia glanced at the canvas tote containing Harris's painting. "Walk time, Captain," she told Haviland and jogged upstairs to put on a pair of shorts and a T-shirt.

Outside, the air bore all the signs of summer. The edge of crispness lent to the breeze by spring had been replaced by the heavy breath of humidity. Memorial weekend was supposed to be hot and sunny, and Olivia predicted that both of her eateries would be packed with tourists.

She gazed out at the sparkling ocean as she walked, feeling incredibly distanced from yesterday's highways and hospital rooms. Haviland splashed about in the surf, eagerly searching for gulls or crabs to chase, but the beach was quiet, as though its creatures still slumbered in their burrows of damp sand.

Reluctant to disturb the serenity, Olivia took out her cell phone and dialed Harris's number. When he picked up, he shouted a hello over the throb of hip-hop music. "I'm heading to work!" Abruptly, the music stopped. "Sorry, this is how I get fired up for the day. A cup of joe and some P. Diddy."

Having no idea who P. Diddy was, Olivia repeated what she'd learned during her visit with Shala Knowles.

"Holy crap!" Harris exclaimed. "Good thing I'm at a red light or I might have just driven into the ditch! That little winter scene could be worth twenty grand?"

"Yes. In fact, I believe the curator was being cautious in her estimation. She indicated that if the painting were sold at auction, it could bring even more." Olivia grinned, imagining her friend digesting this bit of happy news. "What are you going to do?"

Harris exhaled loudly. "Dunno. I wouldn't even know which auction company to take it to."

"The curator gave me a name. Before you sell the painting, however, she and her colleagues would like to examine it further. They're also willing to give you a document stating that they believe the artist is Heinrich Kamler."

"Sweet!" Harris declared. "I've got to tell Nick about this! He probably knows all about this guy after researching him for *The Barbed Wire Flower.*"

Olivia's mouth curled into a wry smile. "I'm headed to his place as we speak. I didn't think you'd mind if I let him have a look at your soon-to-be-famous painting."

"Not at all," Harris stated with his customary affability.

Leaving her friend to his rosy visions of newfound wealth, Olivia pocketed her phone and picked up a stick. She hurled it into the water and watched Haviland lunge into the waves in pursuit.

As she paused to wait for the poodle, a memory of her return home after her father's death crept into her head. Once her father was gone, Olivia had fled Okracoke Island immediately. She'd called Rawlings and asked him to meet her on the beach in front of the lighthouse. Without requiring her to explain where she'd been, he'd simply registered the need in her voice and had been there, waiting for her.

She remembered seeing his figure in the shadow of the lighthouse and feeling such a burning impatience to reach him, to be held by him, that her longing felt like pain. In fact, when the shoreline was close enough, she'd swung her leg over the side of the boat and leapt into the sea. Rawlings had rushed toward her at the same time, and their bodies met, knee-deep in cold water. Wet and shaking, they'd grabbed hold of each other and kissed hungrily, tasting salt on each other's lips.

They'd ignored Haviland's barks and the shouts of the boat captain, pressing ever closer together, their melded bodies illuminated by a swath of moonlight. In that moment, the police chief who wore tacky Hawaiian shirts, drank chocolate milk, took up oil painting as a hobby, and lost his wife of over twenty years to cancer had filled up the emptiness in Olivia's heart.

Now, standing near the spot where he'd waited for her that night, Olivia knelt down and scooped up a handful of warm sand. She watched it flow from her palm, the warmth as fleeting as those hours she'd shared with Rawlings.

Wrapped in blankets, they'd curled up on her living room sofa. As the fire in her stone hearth crackled, she'd told him everything that had happened on Okracoke. She described her father's death, the pain he'd caused her when she was a child, and her discovery that she had a half brother.

Rawlings had listened silently, stroking her hair as she spoke. She found comfort in his scent of soap and sandalwood and paint thinner, in his broad, solid chest and the tenderness of his fingers.

The next morning, she'd sent him on his way with a thermos of hot coffee and her thanks.

And she hadn't let the chief get close to her since.

"I miss him," Olivia confessed to Haviland, who had retrieved the stick and brought it back for another round of fetch. Standing up, she shouldered the canvas bag again and tossed the stick for the last time. She then increased her pace and traversed a series of dunes obscuring the path leading to Nick Plumley's rental property.

If the author had been in search of both privacy and luxury, he'd chosen the perfect house. Olivia had been inside when it had first been built and thought it magnificent, but too pretentious for her tastes. Of contemporary design, the house had been constructed with one thing in mind: the view. One could see the ocean from three of four sides. Instead of walls, the exterior was composed of floor-to-ceiling windows. The interior floor plan was also exaggeratingly open. The entire first floor was a single room interrupted by only support beams.

Olivia rang the doorbell and waited. When she heard no movement from within, she peeked in through the clear panes, but Nick Plumley didn't appear. She could easily see into the kitchen and noted the evidence of the author's breakfast—half a bagel, an apple core, and a coffee cup.

"We hardly want to start banging away if he's in the shower," Olivia said to Haviland and decided to wait for Plumley on the back patio.

After placing the canvas bag containing the painting on a wooden dining table, she settled onto a cushioned chaise lounge, crossed her legs, and sighed.

"Maybe I can come up with ideas for the rest of my chapter," she told Haviland, who had begun a round of investigative sniffing.

Ten minutes later, Olivia became too impatient to remain seated. When the doorbell went unanswered once again, she decided to peer in the windows on the side of the house, allowing her a glimpse of nearly every square foot of the lower level.

With her inquisitive poodle at her heels, Olivia followed a flagstone path around a group of low bushes, walked over a bed of raked gravel, and blatantly stared into the house.

Her eyes were immediately drawn to a splash of blue in the middle of the bleached pine wood floor. It took her a moment to understand what she was seeing, but when it became clear, she sucked in her breath and jumped away from the window.

Fumbling in her pocket, she withdrew her cell phone, cast a frightened glance over her shoulder, and dialed Rawlings' direct line.

"Good morning, Ms. Limoges," he said cordially.

"Chief, you need to get down to Nick Plumley's rental house. I think he's dead."

She took a step closer to the window and then hastily stuck the phone back in her pocket, cutting off whatever Rawlings had started to say.

Olivia raced to the front door and grabbed the handle, but the door was locked. She ran to the back door, adrenaline surging through her, but experienced the same result.

Sensing her agitation, Haviland began to bark.

"He could still be alive!" Olivia yelled, searching the ground for a large rock. There was nothing but gravel.

Desperate, she grabbed one of the patio chairs, dumped the cushion on the ground, and raised it waist high into the air. Made entirely of metal, it was cumbersome, but Olivia smashed it into the glass door with all the force she could muster.

The glass splintered but didn't break. She heaved the chair against the fractured door again and again until it crashed inward, chunks of ragged glass scattering across the floorboards, shards lethal as icicles raining everywhere.

"STAY!" Olivia shouted at Haviland and, only after being certain that he would obey, darted inside and fell to her knees alongside the prone writer.

Gently, she rolled him over and then cried out in shock. Covering her mouth with a trembling hand, she retreated.

"Too late," she whispered, her voice echoing in the light-riddled room.

Chapter 7

*Words have no power to impress the mind
without the exquisite horror of their
reality.*

—EDGAR ALLEN POE

Nick Plumley's glassy eyes were fixed on the ceiling. His mouth was misshapen, stretched unnaturally like a python expanding its jaw in order to swallow a fat rabbit. His lips were blue. A wad of paper filled the entire cavity of his mouth.

Olivia knew she should go back outside. There was nothing she could do to help the dead man, and though every fiber of her being longed to remove the papers crammed into his mouth, she knew that an influx of fresh air would provide him no relief. His lungs would never again expand or contract. They would no longer be invigorated by the sea breeze or by the sharp wind that raced ahead of a thunderstorm. The smoke from wood fires wouldn't irritate the sensitive bronchioles. They'd never feel the keen ache of being outside on a frigid February morning or tingle as they were infused by the magic of the season's first snow.

Exhaling slowly, as though she feared her own body

might be affected by the writer's immobility, Olivia tore her gaze from Nick Plumley's frozen expression of agony. As her eyes traveled down the length of his body, she noticed an angry red welt encircling his neck, just above the larynx.

Plumley was clad in a cotton robe of blue and white checks and matching boxer shorts. He was barefoot and smelled of soap. Olivia noticed that he'd yet to put on his watch and that his hair was still wet. As her eyes returned to his face, she noticed a bead of dried blood on his chin, indicating that he'd cut himself shaving.

Olivia stared at the bright red drop. It was too vivid on a face that had already taken on the waxy pallor of death. She imagined him at the mirror, a handsome man in his midfifties, wiping away the fog with the corner of a towel. After squirting a cone-shaped measure of shaving cream into his palm, he'd have spread the foam over his face, noting the contrast between its whiteness and his tanned skin. Pivoting from side to side, he would have performed the daily ritual he'd begun many years ago as a shrill-voiced, lanky teenager. He would have winced at the cut, briefly, more irritated than injured, and stuck a shred of toilet paper on the wound to soak up the initial rush of blood.

"And then someone came to the door," Olivia mused aloud. "And you let them in dressed like this. Did you recognize the killer?"

Knowing her proximity to the body could contaminate the crime scene, she tarried only long enough to examine the hardcover resting near Nick's right arm. The book had been opened toward the middle and a handful of pages had been roughly torn from the binding. The header on an intact page identified the book as *The Barbed Wire Flower*. Nick Plumley's mouth had been stuffed with pages from his own bestseller.

"Jesus," Olivia whispered and stood up. Carefully maneuvering around the shards of glass, she returned to the patio. The force of the sunshine burned her eyes, but she was grateful for its heat. The wash of light made her acutely aware of her vitality, and she threw her arms around her agitated poodle.

"It's all right," she murmured as he bathed her face with kisses. "The chief's on his way."

Olivia and Haviland walked around to the front of the house. In the lee of a nearby sand dune, they waited for the police to arrive.

Rawlings was in the lead car. He jumped out, readjusted his utility belt, unclipped his holster with the practiced flick of a finger, and strode up to Olivia. Echoing her words to Haviland, he issued a firm command. "Stay here." He then signaled to one of his men. "Please wait with Ms. Limoges."

The officer in question tried to conceal his disappointment over having to babysit a civilian, but Olivia rendered his assignment void the moment she rushed after the chief. "The front door's locked. I had to break a window around back to get in."

Rawlings stopped and turned, blood rushing to his face. "And you did that because?"

"I had to see if I could help him," Olivia stated with a calm she didn't feel. "I couldn't just sit on the patio and wonder if the man inside could be saved by CPR."

Mumbling under his breath, the chief gestured at the officers following in his wake and jogged around the side of the house. Olivia glanced at the uniformed watchdog standing beside her and said, "I'd better show the chief what I touched in there."

The young man was too eager to argue. He led the way with Haviland shadowing after him. Like most of Oyster Bay's police force, the policeman had seen the poodle inside the station several times and knew he posed no threat. "How did you end up finding the body?" he asked Olivia.

"I walked over from my place to show Mr. Plumley a painting," she explained.

The officer nodded. "And did your dog sense anything when you got here? Did he bark or seem nervous?"

Olivia reached out and touched Haviland's head. "That's an astute question, Officer . . . ?"

"Gregson, ma'am."

They rounded the corner of the building, and Olivia stopped at the edge of the patio. "Haviland didn't act like there was a malevolent presence nearby. If he had sensed any violence within the house—shouting or a physical altercation—he would have barked out a warning to me. But he didn't and that makes me think the killer was well away before we arrived."

Gregson's brows rose. "The killer, ma'am?"

Olivia pointed to the shattered door. "You'll see." She sank into a lounge chair and invited Haviland to sit in the shade of the patio's umbrella. "Don't worry, I won't move from this spot."

During the course of the next hour, officers filtered in and out of the house. Olivia listened to the sounds of their work: the rapid-fire clicking of a camera, the crackle of radios, and the slap of measuring tape laid against the bare floor.

The men and women of the Oyster Bay Police kept their voices hushed, following the chief's example. Olivia had witnessed Rawlings' demeanor at crime scenes before and knew that he demanded respect be shown to the victim at all times.

Even now, she could picture him reservedly turning out the pockets of Nick Plumley's robe or touching the stretched skin of his cheeks with his surprisingly gentle, bearlike hands.

Eventually, the coroner arrived and the body was removed. A pair of officers left to interview the neighbors. With half an acre separating the homes, Olivia doubted the men would glean any useful information, but Rawlings was methodical. Everyone living on the Point would be interviewed right away and then, when no clues were discovered, the chief would begin to widen his circle.

Impatient to provide him with her own statement, Olivia peered inside the house and saw that Rawlings was alone. He stood in the middle of the room, arms folded across his chest, head bent. He appeared to be staring at the damaged copy of *The Barbed Wire Flower*.

Car engines started in the driveway, and Olivia knew that a lone officer waited inside the remaining sedan. He would be sitting in the car for a long time, as Rawlings always lingered at a crime scene long after everyone else had left. He doled out assignments and his team leapt to work, but he chose not to focus on the raw data in the beginning of a case. His interest was in the story behind the crime.

He'd stand without speaking for a full thirty minutes in the place where violence had occurred. Whether a dank alley or a million-dollar home, he would become as still as a stone, close his eyes, and feel his way through the events leading to the crime.

Olivia watched him in silence and then eventually picked up the canvas bag containing Harris's painting and stepped across the threshold of the open door. "I moved him," she said softly. "He was facedown and I rolled him over. I couldn't know that he was beyond help until then."

He nodded, his gaze still on the book.

"May I come in?" she asked, examining the evidence of the police work. The body outline, the measurement marks on the floor, fingerprint and shoeprint dust, a scattering of sand.

"You seem to have a magnetic pull toward dead bodies, Ms. Limoges," the chief remarked, his tone unbendingly formal. "Tell me what happened."

They moved to Plumley's kitchen, and Olivia began her recitation by describing how she'd first met Nick at Grumpy's and continued by explaining the author's unusual interest in Harris's house.

"So your plan was to bring the painting here in order to elicit a response from Mr. Plumley?" Rawlings inquired.

"Yes," Olivia answered. "By this point I'd put aside the theory that he had sinister motives. In fact, I felt guilty for assuming that he wasn't sincere in his offer to help Harris polish his manuscript or provide the rest of us with tips on becoming published authors. Bringing the painting here was a peace offering, though Nick wouldn't have realized that's what it was meant to be. I did want to know whether it was pivotal to his research pertaining to the sequel to *The Barbed Wire Flower*, and if so, why hadn't he just admitted that to Harris?"

Rawlings grew quiet, absorbing what she'd told him. He then unzipped the tote bag and spent a long time studying the winter scene.

Olivia was ready to get away from the beach house. The delayed shock of leaning over Plumley's distorted face asserted itself now, turning her palms and forehead clammy. Unbidden, her mind flashed on a vision of her nephew lying in his incubator. A strange and unfamiliar emotion welled inside her, and she sucked in a deep breath to force it back down. Tiny babies, Plumley's tortured corpse—those images didn't belong on Olivia's agenda. She should be concentrating on the hundreds of small details she needed to see to before Friday's grand opening, but she couldn't. Olivia squeezed her eyes shut, trying to focus all of her senses on the feel of the cool glass tabletop beneath her palms.

"Hey." Rawlings reached over and touched her wrist. "Are you okay?"

She flipped her hand over in order to grab hold of him. His skin was warm and solid beneath her touch. It calmed her instantly. "Sawyer, the last twenty-four hours have been hell."

Rawlings listened as she told him about Anders, his hazel eyes softening as he witnessed her relive the fear and worry. When she had finished, his mouth curved into the hint of a smile. "This kind of emotional display could damage your ice queen reputation, you know."

Pushing her chair away from the table, she put a hand on each of his cheeks and, after drinking in his scent of aftershave and coffee, leaned over and kissed him. "With your help, I may defrost yet," she whispered, relishing the feel of his rough skin under her hands.

Carefully and with infinite tenderness, Rawlings pushed her away and rose to his feet. "I need to concentrate, Olivia."

She nodded, unashamed, and pivoted until she faced the spot where Nick's body had lain. Just touching Rawlings had brought her back to herself. She felt grounded again, in control of her feelings and ready to help him work through what had occurred in this living room.

After packing up the painting, Olivia said, "Plumley must have known his killer, to have invited someone in while wearing only a robe and boxer shorts." She took a few steps forward and pointed at the book. "This was personal. Someone took pages from Nick's own work and forced them into his mouth." She hesitated and then asked, "Is that what killed him?"

"The medical examiner thinks he was strangled first. From behind. The pages were put in posthumously. That will have to be verified, of course, but that's his initial assessment."

Olivia felt a shiver of trepidation. "Feels like a crime of passion to me. The murderer choked the life out of Nick and then stuffed this own writing down his throat."

"Made him eat his own words," Rawlings declared solemnly. "Leaving us with the most significant question unanswered: Why? Who hated this man or his work enough to stop him from writing another word?"

There was no ready answer, of course. Olivia and Rawlings stood side by side for a long moment, and then he gave his gun belt a tug and gestured at the front door.

"I'd prefer your exit be less dramatic than your entrance," he said with the ghost of a smile. "You made the right choice, Olivia, in coming to Mr. Plumley's aid, but his killer could have still been inside. I wish you'd learn to curb your impetuousness."

Olivia waved off his concern. "Haviland would have rescued me from harm, even if it meant shredding his paws on broken glass. I have complete faith in him." She touched the chief's shoulder before stepping outside. "And in you too."

Pleasure flitted across the chief's face, but he quickly hid it by sliding on a pair of mirrored sunglasses. The pair stepped outside, and Rawlings raised a hand at the officer waiting in the police cruiser. He then asked Olivia if she'd like a ride.

"No, thanks. I'll provide an official statement when I come into town. I need to get to the hospital by eleven to give Hudson the key card for the hotel in Greenville."

"You're the only person in Oyster Bay who dictates when they'll show up at the station." Rawlings shook his head in mild exasperation. "Still, I know you'll fit us into your schedule. And, Olivia, I might call on you to help dig up information on the previous inhabitants of Harris's house." His sunglasses glinted in the light. "I want to know what connection, if any, they had to that painting and, possibly, to Mr. Plumley."

While Rawlings had been speaking, the other officer had eased out of the car, leaving the driver's door open and the engine running. Obviously, it was now his task to watch over the house until it could be properly sealed, but he kept his distance until Rawlings made it clear that he was ready to leave both the crime scene and Olivia behind.

"I'd be glad to help, Chief," Olivia replied, pleased that he'd asked. She kicked at some loose gravel, reluctant to part from Rawlings.

At that moment, Haviland ambled around the house from his napping place under the chaise lounge. He glanced at the chief and yawned widely, his white teeth gleaming in the midmorning sun.

Rawlings gave the poodle an affectionate pat on the flank.

"Keep her safe, Captain," he murmured just loud enough for Olivia to hear. And with a professional nod in her direction, he climbed into the car.

Olivia watched the sedan reverse down the driveway in a cloud of sand-infused dust, gave a friendly but fatigued wave to the officer left in charge of the house, and climbed over the dunes toward home.

Standing in her kitchen, Olivia surveyed the three objects on her kitchen table. Her fingers moved past the canvas tote bag containing Harris's painting and the hotel key card she needed to deliver to Hudson within the hour, to a tumbler filled with two ice cubes and an inch of Chivas Regal. She preferred to consume the twenty-five-year-old blend of Scotch whiskies before dinner, but her thoughts were too fractured, too frenzied for her to continue on with the day's plans. Downing the contents of the glass in one gulp, she felt a rush of steadying warmth flow through her.

"That's better," she told Haviland, who was busy consuming his second breakfast.

She refilled the tumbler with tap water and drank it with more deliberation. Her hands stopped trembling and the tumultuous images swirling in her mind separated into cohesive, orderly thoughts.

Rawlings needed her help. She'd be no good to him if

she couldn't find the time to research the families who'd lived in Harris's house.

Decisively, Olivia grabbed her car keys and the other items off the table and drove to the hospital. She told Haviland his wait would be brief and called Hudson from the lobby. Olivia wasn't ready to see Kim today. She just did not possess the strength or the proper words to comfort a woman separated from her newborn son.

Hudson was as taciturn as always. He took the key from Olivia with mumbled thanks and then told her he was sorry to be missing the staff meeting at The Bayside Crab House.

"You don't need to be there. You've got everyone trained perfectly and this isn't my first rodeo, Olivia assured him. After all, she was well accustomed to giving orders to the staff and supervising their practice runs. For the soft opening tonight, a motley assembly of diners had been hand-selected to test the wait and kitchen staff. Dixie and her husband were among them, and Olivia had made special arrangements with her friend. In other words, she'd asked Dixie to be curt, picky, and demanding.

"Test their mettle," Olivia had told her bemused friend over the phone. "Request extra lemon wedges and butter sauce and send back a dish because it doesn't taste right. Spill your wine and complain about spots on the flatware. I want to know that they can handle belligerent customers."

Dixie had been delighted by both the assignment and the chance to share a free seafood feast with Grumpy. "If you really want to see what your employees are made of, let me bring my kids. You'll get yourself a pack of fussy eaters, a whole lotta extra noise, and crab claws a-flyin' every which way. Your poor waiter might just quit before dessert."

"I love the idea, Dixie. Most of the tourists will have families in tow, and some of them may very well be boisterous or superfinicky." Olivia had grinned. "Tell your brood to let loose."

"You do *not* know what you're sayin', 'Livia, but for the record, I'm not responsible for the dischargin' of fire extinguishers or any structural damage," Dixie had stated seriously before hanging up.

Now, standing in the hospital's lobby, Olivia tried to convince her brother to forget about the restaurant and focus on his family, but no matter what she said, he refused to take a week off to be with his wife and daughter. She knew fear kept him from making the right decision. Not only did Hudson fear his newborn son's fragility, but he was clearly terrified that the restaurant would fail and he'd have moved his family to Oyster Bay for nothing. And though Olivia understood both fears, she still chastised him for putting his job ahead of his family. He stood firm though.

Eventually, he did accept the key card but made no move to return to his wife's room. "I know what I'm doing in the kitchen," he muttered miserably. "I belong there."

An image of Anders' little face, his translucent skin covering the rivers of blue veins carrying fresh blood from his newly stitched heart flashed through Olivia's mind. She narrowed her eyes in anger. "You *belong* with your son. And with your wife. It's probably killing her that she can't be at that baby's side. You might not know how to handle this, but you're going to figure it out. You're a father to two children, so start acting like one."

Her tone allowed no argument. She handed him a slip of paper. "That's the combination to the hotel room's wall safe. If Kim and Caitlyn are going to live there for the next two weeks, I want them to be comfortable." Her brother looked so terrified that she relented a little and gave his thick shoulder an affectionate squeeze. "I'll see you tomorrow, *after* you get back from driving your family to their temporary home."

Nodding in compliance, Hudson grabbed her hand and clung to it for a moment before walking away.

Olivia watched him go, imagining how tomorrow morning would pass for the Salters. Kim would be taken by wheelchair to the hospital's front door. She'd climb out of the chair, the pain in her belly from her cesarean forcing her to cringe, and get into Hudson's car. She'd sit in the back, holding her daughter and comforting her as she and Hudson spoke of the future. Kim would try to keep everyone's spirits up while silently noting the passing of every mile marker, her hands clenched in impatience as the distance closed between her and her tiny son.

"Enough with the maudlin imagery," Olivia chided herself, got back in the Range Rover, and headed for the office park east of town.

Harris worked in a three-story concrete box that was completely unremarkable except for the Yoda replica in the lobby. The green-skinned, elfin-eared Jedi rested on a podium in the middle of a fountain surrounded by tropical plants. He welcomed visitors with a wise and wrinkled gaze and a plaque bearing the company logo.

Olivia glanced at the statue in puzzlement and then turned her attention to the young receptionist who was jotting a message onto a pink memo pad. She recognized the girl's pretty face immediately.

"Hi, Estelle."

Estelle beamed as though the very sight of Olivia had made her day. "How *nice* to see you here! And your cute doggie came too! Are you visiting Harris?" Her words tumbled forth rapid-fire, every syllable infused with a shrill energy. Before Olivia could answer, the phone sitting directly in front of Estelle began to ring and she answered it with a lengthy, well-rehearsed greeting. She filled out another sheet on the pink memo pad and then, as the caller continued talking, her hand drifted to a massive desk calendar, where she idly drew a series of small hearts around Harris's name.

Finally, she said good-bye and replaced the receiver. She was about to speak to Olivia when the phone rang again. Estelle held out her index finger, signaling for Olivia to wait until she finished with her next caller.

"Could you just tell me where to find Harris? It's important," Olivia said, placing her hand on the edge of Estelle's desk. The phone continued to ring.

Something ugly flickered in the young woman's eyes, but she blinked it away and pasted on a bright smile. "Don't worry, I'll call him for you. But I've got to answer this first."

Tucking a strand of hair behind her ear, she repeated the extensive greeting she'd used on the previous caller, her pen poised over the memo pad.

Annoyed, Olivia covertly examined Estelle's calendar. To her surprise, she saw that Estelle had added Harris's last name to her own and had practiced the signature over and over in the margin. Wedding bells and tiered cakes danced along any available white space, and plump hearts were scattered about.

This evidence of Estelle's vision of her future with Harris didn't please Olivia at all. Harris would make a wonderful husband someday, but Olivia didn't think that Estelle was a suitable life partner for her friend. In her mind, Estelle was merely one of the girls Harris would date to discover exactly what he was looking for in a spouse. Estelle was pretty, sweet, and bubbly, but she was about as deep as a puddle.

She was practice for the real thing.

And then there was Millay. The tension had been escalating between Harris and Millay ever since Estelle had entered the picture, and Olivia knew that it stemmed from the fact that the two young writers were attracted to each other. Millay had dated dozens of men, from bikers to stockbrokers, but she'd never stayed with anyone long enough to form a genuine relationship. Though Millay had an undeniable connection with Harris, Olivia knew that Harris hadn't ripened into the man he needed to be in order to capture the beautiful bartender's heart. He was getting closer, but he wasn't quite there. He needed another dose of confidence, a dash of bravado, and a bit more worldly experience before he had the necessary ingredients to woo his fellow writer.

Olivia was positive that Harris was precisely what the fearless bartender needed: someone to challenge her on a mental level, treat her tenderly, and win her respect not by possessing a muscular physique or fat bank account, but with a sharp wit and ready humor.

"I'll ring Harris's extension now, but I'm not sure what the company policy is about having dogs in the building," Estelle said, a jester's practiced smile stretched across her face. "And what can I tell him this is about?"

"It's personal," Olivia said flatly. "And you have my word that Haviland won't soil the carpet."

Again, that flicker of hostility appeared in the young woman's eyes, but she looked down at the phone and pressed some keys with manicured nails. She baby-talked into the receiver until Olivia had to step back lest Estelle see the disgusted curl of her lip.

Harris jogged into the lobby less than a minute later. "This is so cool!" He exclaimed to Olivia. "I've never had a friend visit me at work before!" He scratched Haviland on the head and then noticed the canvas tote bag. "Whoa. Is that the painting?"

Olivia nodded. "Can we go sit somewhere? An empty conference room or staff lounge?"

"Sure." Harris waved at Estelle. "Thanks for paging me."

"Anytime, sweetie," she cooed. "And I won't tell anyone that you've got a dog back there with you." She drew a finger across her lips to seal in the secret.

Flushing, Harris led Olivia through a warren of hall-ways. He poked his head in a small conference room and signaled for Olivia to enter. "This one has food left from the bigwig's lunch meeting. I don't know about you, but I'm starving." He gestured at a sandwich plat-ter flanked by a bowl of red apples and a row of soda cans and snack-sized bags of potato chips. "It doesn't look like much, but this is the best chicken salad you'll ever eat."

Olivia raised her brows. "You do recall that I own a five-star restaurant?"

"I *know*!" Harris enthused. "That's how good it is."

He loaded two sandwiches, an apple, and a bag of Fritos onto his plate.

Olivia carefully laid the tote bag on the conference table and then idly chewed on an apple as Harris devoured his lunch. They small-talked about their writing and Harris's current software project until he finally pushed his plate away.

"It was totally nice of you to bring this here," he said. "But it wasn't necessary."

Exhaling, Olivia touched the canvas bag. "There's a reason I came to your office. Harris, this painting may be more important than any of us can comprehend. In fact, it may figure into a murder investigation."

Harris blanched. *"What?"*

Gently, for she knew that her young friend idolized Nick Plumley, Olivia told him that the writer had been killed that morning.

"How? *Why?"* Harris stammered, clearly shaken.

After admitting that she didn't know the reason, Olivia hesitated and then softly explained that Plumley had been strangled.

"Harris, this is going to sound strange, but did Nick poke around your house the day you two were painting the living room?" Seeing the confused look on her friend's face, she went on. "Was he especially interested in loose floorboards or in seeing the attic? Did he ask if you'd discovered any hidey-holes?"

Harris's eyes widened. "Yeah, he did. He was telling me about this old house north of Beaufort he'd visited a bunch of times. It had a hidden space behind a wallboard in one of the closets and a niche carved from an exposed beam in the kitchen. Nick asked if I'd found any secret hiding places in my house, but I told him

I doubted there were any." He shook his head in befuddlement. "It's not that old of a building. And except for being moved a few decades ago, it wasn't important, historically speaking."

"But what if it wasn't the house that captured Nick's interest?" Olivia wondered aloud. "What if he wanted to find *this* painting all along? Maybe the message on the back indicates that there's more to Heinrich Kamler's story. What if Nick believed he could track Kamler through this painting? Could you imagine the book he could write?"

Harris touched the canvas tote bag possessively. "Why didn't Nick just ask me? I would have fessed up that I hadn't found anything but would gladly show him if I did." A hurt look crossed his features. "He never cared about my manuscript, did he? I bet he never read it."

"That's his loss, Harris." Olivia gave her friend a fond smile. "If it's any consolation, I believe he genuinely liked you and would have helped you with your writing, but for some reason, he wanted to keep the knowledge of this painting to himself."

This notion seemed to trouble Harris. "What makes you say that?"

"When I called him this morning and told him about the painting's existence, I could practically feel his desire to see it surge through the phone line. The emotion was so strong that I could picture a pair of hands reaching out to me." She shook her head at the theatrical depiction. "Okay, that's a bit much, but it meant a great deal to him."

Crushing the remaining Frito on his plate into corn-colored bits, Harris's expression grew thoughtful. "If you hadn't just told me that Nick was dead, I'd assume the watercolor was important to his research and that he wanted to use it as a plot device in his sequel. But now . . ."

"Now?" Olivia prodded.

Harris pushed the bag toward her. "You'd better keep this. It would be safer at your restaurant or in a bank vault or something. Give it to the cops. Don't even tell me where you put it, just take it away."

It was unlike Harris to be dramatic, and Olivia frowned, but she'd just told him that his potential mentor had been murdered and he had every right to be upset. "All right, I'll see to it."

"Listen, Olivia. The killer stuffed Nick's own book pages into his mouth. That means not only is it likely that some homicidal maniac had cause to hate *The Barbed Wire Flower*, but also didn't want Nick to write the sequel." Harris's face was pink with anxiety. "This painting might be a pivotal part of the book Nick planned, so it might be important to his murderer too."

Nodding, Olivia fed Haviland a few hunks of chicken. "I've been concerned about the same thing, but we could be blowing this out of proportion. We have no facts as of this point, and we need to gather some quickly."

Harris opened a can of Fanta and drank a swallow. "Yeah, because I don't want any of us to end up with pages of manuscripts crammed down *our* throats." He ran his hands through his ginger-colored hair. "We need to figure out why Nick's research set the killer off. If we don't, *I* could be the next victim. This lunatic might come to my place in search of the painting or whatever connection Nick thought my house had to his story."

Olivia saw the fear in her friend's face. "Chief Rawlings has asked me to investigate the history of the families who used to live in your house, and I intend to begin this afternoon. Harris, I will do everything in my power to figure out this riddle. Millay and Laurel can assist me. Laurel can dig through the newspaper archives, and Millay can help me sift through the records at town hall."

"I can't just send my female friends all over town to solve this mystery while I design a fairy forest for some stupid computer game." Harris squared his shoulders and sat up a fraction straighter. "I need to get my hands on Nick's computer. There's got to be a clue in his files as to why someone wanted to silence him before he could publish that sequel."

"Talk to the chief." Olivia rose and carefully shouldered the tote bag. "And forget about critiquing my chapter on Saturday. We've got more important things to do."

Harris absently put a hand to his throat. "Like staying alive."

Chapter 8

Olivia and Haviland trotted down the stairs lead-ing to the windowless lower level of the town hall building. The woman in charge of the register of deeds was examining a stack of forms when Olivia appeared at her desk. Her eyes went wide when she noticed the poodle and then her face closed off and she smacked the piece of paper in front of her with a rubber stamp.

"You can't have a dog down here, ma'am." She slammed the stamp down on another piece of paper and continued her work without looking up.

Glancing around the empty room, Olivia was about to point out that there was no one around to be troubled by Haviland's presence, but she sensed that the govern-ment employee, with her taut ponytail and humorless eyes, was a stickler for rules.

"He accompanies me for medical reasons," Olivia whispered and then cleared her throat, as though it shamed her to admit to having such a serious health problem. "Hopefully, I won't have an *episode* while I'm here, but I'd best not waste time. My dog is trained to seek help should I start convulsing." She handed the skeptical clerk a slip of paper bearing Harris's address. "I need the names of all of this home's previous owners, please. And I'll need to make copies of every deed pertaining to this address."

The woman hesitated, clearly debating whether it would require more effort to toss Olivia out or simply fulfill her request. Sighing heavily, she turned to her computer and began to type in the address on Oleander Drive.

It wasn't long before she presented Olivia with several pages, still warm from the printer. "Anything else, ma'am?" she asked, her mouth puckering as though she'd bitten into something sour.

Olivia read through the sheets, recognizing names from her conversation with librarian Leona Fairchild, including the Carters and the Robinsons, the couple that sold the house to Harris.

"There's an owner missing from this pile," she murmured and then retrieved a small notebook from her purse. "The White family lived there as well."

The clerk crossed her arms over her chest. "Not according to my records."

"Can you check again?"

At this request, the woman's lips compressed into an angry, thin line. She jabbed a few buttons on her computer keyboard and gestured at the screen. "There were no owners by the name of White at the address. Perhaps you're mistaken."

Suppressing a surge of annoyance, Olivia stared at the street address and then shook the pages in her hands like they were pompoms. "You're brilliant!" she told the startled clerk. "The house was moved during the highway expansion project. This address is only current for the past fifty years or so."

"I'm not old enough to remember the date of that event," the woman declared smugly. "You'll have to come back when you have an accurate address."

Olivia recalled Harris telling the Bayside Book Writers that Nick Plumley had found a copy of the newspaper article describing the move and, therefore, Laurel could easily get ahold of the same information. Thanking the clerk, Olivia jogged upstairs and called her friend.

"Olivia! I was hoping I'd have an excuse to take a break," Laurel said. "I'm working on this yawn-inducing piece about average household incomes and—"

"I need you to find an old article for me," Olivia cut in. "It's urgent." She explained what she needed. "Could you bring it by The Bayside Crab House as soon as you find it?"

There was a pause. "Is something going on with Harris? What's wrong, Olivia?"

Silently berating herself for assuming that Laurel wouldn't ask why the information was so crucial, Olivia promised that Harris was fine and that she'd fill Laurel in when she delivered the article. Olivia was quite surprised that Nick Plumley's death hadn't been leaked to the press yet and wondered if Rawlings had kept his team so busy that not a single officer had been able to contribute to the famous Oyster Bay gossip chain. It would certainly be a coup for Laurel to break the news first, especially since she'd established her reputation as a respected local journalist based on her articles on the Cliché Killers.

"Just do this for me," Olivia coaxed. "And I'll tip you off on what's to become the biggest story of the summer."

Laurel sucked in a quick breath. "I'll take the tip. It's been mighty sleepy in the news department."

"That's about to change," Olivia stated solemnly and hung up.

An hour later, she was well into her speech on treating customers like royalty, the employees of The Bayside Crab House listening to her every word with a mixture of trepidation and awe, when Laurel arrived.

Olivia wished her staff good luck, cautioned them that the first guests would be arriving at five, and led Laurel into the manager's office.

"Is this yours?" Laurel asked, taking a seat and glancing around the space with interest.

"It's really Kim's domain. She's in charge of supplies and bookkeeping. Once we have an established routine, I'll only come in to sign checks."

Laurel frowned. "But what will Kim do with the baby? You're their only family in Oyster Bay, right?"

Having no desire to introduce the emotionally charged subject of Anders, Olivia shrugged. "I suppose she'll bring the baby with her. Caitlyn's going to day camp this summer and Kim's hours are fairly flexible. She'll be home when the kids are home. I agreed to that arrangement from the start."

"What a boss," Laurel said with a wistful smile. "Wish you ran the *Gazette*. I have been allowed to work from the house more and more, but it's so hard to get anything done. The twins have entered a seriously brutal rivalry phase. They're like two Roman gladiators, destroying anything in their path." She shook her head hopelessly. "Enough about my boys. Why did you need this?"

Olivia accepted two sheets of paper from Laurel and quickly scanned the article. Before the houses were moved and the two-lane road became a highway, it was called Stillwater Street. The article described the complexities of the expansion project and featured a photograph of a bungalow atop the flatbed of a tractor-trailer. Even from the grainy black-and-white image Olivia could tell that the house wasn't Harris's. It was smaller and had a slightly different roofline. A group of people clad in their Sunday finery was gathered around the truck. The women were impeccably turned out in tailored skirts, hats, and gloves; the men were in suits and felt fedoras; the little girls looked angelic with their curled hair and crinoline; and the boys wore high-waisted shorts with suspenders and argyle knee socks.

The caption listed the names of the four men grouped together near the left side of the trailer. "There! Frank White must have been the original owner of Harris's house. Now I just need to search for the deed for Stillwater Street."

Laurel drummed her fingers on the arms of her chair. "You're killing me, Olivia! What is going *on*?"

Olivia dropped the paper onto the desk and sat down next to Laurel. "By now, Chief Rawlings will probably have a press release ready, but let me tell you what happened from my point of view and then you can zoom over to the station to get a quote. And, Laurel, we can forget about critiquing my book on Saturday."

"Why?"

Gesturing at the newspaper article, Olivia said, "Because we need to help the police track down a murderer instead."

While the employees of The Bayside Crab House began their trial run, Olivia made phone calls to Harris and Leona Fairchild. Without telling the librarian why she wanted to dig deeper into the background of the former inhabitants of Harris's house, Olivia asked her how to find out more about the families. The computer-savvy librarian provided her with a simple solution.

"These days, most public records are available online. You can look up birth, marriage, and death certificates, criminal records, background checks, property values, and even the names and ages of other residents in the household. The further back you go, the fewer the details, but it's a start." She gave Olivia the URL. "You can often pay to get more information, especially from some of the genealogical sites. I'll give you the one I prefer."

Armed with this information, Olivia began to delegate tasks. She asked Millay to research the White, Carter, and Robinson families during her shift break at Fish Nets, and if she couldn't complete the task that night, to return to it the next day. Millay had heard of Nick Plumley's death only moments before Olivia's call, but she had no idea that foul play had been involved.

"How is Harris taking it?" Millay inquired with marked indifference, but Olivia wasn't fooled. She knew her friend was genuinely concerned.

"He's understandably disturbed. After all, the painting came from his house, and Plumley had clearly been searching for it there. Harris is worried that the killer might come looking for it too."

Millay was silent for several moments. "Someone needs to find out more about Plumley. So he wanted this painting. Whatever. He didn't even have it in his possession when he was killed. There's more to this murder than some old piece of art. It's got to be about Heinrich Kamler or Plumley. And I mean the man, not the writer. We need to know *his* background as well as getting the four-one-one on the people who used to live in Harris's house."

"Agreed," Olivia answered readily. "I'm putting Harris in charge of that. He has the necessary computer skills to hunt for the sort of biographical tidbits not included in the inside flap of *The Barbed Wire Flower*'s book jacket."

By the time the grand opening celebration of The Bayside Crab House got under way Friday night, Olivia was already exhausted. During yesterday's trial run, both the wait and kitchen staff had made inexcusable blunders, and Olivia could only pray that having Hudson back in the kitchen, working his magic amid the cacophony of shouting, chopping, and sizzling, would eradicate some of her stress. In fact, when she saw him that afternoon, his face flushed by a geyser of steam billowing from a lobster pot, he was the picture of contentment.

"How's Anders?" she asked.

He gave her a small smile as he dumped a load of crabs into a steamer basket. "He's doing fine. Thanks . . . for being with him. I'm . . . You're a good sister."

Olivia was spared from having to respond because,

at that moment, a flustered waitress burst through the kitchen's double swing doors, leaving them to flap in her wake like untethered sails in a squall. "Ms. Limoges! The bar's totally *full* and it's only five thirty! We've got a *huge* line of customers waiting outside. What should we do?"

Hudson and Olivia exchanged satisfied looks. "Pace yourself, Angie," Olivia told the girl. "It's going to be a long and profitable night."

Her prediction was correct. The restaurant was packed from the moment it opened until well after midnight. Olivia helped out wherever she could; refilling empty glasses, clearing tables, and making small talk with customers. Despite the crowd, the kitchen stayed on top of all the orders, and every dish was presented before the expectant diners warm and fragrant with freshness.

Olivia's feet were throbbing by the time the last patron left. While the weary waitstaff began their closing duties, she took a seat at the bar and sent one of the waiters to ask Hudson to join her.

"Chivas Regal over ice." Julesy, the bartender, put Olivia's drink on a white paper napkin featuring The Bayside Crab House logo and then started to clean off the bar with quick, efficient strokes.

"Another for the chef, if you would," Olivia said, envying the girl's energy. She didn't seem tired at all, even though she'd been racing from one end of the bar to the other all night, serving glasses of frothy microbrews and an array of colorful frozen cocktails. Julesy was Gabe's cousin and had the same all-American good looks as The Boot Top's barkeep. With her sunstreaked hair, tanned skin, athletic figure, and sincere smile, she'd been an immediate hit with the crab house clientele.

"Let's pour a round for the staff," Olivia suggested to Julesy's barback, a reserved Hispanic man in his early twenties. "I'd like to raise a toast to an amazing night."

Julesy nodded in approval. She and Raulo began to line up pint glasses and fill them with a light summer wheat beer. The color was beautiful, reminiscent of sunrise at the beach or the vibrant gold of crisp corn.

Olivia kicked off her pumps and curled her toes over the rung of the barstool. The live band, which had played Jimmy Buffett and Bob Marley songs for the past three hours, had mercifully turned off their amps and mics. They'd have to return tomorrow night and perform the entire set again, yet they seemed in no hurry to leave. In fact, the atmosphere in the restaurant was downright festive. Even as the bone-tired waitstaff wiped tables and swept the floor, they laughed and chatted animatedly as though they hadn't just pushed their bodies to the limit over the past eight hours.

When Hudson entered the bar area, he was met with a round of applause and shrill whistles. He waved off this show of praise, his dark eyes glimmering with pleasure. He clinked glasses with Olivia and took a generous swallow of Chivas Regal.

"Best tips I've ever made," the waitress named Angie told one of her coworkers. "If every weekend's like this, I'll be able to pay for graduate school."

"And I can quit the gym," the waiter replied, and the pair raised their pint glasses in Olivia's direction. She gave them a regal nod over the rim of her tumbler.

Confident that her employees could finish closing the restaurant without her watchful eye, Olivia picked up her shoes, said good night to Hudson, and collected a groggy Haviland from the office. At home, she managed to brush her teeth and wash her face before falling into bed. She slept, but her dreams were filled with images of lobster claws and paintings of a forest in winter.

The next morning, Olivia woke late, filled a thermos with coffee, and took Haviland down to the beach for a walk. Saturdays were traditionally treasure hunt days, but her muscles still ached from last night's exertions and she didn't feel like toting the metal detector or trench shovel.

After the leisurely stroll, she showered and dressed in a gauzy cotton sundress in an indigo hue and a pair of silver sandals and headed into town for brunch at Grumpy's. She brought her laptop along out of habit but never actually removed it from the case. Her meal of eggs Benedict with a side of sliced strawberries was constantly interrupted. By this time, word of Nick Plumley's death was all over town, and Dixie wanted to hear every detail. The Oyster Bay gossip chain had somehow gotten hold of the fact that Olivia had discovered the body.

Cautioning her friend that the writer's demise was still under investigation, therefore preventing her from sharing certain aspects of the case, Olivia managed to satisfy Dixie's curiosity by describing how she'd smashed the window with Plumley's patio chair. "But there was nothing I could do to revive him."

At that point, Olivia abruptly stopped speaking. There was no way she was going to mention the book pages stuffed into the writer's mouth.

Dixie, who was clad in a frayed denim skirt, rainbow tube socks, and a T-shirt reading, "Ms. Pac-Man for President," dropped into the seat opposite Olivia. Using a spoon, she examined her feathered hair in the reflection and flattened a stiff, heavily gelled lock back into submission. She then studied Olivia with a solemn expression. "You're just one of those people, 'Livia."

"What does that mean?" Olivia growled.

Dixie shrugged, never the slightest bit flustered by Olivia's gruffness. "Things happen to you. Things that make most folks crumble into tiny pieces. Maybe that's why death hangs 'round you. He knows you're a match for any man, even one with a scythe."

Olivia pressed her palms against her coffee cup, intent on the warmth seeping into her skin. "That shadow has been hanging over my shoulder for a long time. If my mother hadn't died the way she did—trying to make me happy—my life would have been different." She took a sip of her coffee and glanced out the window. The sidewalks were bathed in strong light, and the streets were crowded with sunburned tourists and merry locals. "It was like the storm that ended her life left a mark on me, like a tattoo that no one can see."

Dixie was silent for a moment. A customer in the *Phantom of the Opera* booth signaled for his check, but the diner proprietor made no move to serve him. "Girlfriend, you've just dug on down to the heart of your own biggest problem."

Olivia cocked her head quizzically. "How so?"

"You find a man that really sees you, shadows and all, and you'll have the power to burn away the past. Take a match to it, light it up like a forest fire in July, and blow away the ashes." Dixie scooted out of the booth, bent over, and retied the sparkling lace of her left roller skate. "You let that man in, and he'll beat the past away with his bare hands. That's what Grumpy did for me. It's why I know our lives were meant to intertwine—we're like a kudzu vine and a big ol' pine tree."

"That's a very romantic image, Dixie," Olivia quipped in an effort to erase her momentary display of vulnerability. "So your advice is that I should go out in search of a tree? Unbending to the wind, unburned by the sun, dependable, and strong. Sounds like a rare find."

"Oh," Dixie said as she began to skate backward toward her waiting customer. "I reckon you've already found him. You're just too scared to invite him in. Get over yourself, 'Livia. It's about damn time you did."

Olivia didn't have the chance to be amazed by her friend's perceptiveness, for while she was still digesting Dixie's words, Millay entered the diner. She spotted Haviland snoozing on the floor of the window booth and took the seat Dixie had vacated seconds earlier.

Millay's short, black hair was relatively monochromatic this morning. There were three parrot green streaks in her bangs, but she wore less makeup than usual and had clearly not bothered to put on her rows of hoop earrings or cover both wrists with dozens of rubber bracelets. "Get this," she began without preamble. "I was just at Bed, Bath and Beyond buying some storage containers and who should I see there but Miss Bubble Head."

Recalling that Miss Bubble Head was the moniker Millay had assigned to Estelle, Olivia grinned. "And?"

"She was buying a set of bathroom towels with lace trim and embroidered seashells. Total Southern-princess-type crap." Millay helped herself to Olivia's water glass. "One of those furry toilet seat covers too. I thought only old people used those things."

Olivia pivoted in order to catch Dixie's eye and then faced Millay again. "Admittedly, that style doesn't appeal to my taste, but it's Estelle we're talking about. What do you expect? Her cell phone is covered in pink and purple rhinestones."

"That's the thing!" Millay's dark eyes narrowed dangerously. "She was buying that stuff for *Harris's* house. I heard her talking to someone on her blinged-out Lady Gaga phone, and she said, and I quote, 'I might as well buy what *I* like because it'll be my house soon enough.'"

Olivia's expression of condemnation was interrupted by Dixie's arrival with a pot of coffee for Millay. As she filled Millay's mug, the diner proprietor gave her an indulgent smile. "What are you doin' awake this side of noon, girl?"

Millay took a grateful sip of black coffee and then pointed at the stainless steel carafe. "I don't know what illegal drugs you put in your joe, Dixie, but you brew the best fuel in town. Bagels 'n' Beans is good too, but you actually make it worth my while to be outside when the tourists are prowling the streets."

Dixie laughed, pleased by the compliment. "You make them sound like zombies comin' to overtake Oyster Bay."

"Hey, as long as they stuff my tip jar, they're free to feed on some of my least favorite townspeople. I have a nice, ripe bimbo I'd be glad to toss their way," Millay murmured and then ordered a bacon cheeseburger with onion straws and slaw.

Once Dixie had zipped off to place Millay's order,

but not before slipping Haviland a sausage link hidden in her apron pocket, Olivia waved aside the subject of Estelle. "She's only temporary. He'll tire of her soon enough. In any case, Harris has more significant problems at the moment. How did your research go?"

"Laurel had some luck with the newspaper's archives," Millay answered, rummaging around in a black messenger bag covered with Japanime characters. "She didn't have a ton of time because she had to finish an article, pick up groceries, and be home in time to clean the whole house. Man, how I'd like to shove her husband's dental drill up his chauvinistic—"

"Not very hygienic, I'm afraid," Olivia interrupted and gestured at Millay's bag. "Show me the goods."

Millay withdrew a notebook covered with pirate skulls and flipped open to a page covered with her angular scrawl. "We can forget about the families who lived there after the house was moved. They're squeaky-clean, law-abiding, church-going drones. No criminal records, no tax evasion, no outstanding debts, nothing. Trust me, they're a dead end."

"Interesting word choice," Olivia said with a sigh. "And the White family?"

Millay unfolded a sheet of paper showing a black-and-white photograph of a teenage girl standing on the porch of Harris's house. In the background, the heavy machinery required to lift the home onto a trailer hovered over the roof, throwing shadows across the ruined lawn and crushed flowerbeds no doubt once lovingly maintained by the girl's mother.

Olivia removed the magnifying glass she kept in her purse and placed the circle over the girl's face.

"Forget that. I enlarged this copy on Laurel's Xerox

machine. It's a little blurry, but I want to see if you'd react the way I did when I really looked at her." Millay's expression was unreadable, so Olivia merely accepted the paper she offered.

Immediately, Olivia was struck by the girl's eyes. They were the eyes of an old woman, filled with resignation and sorrow, yet still clinging to a delicate thread of hope. The knowledge emanating from those depths was a contradiction to her plain dress, ankle socks, and the corkscrew curls pulled off her forehead and secured with a large silk bow. She looked as though she should be clutching a lollipop or a bouquet of wildflowers with both hands. Instead, she had her arms wrapped around the porch post, as though the moving of the house was something she greatly dreaded.

"It's like this is too big a change for her," Olivia whispered, noticing the girl's name in the caption. "Evelyn White, age sixteen. What else happened to you? Why are you so filled with fear?"

Millay put a finger on the photograph. "The country was at war, but I think kids her age are pretty adaptable. Her father didn't enlist and she was an only child, so no brothers were sent off to fight. Friends, maybe. Or possibly a boyfriend. She *was* pretty."

"If she had a boyfriend, then something must have happened to him," Olivia remarked softly. "I know that look. That's grief. She's lost something precious to her and now her house is being torn from the ground right in front of her. Nothing is stable. She feels totally lost."

The two women stared at the young girl, this beautiful, fresh-faced stranger in a checkered dress, and found they no longer felt like talking. Millay drank her coffee as she watched strangers parade past the diner window, but Olivia couldn't take her eyes from Evelyn's face.

She didn't even hear Dixie skate over with Millay's cheeseburger.

"Could I get that in a takeout box?" Millay asked sheepishly. "I'm not hungry anymore."

Dixie gave her a maternal pat on the cheek. "'Course you can, sugar. Your schedule's not the same as most folks, now is it?" She handed Olivia the check and then caught sight of the photograph. "Good Lord, who is that child?"

"A girl who used to live in Harris's house," Olivia replied.

With a sympathetic shake of her head, Dixie whispered, "She'd make a helluva ghost. There she is, a livin' and breathin' young girl, but she already looks like she's got a foot in the next world. She's grabbin' on to that porch post like her life depends on it. Her face is pinched like she hasn't eaten for days, and her eyes, they're so . . ." She trailed off, searching for the perfect adjective.

"Haunted," Olivia completed the thought.

Dixie swallowed hard. "That's it. That poor girl is haunted."

Chapter 9

Olivia stopped by both of her eateries before going home to prepare for the meeting of the Bayside Book Writers. She collected the printouts of the deeds for Harris's house and pages of background check documents on the residents. Like Millay, she'd found nothing unusual about them, but her picture of the White family was incomplete. One of the genealogy sites she'd used to search for more information on Evelyn White and her parents indicated that the forms she'd requested would be e-mailed to her as a PDF file by the end of the day on Monday at the earliest. Until then, she'd have to wait.

This was frustrating because she'd been hoping to have a tangible lead to share with her fellow writers. Now, she not only had nothing of interest to impart, but she'd found herself absorbed in another and even more obscure mystery than Nick Plumley's murder: the story behind the beautiful and troubled Miss White.

Laurel and Millay hadn't come across any useful data either. Facing a deadline and a visit from her in-laws, Laurel had turned the assignment over to Millay. She'd spent hours searching through book after book of bound newspapers, but the *Gazette* archives revealed no other photographs of the house or its occupants other than the images from the relocation and the impromptu church service held when the tractor-trailer broke down on Main Street.

As Millay adeptly decanted the bottle of wine on the cottage's countertop, she declared that someone owed her a hot stone massage. She then poured a glass for Laurel, knowing that Olivia would see to her own cocktail.

"I hope Harris has had more luck," Laurel said with a weary sigh.

Millay handed her the glass of wine. "Take a slug of this and relax. You look wrecked."

"I am," Laurel confessed. "I thought the energy I'd need to be a mom and a career woman would be my biggest challenge, but it turns out that I can handle that just fine. What I can't handle is that Steve and his parents make me feel like a stranger in my own house."

Olivia fixed herself a drink and then took a seat across from Laurel. "Steve *still* doesn't support your decision to be a journalist?"

Laurel shrugged. "In front of company he does, but if it's just us, and he finds so much as a dirty dish in the sink, he points out that our family was in better shape before I decided to go all 'Clark Kent.'" She drank half of the fruity zinfandel blend in one gulp.

Millay frowned in disapproval. "I know his hands are delicate instruments and all, but come on. Make him do the dishes."

"I doubt that would solve the problem," Olivia remarked as Millay pulled a bottle of beer from the fridge. "Is it possible he's jealous of you, Laurel?"

"*That* would be a first," Laurel replied wryly.

Using the shark-shaped opener that hung from her keychain, Millay popped the cap off the Heineken bottle and tossed it in the trash can in one fluid motion. "Olivia might be onto something. Your man has always been the Big Cheese at home. Mr. Breadwinner. Mr. Head of the Family. Then you go and land your dream job, instantly becoming a local celeb. Stevie Boy probably doesn't feel as macho as he did before." She sank gratefully onto the sofa and pointed at Laurel with her beer. "He needs a testosterone jumpstart."

"Maybe you're right." Laurel sipped at her wine, her gaze fixed on the glasslike ocean beyond the windows of the lighthouse keeper's cottage. "He's been keeping really long hours at the office. He probably feels like we're in some kind of competition." She blinked and her face seemed to regain a fraction of its customary brightness. "At least having a double income means that our piggy bank is getting nice and fat."

"Those are two words I've never heard a woman use together before," Harris stated as he entered the room. He headed straight for the refrigerator and helped himself to a beer. Flopping onto the sofa next to Millay, he spread out his long arms and let his head sink into the cushions. "What . . . a . . . week."

Millay prodded him with the toe of her black boot. "Don't play coy. Did you dig up anything important on Plumley or what?"

He pointed at her footwear. "Do you sleep in those things?"

"Wouldn't *you* like to know." She gave her bootlace a saucy twirl.

It took Harris a moment to break eye contact and turn his attention to his laptop case. He placed his iBook on the coffee table and pointed at the document on the screen. "I learned quite a few interesting things about Plumley, but most of the data I came across in my cyber search focused on his post-publication years. Biographically speaking, it's like he didn't exist before *The Barbed Wire Flower.*"

"Is Nick Plumley a nom de plume?" Olivia asked.

Harris shrugged. "It must be, but if that's the case, I can't find his real name anywhere. However, I discovered that he lives, ah, lived, in Beaufort."

Laurel looked confused. "But that's so close. Why would he want to move here when he already had a home in a quaint seaside town?"

Recalling Plumley's declaration that he'd come to Oyster Bay in search of anonymity, Olivia repeated the conversation she'd had with the author in Grumpy's. "At the time I believed him."

"I don't buy that explanation for a second," Harris said. "I had to jump through a dozen cyber hoops locating the guy's permanent residence, and *I* know how to find people on the Internet. Nick spent so many days of the year on tour, both here and in Europe, that he was rarely in Beaufort. In fact, more than one state claims him as one of their resident authors. Trust me, he was *not* getting hounded by the paparazzi in Beaufort, North Carolina."

Examining the diminished ice cubes at the bottom of her glass, Olivia walked into the kitchen to fix herself a second drink. "In my opinion, this strengthens the theory that he came to town in search of your painting, Harris."

"I still haven't seen this masterpiece," Laurel said with a pretty sulk. "And I don't get why he wanted it so badly."

Harris shook his head. "I'm stumped on that question too. Obviously, Nick was interested in the connection between the artist, Heinrich Kamler, and the New Bern prison camp. Oyster Bay's at least twenty miles away from New Bern, so he didn't pick our town because of its proximity to the POW camp. There's got to be something we're not seeing clearly. If only I had his laptop. There must be a clue embedded in his manuscript."

"I'd let you see every file on Mr. Plumley's computer," a deep voice stated from the doorway. "If only we'd found one."

Chief Rawlings smiled at the writers. "It's my dinner break. I decided that discussing certain elements of the case with you four would be more productive than staring at the ME's report for the hundredth time while choking down a burger."

"Nick's laptop was stolen?" Harris looked stricken. He, Millay, and Laurel began to exchange thoughts as to where else Plumley might have backed up his work while Olivia watched Rawlings assemble a sandwich from the platter of sliced rolls, meats, and cheeses she'd picked up from The Boot Top's walk-in fridge earlier that afternoon.

He carried a thick sandwich made of prosciutto, smoked Gouda, red onions, and mustard on a crusty roll to one of the wing chairs. The writer friends waited with barely concealed impatience as he took a large bite. Influenced by the sight of Rawlings' supper, Millay began to assemble a sandwich of buffalo mozzarella, sliced tomatoes, and pesto spread. No one else seemed eager to eat.

"There were no computers in Mr. Plumley's house or car," Rawlings stated. "There were also no printouts, no file folders containing outlines or notes, not even a journal. Nothing. I expected to at least discover correspondence with his agent or publisher, but even his phone records are sparse. Too sparse."

Laurel cocked her head. "What do you mean?"

"Mr. Plumley and I both live alone, but I probably made four times the phone calls he made last month. Think about your average day. You speak with friends and family members. You contact businesses." He put down his sandwich, too engrossed in the topic to continue eating. "There were many days when Mr. Plumley neither made nor received a single call. Even for a writer in search of privacy, that strikes me as unusual."

Harris slowly made his way into the kitchen, his expression pensive. "He might have done most of his communication via e-mail. If so, it'd be another reason for the killer to steal Nick's laptop." He began to build a tower of Genoa salami, pepperoni, Soppressata, and provolone. "What about his place in Beaufort? Any computers there?"

Rawlings, who was about to take a sip of light beer, froze, and then lowered the bottle like an automaton, his eyes never leaving Harris's face. "How did you know about Mr. Plumley's permanent residence?"

Instead of answering, Harris pivoted his laptop screen so the chief could read the results of his research.

"As you can see, I hit a wall. Prepublication, the man's a ghost. I figured Plumley was a pen name, but couldn't find his real one no matter where I looked."

"It's Ziegler. Nick Ziegler."

With a grin, Harris saluted Rawlings with his massive sandwich. "Point scored by the blue team."

Millay leaned forward eagerly. "So what's shady in Ziegler's past? Drug deals? Child porn? A penchant for farm animals?"

Rawlings raised a brow at the last phrase. "The fact of greatest interest was that he was married. His ex-wife, Cora, is sitting in our interview room as we speak."

"Is she a suspect?" Olivia asked.

"Mrs. Ziegler, excuse me, she's Mrs. Vickers now, is the sole beneficiary of Mr. Plumley's life insurance policy. We don't have a full picture of the victim's financials, but there was an insurance card in his wallet. We spoke to his agent, who put us onto the ex-wife." Finished with his sandwich, Rawlings wiped his hands on a paper napkin and then began to steadily wind it around the first two fingers of his left hand. "If she hadn't been vacationing at Emerald Isle with her new husband at the time of the murder, she wouldn't have raised my suspicions."

Laurel motioned for Millay to pass her the wine. Olivia observed her friend pour herself another generous glass. It was unlike Laurel to consume more than one serving per evening, but tonight, she was drinking zinfandel like a marathon runner chugging water at the end of a race. Millay shot Olivia a concerned glance and, in an exchange of unspoken agreement, Olivia began to fix Laurel a plate of food.

"Two husbands, huh?" Laurel snorted ruefully. "When did she and Plumley or Ziegfried or whoever he was break up? And did she wait until he was rich and famous to dump him so she could live happily ever after with another man?"

Rawlings stared at her in bewilderment for a moment before answering. "According to Mrs. Vickers, she and her former husband had an amicable parting years before his novel was published. During most of their three-year marriage, Mr. Plumley had worked as a free-lance journalist and photographer. He traveled often, leaving Cora alone and unhappy. One day, he returned from an assignment and she told him that their marriage was over. He took the news well, they divided their things, and Cora moved to the western part of the state. She's been living there ever since."

"Yet she brought her new husband to Emerald Isle? That's right near Beaufort. Why would she vacation so close to where she and her ex lived?" Harris inquired before attacking his sandwich again.

"Cora and Boyd were married the day before Mr. Plumley was murdered. We've confirmed the details with both the officiant and their sole witness. The Vickers claim to have come to the coast because they wanted a beach wedding and both swore in separate interviews that they spent most of the hours following their nuptials inside a rental cottage. Celebrating." Rawlings sighed and ran a hand through his salt-and-pepper hair. "The reason Mr. and Mrs. Vickers have been questioned for the past four hours is that Emerald Isle is an easy drive from here and the Vickers are broke. And in my experience, very few divorces are truly amicable."

Millay held up an index finger. "Motive." She then raised her thumb. "Opportunity." She fired her air gun while whistling the first three notes of Beethoven's Fifth.

"It's not that simple, I'm afraid." Rawlings glanced at his watch. "Without any tangible evidence, we're going to have to let the couple go." He stood up and carried his plate to the sink. "This is where I could use some unofficial help."

Olivia grinned. "We thought you'd never ask."

"The two of them are hiding something. I don't know what it is, and my hands are tied. I've questioned them, they've been relatively cooperative, and their statements match. Their alibi is weak, so I've sent officers to Emerald Isle to confirm the few facts that *can* be confirmed. That's all I can do for now." He looked at Olivia. "They plan to have a meal at The Bayside Crab House before driving back. It was my hope that you could see to it that their drinks were poured with a very liberal hand and that someone"—he cast a meaningful glance at Laurel, Millay, and Harris—"could strike up a casual conversation with them."

Harris rubbed his hands together. "Recon! *Sweet.*"

"If possible, find out why they don't have any money. Boyd's a personal trainer and Cora's an interior decorator. I don't expect them to be rich, but it looks like Boyd's maxed out his Visa card with this vacation and Cora's credit has been shot for years. They'll certainly benefit from the insurance payout." He paused. "Just try to get a sense of what makes them tick. Are they greedy? Compulsive? Jealous? There was more than a trace of ire on Mrs. Vickers' part when I questioned her about her ex-husband's literary success. I got the sense that she feels she was owed a piece of Plumley's earnings even though the book was published long after their divorce was final."

Laurel drained her glass and set it so roughly on the coffee table that it tipped over and rolled onto the floor. Rawlings scooped it up in his large hand and quickly dabbed at the splatters on the rug with a napkin. "I'd better drop you off on my way back to the station," he told her gently.

"I'm *fine*," Laurel argued with a noticeable slur.

Olivia touched Rawlings on the arm. "I'll take her home. I need to get going anyway if I'm going to talk to my staff about treating the Vickers like royalty tonight."

Rawlings took a step closer, as though trying to transmit his reluctance to move away from her touch. "Thanks. Let's meet for coffee at Bagels 'n' Beans tomorrow morning. I know you'll have something to tell me."

"I'll be there at nine." Olivia dropped her hand. "What angle will you be running down in the meantime?"

The chief shifted his gaze toward the placid ocean. "I'll be spending the rest of the evening reviewing Mr. Plumley's financial records. Murder is usually about money, and I need to see what he was doing with his."

"Well, if *I* don't show up for my shift, I won't be making any," Millay said with an unhappy frown. "But I can't leave this to you and Harris. You need me behind the bar."

Olivia considered the dilemma as Rawlings walked out of the cottage. "Call in sick to Fish Nets. I'll need your special talents tonight and will double your regular Saturday-night salary. And don't worry, I'll make certain Cora and Boyd end up seated in front of you." She turned to Harris. "Carry a copy of *The Barbed Wire Flower* with you. Don't talk to the newlyweds until Millay gives you the signal. I'm willing to gamble that once she works her magic, they'll be falling all over themselves to talk about Nick Plumley and a whole host of other intimate topics."

"I just hope you don't have some dorky dress code," Millay mumbled. "I am *not* wearing a white shirt and bowtie or anything made from a polyester blend."

Olivia grimaced. "It's not a T.G.I. Friday's. You have to wear a Bayside Crab House T-shirt, but you can stay in your boots and skirt. Just don't give away liquor and food to anyone but the Vickers." She smiled indulgently at Harris. "Notwithstanding a beer or two for this one."

"What about me?" Laurel whined.

Millay slung a shoulder around her friend and helped her to stand. "You're cut off, lady. You and Bacchus got a bit too hot and heavy tonight."

Harris took Laurel's other arm, and together, he and Millay escorted her to Olivia's Range Rover. Haviland jumped to his feet and gave Olivia an inquisitive look. She told him that they were going to work and he was out the door in a blur of black fur, undoubtedly envisioning bowls of butter-drenched seafood or cubes of choice beef steeped au jus.

After promising to meet Millay and Harris downtown, Olivia drove Laurel home in silence. When she and Haviland were alone, Olivia preferred to listen to an audiobook or to put all the windows down, inviting the whirl of the wind to fill the void within the Range Rover's cabin. Now, the humming of the road moving beneath the tires seemed poignantly loud.

"Do you want to talk?" Olivia asked, desperately hoping Laurel wouldn't take her up on the offer. She had enough on her mind without having to listen to her friend's marital woes.

Laurel was quiet for so long that Olivia began to believe she'd be spared, but finally, her friend released a mournful sigh and pressed her cheek against the window glass, as though welcoming the coolness against her skin. "You can't have it all, you know. The media makes it look like any woman can have well-adjusted kids and a happy marriage and a successful career, but that's total crap. The most we can hope for is kids who won't grow up to be serial killers, a marriage that exists out of habit, and a career where you take on more than you can handle because if you don't, you look weak."

"So which part of living an imperfect life bothers you the most?" Olivia glanced at her friend in the rearview mirror.

Laurel's voice quavered. "Not being a good mother. Nothing matters more to me than those boys."

"And quitting your job? Will that make you a better mother?"

"I don't know," Laurel whispered after a lengthy pause.

Olivia could hear the pain in her friend's voice but was unsure how to console her. After all, she had no experience juggling a family and a career. She'd never had to worry about her checkbook balance or raise children or hold the interest of any man for more than a few months. Yet she firmly believed that everyone deserved their share of happiness as long as they were working at fulfilling their dreams. Laurel was a fighter at heart, and Olivia disliked seeing the younger woman so deflated.

"As you may know, my mother worked at the local library," she spoke softly and put one hand on Haviland's neck, her eyes locked on the road. "Some of my fondest memories were of her packing our lunches each morning—hers for work and mine for school. I'd sit in the kitchen and watch her get ready for the day while I ate breakfast. I remember how carefully she'd iron her blouse and that her hair looked so professional pinned up away from her face. She'd hum as she got ready for work, and I knew she looked forward to it every day." Olivia paused, reveling in the memory.

With the smoke gray road in front and a washed-out sky overhead, it was easy to become lost in the cozy scene. Olivia could almost smell the oatmeal cooking on the stovetop, hear the bustle of her mother's skirt as she moved about the room, and feel the sunbeams coming in through the window over the sink, marbling the table with warmth. With her father at sea, these mornings with her mother were filled with a simple kind of peace, and Olivia held on tightly to the vision until the lights of town seemed to burn it away.

"The point I'm trying to make is that I noticed the pride my mother took in her work. She loved her job. It was important to her. It helped to define her. As her daughter, I took note of how she felt, and I wanted to grow up to be just like her—a working woman." Olivia glanced back at Laurel. "I was proud of my mother, and your boys will be proud of you. If you slink off to the paper with the weight of the world on your shoulders, you're teaching them that work is misery. Yet I've seen the glimmer in your eyes when you're running down an exciting story, and the twins will see it too, if you'd only show it to them." She turned down Laurel's street. "You can be an inspiration to your children, Laurel. Frankly, I can't imagine a better gift."

Olivia pulled in front of Laurel's charming Cape Cod–style home and put the Range Rover in park. She kept the engine running.

Laurel looked at the illuminated windows, which bathed the lawn and flagstone path with a soft white light, and put her hand on the door handle. She did not get out of the car. "Everything I love is in that house, so why don't I want to go in?"

Pivoting in her seat, Olivia asked, "Because you feel that your love is not equally returned?"

Swallowing hard, Laurel nodded.

"Then tell that to the person who needs to hear it," Olivia ordered. "No fairy godmother is going to swoop down and make your problems disappear. Get in there and go to work. You love your job? Fight for it. You love your husband? Fight for him. You want your family to be united? Unite it!"

Laurel opened the door. "Okay, okay, I will. But first, I'm going to have another glass of wine."

And with that, she tripped up the walk and disappeared inside.

At The Bayside Crab House, it was clear that Millay and Julesy were hitting it off, despite their markedly different appearances. Julesy was tall and tan and towered above the petite Millay. Millay's black hair was streaked with scarlet and her dark eyes were accentuated with a plum-colored shadow. Julesy was pretty and outgoing, like a daisy growing in a sun garden, while Millay was more of a rare orchid, blooming only at night beneath a swath of pallid moonlight.

The hostess had been instructed to obstruct the two stools at the end of the bar using stacks of plastic booster seats. When Cora and Boyd arrived, the items would be whisked away and the couple would be led straight to the bar, where Millay would immediately serve them a round of drinks. Harris would already be established on a stool to the right, reading away while nursing a beer and picking at a basket of fried calamari. Olivia had staked out a small table behind the newlywed's assigned seats. She'd spread out a fan of paperwork and opened her laptop, but instead of focusing on the screen, she'd be watching the Vickers' facial expressions and body language in the bar's horizontal mirror.

Fortunately, the restaurant was packed by the time the couple arrived, looking haggard and cross from an afternoon spent in separate interviews with various members of the Oyster Bay Police Department.

Carrying out Olivia's instructions flawlessly, the hostess added the newlyweds to the wait list and then made a big show of clearing off the pair of unoccupied barstools and introducing them to Millay.

"If your name isn't called in the next thirty minutes, we'd be delighted to offer you a free appetizer platter. Many of our customers just end up eating dinner at the bar. If you choose to stay, Millay will provide you with place settings and excellent service." The young woman issued her broadest smile, her face dimpling prettily. "Enjoy our selection of microbrews on tap, our signature cocktails, or pick from our extensive wine list."

As soon as they sat down, Cora and Boyd showed subtle signs of relaxation. Millay set coasters in front of them and pointed out various drinks on the menu, and Olivia could see Boyd's tense shoulders loosen a bit. Cora asked Millay if she'd recommend the Lemon Drop Martini and was given an answer that obviously pleased her.

"The Lemon Drop is totally delicious," Millay said.

"But my favorite is the Melontini because it's *so* incredibly refreshing. If you're on vacation, you should have both. And if you're not, then you deserve both even more. And we've got a two-for-one bar special going on."

This earned Millay a small smile from Cora, who ordered a pair of cocktails and then looked at Boyd expectantly.

"I don't suppose a boilermaker would be included in the special," he grumbled.

Millay shrugged. "I don't see why not. We're a new business, so it's our job to impress first-time customers." She winked at Boyd. "Which beer would you prefer?"

Boyd made his choice and Millay poured the golden liquid from the tap into a pub glass, allowing a perfect crown of foam to form on the top. She set the glass in front of Boyd and then, instead of serving him a shot glass filled with whiskey, poured two fingers' worth of Johnnie Walker into a tumbler. Her generosity clearly impressed the couple, and they exchanged looks of pleasant surprise while Millay's back was turned. Within the next minute, she presented Cora with two martinis. The first glowed like liquid sunshine and was garnished with a sugar rim and a curl of lemon peel. The second, and the one Cora instantly reached for, was the soft pink of a watermelon. A pair of translucent kiwi slices balanced on the rim.

Cora popped a kiwi into her mouth and then took a dainty sip of the Melontini. She took a longer, greedier sip and then sighed. Olivia couldn't hear the sigh, but she saw Cora's body deflate as the air was pushed from the woman's lungs.

The couple, having angled their bodies in order to face each other, was unlikely to notice Harris or the book he'd laid on the bar by his right elbow. Olivia wasn't worried. If the Vickers stayed at the bar for the length of their meal, they'd eventually shift positions and hopefully fall into conversation with their neighbor. For his part, Harris was wisely drawing no attention to himself. He'd let Millay exert her charms and get enough alcohol into the couple's systems before she eventually included him in the conversation.

The newlyweds, now significantly more relaxed than they'd been upon their arrival, smiled at each other, chatted with Millay, and worked on their drinks. The moment Boyd's whiskey glass was empty, their attentive bartender appeared like a bottle-welding jinn to refill it.

"This is your free one," Millay announced with a friendly dip of her chin and poured two more shot glasses worth of whiskey into Boyd's tumbler. She then placed a brand-new beer alongside his pub glass, correctly assuming that the presence of the fresh pour would encourage him to drink down the rest of the first beer in a few gulps.

By this time, Cora had finished her first martini and was studying the menu. When her second martini was half done, Millay told the Vickers that the wait list was moving along at a snail's pace and that she'd be bringing them a complimentary appetizer platter within a few minutes.

"Do you want to dine here or would you prefer to continue waiting for a table? I'd like you to stay, of course. I prefer a polite couple like you two to a bunch of horny golfers on a weekend trip away from their wives. I had to deal with enough of *that* sort last night." She smiled, her beautiful face captivating the tipsy couple.

Cora laughed. "Don't worry, we'll eat here. It looks like the band is back from their break. We've got great seats for listening to the music and won't have to wait around for a waitress to bring us drinks."

"That *is* a plus," Millay agreed and disappeared into the kitchen to fetch their appetizer.

Olivia started in her seat when the band, a group of good-looking high school boys led by front man Cody Rigod, Chief Rawlings' nephew, began the second half of their set with a rowdy rendition of "Get Off of My Cloud" by The Rolling Stones.

It was now impossible to hear what anyone in the bar area was saying, and Olivia was reduced to casting covert glances at the Vickers as they devoured their appetizer and started in on their third round of drinks. However, it was plain to see that Millay was winning their trust. Judging by the way she leaned over to listen to what they were saying, Olivia assumed they were complaining about their afternoon.

Then Millay's eyes opened wide in shock and she pointed at Harris. He blinked in confusion and stared stupidly from his copy of *The Barbed Wire Flower* to the Vickers and back to the book again. Soon, all four of them were huddled together, trying to converse over the din.

On the sly, Millay poured the newlyweds another round. Olivia noticed that Boyd was given another boilermaker, but Cora had been served a Blue Orange Martini.

"Vodka, blue Curaçao, and Cointreau. Nicely done, Millay," Olivia mused aloud. "You must have had that ready to go in an extra shaker." Signaling for a waitress, she placed an order for scallops with mushrooms in a white wine sauce and asked for a glass of Dr. Loosen Riesling.

Ten minutes later, with the quartet at the bar still oblivious to the rest of the world, Olivia took her wine and went into the office to check on Haviland. He'd been fed a meal by one of the sous-chefs and was now taking an after-dinner nap on the carpet. A note on the desk read:

Ms. Limoges, Michel gave me a few recipes for your dog and told me to take good care of him. Tonight Haviland had prime beef mixed with peas, carrots, and rice. He seemed to like it. Thanks, Danny.

Olivia smiled. "Ah, Michel. I miss you. As soon as Kim can take over here, I'll be back in my little office at The Boot Top where I belong."

Haviland had been dreaming, his paws flexing and shivering in his sleep, but at the sound of Olivia's voice, he opened his eyes and raised his head an inch off the floor. She bent down and kissed his black nose. "Go back to sleep, Captain," she whispered and returned to her table.

The waitress arrived with her meal and fresh glass of Riesling. While Olivia savored the flavorful entrée, Cora and Boyd pushed their empty dinner plates aside and began to indulge in yet another round of drinks.

"I'm going to have to put them up at a hotel," Olivia murmured to herself. "They can't drive back to Emerald Isle. They'll be wrapped around a telephone pole trying to get out of the parking lot."

Suddenly, Millay made a comment and then gave a flippant shrug of her shoulders. Whatever she said had no effect on Boyd or Harris, but Cora's reaction was dramatic. Olivia saw the new bride's stricken face in the mirror and watched as she jumped down from the barstool and lurched through the doors leading outside, Boyd staring after her, his mouth ajar in astonishment. After a pause, he took off in pursuit of his wife.

Olivia waved Harris over. "What happened?"

"Millay made some glib remark about them not having a kid at home to worry about, what with the day they've had. Cora's eyes filled with tears and she tore out of here."

Perplexed, Olivia pressed a wad of bills in Harris's hand. "Drive them to a hotel, would you? They're both blind drunk and I'm responsible for their state of inebriation. Tell them you picked up their dinner tab too. Let them think you're some rich dot-com guy."

With a nod to Olivia and a salute for Millay, Harris dashed outside.

Millay cleared the Vickers' plates and glasses and then sank down in the chair opposite Olivia. "I didn't touch a nerve until I mentioned kids. We talked about the cops, Nick, money, divorce, sex, and God knows what else and didn't get so much as a facial tic. Drop the word 'kid' and Cora looks like she's been kicked in the gut."

"Well played," Olivia told the bartender. "So Cora has something to hide and it has to do with a child." She took a final sip of her wine and stood up, lost in thought. "The question is, what about a child? Did she want a baby? Did she lose a baby? Or did something tragic happen to her child? And if she had one, who's the father?"

Millay fell into step with her as Olivia walked to the office to wake Haviland. "Not Boyd. He doesn't know a damn thing about it."

Olivia paused, an image of Laurel hesitating before entering her own house appearing in her mind's eye. "Married people have secrets too. If Boyd wasn't aware of that before, he is now. Poor fool."

Chapter 10

*I have lived long enough. My way of life is
fall'n into the sere, the yellow leaf, and that
which should accompany old age, as honor,
love, obedience, troops of friends I must
not look to have.*

—WILLIAM SHAKESPEARE

Chief Rawlings showed up at Bagels 'n' Beans wearing a particularly unattractive Hawaiian shirt. Olivia took one look at the yellow and green pineapple print and grimaced. "I take it you're off duty?"

He placed a basket containing a toasted asiago bagel smeared with a generous layer of cream cheese on the table and sank into his chair with a sigh. "For the moment. I'm never really off the clock during an investigation as serious as this. I expect the media to descend on Oyster Bay today." He glanced around the café, quickly assessing whether potential gossipmongers were close enough to overhear their conversation, but most of the eatery's patrons were tourists. His hazel eyes softening, he focused his gaze on Olivia's face. "How'd it go last night?"

Olivia proudly recapped Millay's brilliant performance. "The lovebirds are going to have a hell of a hangover this morning," she declared at the end of her narrative.

Rawlings rubbed his chin, lost in thought. "Cora only cracked when Millay brought up the subject of children. I wonder why."

"I have a theory," Olivia said. "If Cora and Nick had a child, then that kid would surely be entitled to a share in his estate."

The chief took a bite of his bagel and chewed heartily. Then he shrugged. "In that case, why didn't Mr. Plumley name his dependent as a beneficiary on his life insurance policy?" He scribbled a notation in his pocket notepad. "This will have to wait until tomorrow. I'll need to get ahold of Cora's medical records, and without her being an official suspect, that won't be easy."

Taking a sip of coffee, Rawlings pointed at the framed photographs hanging from the brick wall above their table. "What do you think of these?"

Olivia had kept her eyes averted from the images since she'd sat down. The smiling infant faces served as a pointed reminder that she hadn't called Kim to see how Anders was doing. "Wheeler usually displays such tasteful art," she said. "Yours, for example."

"These are more certainly commercial than Wheeler's usual selections, but the photographer isn't without skill." Rawlings grinned. "Still, I'd never have pegged Wheeler as a fan of kittens, puppies, or babies."

Olivia glanced at the photograph hanging above her right shoulder. It showed a toddler with gossamer blond hair being used as a climbing post by a pair of kittens. "All this picture needs is a balloon and a rainbow."

Rawlings laughed. "I bet Laurel would think it's cute."

Briefly, Olivia wondered whether her friend had had any success communicating her feelings to Steve last night. Certain phrases surfaced in her mind, and Olivia realized that the time Laurel's husband spent at the office coupled with his hypercriticism of his wife might have an obvious and unpleasant explanation. "Speaking of Laurel," she paused, wondering how to broach the delicate subject to Rawlings. "Do you remember when you had to question Steve when you were working on the Cliché Killers case?"

The chief nodded and his eyes lost their bemused glimmer and became instantly veiled.

"You checked his alibi without Laurel's knowledge, which was very thoughtful and sensitive, but you also never told me what that alibi was." Olivia left the unspoken question dangling in the air between them.

The chief scraped his chair away from the table and held out his hand for Olivia's empty coffee cup. "I didn't tell then and I'm not going to now. Would you care for a refill?"

Olivia pushed her mug into his palm, her fingertips brushing against his. They smiled at each other for what seemed like a long moment before Wheeler called Rawlings over to the counter to pick up the snack he'd prepared for Haviland.

"That dog gets better service than I do," a sunburned vacationer whined.

Wheeler mumbled, "Reckon it's 'cause he's got better manners," and poured two fresh cups of his Coastal Coffee blend for Rawlings and Olivia. He then pasted on a congenial grin and handed the petulant tourist her order. "Soy latte no foam and an ever-so-gently toasted multigrain bagel with fat-free cream cheese on the side. May I get you anythin' else, ma'am?"

The woman scrutinized her bagel but seemed pleased with its even golden hue. She then took the lid off her to-go cup to make sure that Wheeler hadn't included the offensive froth. Satisfied, she dropped a dollar in his tip jar and walked out the door.

When she was safely away, Rawlings let out a laugh—a deep and hearty rumble that shook his whole entire torso.

Wheeler scowled. "Don't you have criminals to catch, Chief? Go on, now. Drink your coffee while it's hot."

With that reprimand, Rawlings returned to the table and handed Olivia her replenished cup, but he did not sit down. Though his face still held traces of humor, it was evaporating quickly. "He's right. I have a pile of reading to do on the New Bern prison camp and a phone interview with Nick Plumley's agent at eleven."

"Do you have another task to assign me?" Olivia asked coyly.

Rawlings put a finger under her chin, forcing her to meet his stern gaze. "Yes. Don't find any more bodies."

The chief held the door for a family of five and then disappeared into the sunshine. Olivia watched Wheeler and one of the teenagers he'd hired for the summer attend to the hungry family. They ordered breakfast sandwiches, complicated espresso drinks, fresh-squeezed orange juice, pastries, and fruit cups. After collecting their food, the father handed Wheeler a wad of bills and, signaling for him to keep the change, he joined his brood at one of the window tables. Olivia finished her own buttered sesame bagel and observed several more families enter, order, and leave, hands filled with carryout bags.

Eventually, the morning rush eased and Wheeler came out from behind the counter to wipe off the unoccupied tables.

"You're amazing," Olivia told him and studied the old-timer with genuine warmth.

He smiled wanly. "This place keeps me tickin'."

Struck by a thought, Olivia touched his arm as he passed her table. "How long have you lived in Oyster Bay?"

"Seems like my whole life," he replied in a tired voice and then saw that Olivia wasn't satisfied by his answer. "I left a job at a paper mill and settled here in the fifties, a young man with his whole life ahead of him. Worked the docks for a decade, had a warehouse job for a decade, and then got hired here when this place was still a bakery." He gestured at the room. "This was what I always wanted though. A little coffee shop by the sea. Sometimes life deals you a decent hand. Other times not."

Unsure what to make of the cryptic phrase, Olivia put a hand on the rough brick of the interior wall. "And have you always loved art? Not this stuff"—she jerked a thumb at the photographs—"but the things you typically display. You have an eye for talent."

Wheeler's gaze grew distant. "Art's in my blood. It's a way of travelin' to other places, to other times. It lets you forget or remember and it doesn't have to say a word. It's my favorite kind of company to keep."

"Did you know that several of the German prisoners held in the New Bern camp during World War Two were gifted artists? Have you heard anything about the camps or those artists?"

Twisting the damp rag in his age-spotted hands, Wheeler shrugged. "I didn't live here then, girlie, but I heard tell that there were men who could paint, men who could throw a pot, and men who could carve wood with such skill that they got a share of local folks' precious rations in return for a piece of their work."

"It's a wonder there hasn't been a significant exhibit featuring these wartime masterpieces," Olivia mused softly. "What a story it would make." She met Wheeler's pale blue eyes. "I've seen one of the paintings. A snow scene by a man named Heinrich Kamler. Simply executed, yet utterly captivating. I'd never heard of him until Harris found the painting hidden under one of the stair treads of his new house, but I wish I could talk to someone who worked at the camp."

The bell over the front door tinkled and a host of bronze and bare-chested teenage boys in board shorts entered the café, hair slick with water, faces flushed from an early morning spent riding the waves. They spoke in rich baritones and flashed white smiles, enveloped in an air of robust assurance.

Wheeler's gaze fell upon the young men, and Olivia saw a flicker of sorrow or regret cross his wrinkled features. It happened so quickly she wasn't sure what she'd seen, but she looked upon the boys with a brief stab of envy. She'd never known a carefree summer, had never been invited to be a part of a circle of friends such as this group of shining, beautiful boys. Their ability to live wholly in the present was alluring, and Olivia continued to stare at them as they jostled one another amicably to be first in line.

"Not too many old-timers left, my girl," Wheeler said and slowly got to his feet. It was as if the presence of the young Adonises made him feel every minute of his age with painful acuity. "I can recollect what it was to be like one of them boys. Back then we thought nothin' could touch us either. We'd win the war and get the girl, spend the next fifty years drinkin' beer and goin' to ballgames with our best pals, have piles of money in the bank and a real nice car. Maybe a house and a kid or two. But that ain't the way of things. Pennies lose their shine after they've been passed 'round long enough."

Olivia wasn't giving Wheeler her full attention. She was suddenly transported to the moment in Grumpy's Diner in which the school librarian had asked Nick Plumley to sign her copy of *The Barbed Wire Flower*. She'd mentioned that the son of one of the New Bern prison guards had spoken at their annual fund-raiser. Perhaps Nick had tracked this man down. Perhaps the prison guard's relative had become a useful source for the writer. He might unwittingly be in possession of a clue regarding Plumley's murder.

After clearing off her table, Olivia patted her thigh, and Haviland lumbered to his feet, blinking sleep from his eyes. Wheeler was busy filling orders, so she didn't bother to wave to him.

Edging past the chiseled bodies of the young men, she breathed in the coconut scent of their sun lotion and the salt water clinging to their shorts. Pausing, she allowed the pure smell of summertime to wash over her, bestowing upon her tiny particles of youth and promise.

Olivia spent over an hour looking for the name of the prison guard's son on her computer. The school website had no evidence of the event, and she couldn't find a record that anyone had spoken about the prison. The only hits she had involved a history professor at the University of North Carolina who'd posted his research on Camp New Bern on the university's intranet. Olivia didn't have access to his files and would have to get in touch with the professor during his office hours.

Resigned, she called the public library and asked for Leona Fairchild but was informed that the senior librarian never worked on Sundays. That left Harris. Olivia had a feeling that her friend might be spending time with Estelle, and though she didn't mind interrupting the couple's leisurely Sunday, she decided that sending an e-mail would be just as effective as calling. Harris was never far from his computer, and she knew from experience that he kept the volume turned up high enough to be able to hear the ping of an incoming message from any room in his house.

Made restless by her lack of progress, Olivia decided to take a walk on the beach. Donning a wide-brimmed hat and a pair of sunglasses, she gathered her metal detector, backpack, and trench shovel and set out with her grinning poodle. There was nothing Haviland enjoyed more than being given the freedom to rush over the dunes into the shallows, the water parting beneath his paws and splattering his black curls with cool moisture.

He pranced at the ocean's edge, barking happily, until Olivia caught up. She tossed a stick toward the sandbar and watched as he leapt into the waves, his mouth hanging open in anticipation, pink tongue lolling to one side. Smiling, she turned on her Bounty Hunter and began to sweep the head of the detector over the damp sand along the waterline.

She absently listened to the blips and bleeps, her thoughts wandering. Aimless theories concerning Nick Plumley's death darted about like a school of startled minnows until she finally focused on the metal detector's display.

Ignoring the readouts occurring near the lighthouse, Olivia walked farther east where she'd be less likely to encounter bottle caps or soda can tabs. The stretch of beach between the lighthouse and her nearest neighbor had yielded interesting finds in the past, but today her device remained stubbornly mute. After pausing to throw Haviland's stick a few more times, she rounded the jetty and strolled on the sand leading toward Plumley's rental house.

Her Bounty Hunter gave a high-pitched signal, indicating the likely presence of an object made of silver. Tired of carrying the ungainly device, Olivia decided this was as good a place as any to dig and pulled her trench shovel from her backpack.

"Come help, Captain!"

Haviland was pleased to oblige, and together, they dug until they reached moist sand.

"Hold on a sec," Olivia said, wondering whether they'd gone too far. She directed the metal detector at the pile of the discarded sand, but it stayed quiet. Placing it over the hole resulted in a bold chirp.

Discarding the shovel, Olivia used her fingers to comb through the damp sand. Eventually, she felt a tiny object beneath the nail of her index finger and pulled a coin from its cool, dark bed. Sitting back on her haunches, she brushed off granules of sand and held out the find to the sun.

"A dime," she murmured. "But an unusual one."

The coin needed cleaning. Olivia couldn't make out the date, but despite the coating of dirt and grit on its face, she recognized that the profile did not belong to Franklin D. Roosevelt. Plus, it was heavier than a modern dime and felt solid in the middle of her palm.

Olivia slipped the coin into the pocket of her shorts and packed up her shovel.

"I prefer this sort of mystery, Captain," she told her panting poodle. "Let's go home, get you some water, and wash our find. Perhaps the ocean has something to tell me today." She cast a covert glance at the sparkling waves. "It's been a while since I've had a message."

Untying her shoes, she added them to the backpack and waded past the gurgling sea foam, letting the waves lap at her ankles. Olivia walked back to her house this way, reconnecting with the sea like a mermaid who spent far too long on dry land.

Later that afternoon, before she headed downtown to check in at both of her restaurants, Olivia removed the dime from its vinegar bath. When she'd first found the coin, it had the dark gray hue of sharkskin, but now it had reclaimed much of its original silver shade along with a sheen of oil slick blue and green when held directly under the light. A true coin collector wouldn't have cleaned the dime in this manner if they'd cleaned it at all, but Olivia didn't sell her beach finds. They were placed in jumbo pickle jars labeled by the year. In the depths of winter, when it was hard to believe summer would ever return, she'd dump out the contents of a jar onto her living room rug and comb through the relics, rediscovering her simple treasures and reliving the hours having her shoulders doused with sunshine and her lungs infused with sea air.

Olivia carried the dime to her computer and pulled up a bookmarked site on coin identification. She scrolled to the section on U.S. dimes and spotted hers immediately. The female profile on her find was an exact match of the Winged Liberty Head wearing a Phrygian cap pictured on the website.

Haviland sat beside her and gazed at the screen with interest.

"That silly-looking hat is supposed to represent liberty and freedom," she told the poodle. "And that bundle of branches tied together with an ax on the reverse is called a fasces. A Roman symbol indicating power. According to this article, however, it was supposed to indicate America's readiness for war. Combined with the traditional olive branches shown on every dime, it was also supposed to portray our country's desire to acquire peace." She shook her head. "We always did take the other Roosevelt's declaration to 'speak softly and carry a big stick' too much to heart."

She put the Mercury dime beneath the lens of her magnifying glass and searched for the date.

"1941," she read and then tilted the coin so that light from her desk lamp made it appear as though the goddess of Liberty was winking at her with her single eye. "So you were minted during the war. Whose pockets did you travel in? Did some poor fool about to be shipped to the front lose you when he stripped down to take one last swim in his home waters? Did you bear witness to the sinking of the German U-boat and the roundup of the first wave of prisoners? Or were you a little kid's birthday money?"

Olivia glanced out the window, where the hazy, pink sky reminded her that she needed to get going. She turned off the lamp and looked down at the coin before dropping it into this year's pickle jar. Liberty's face was painted in shadow, smudges of dark gray that the vinegar bath had been unable to erase. The goddess looked solemn. Her gaze was firm and unwavering, but her mouth turned down at the corner into what looked like disapproval or even doubt.

"There must be a clue hidden in the past," Olivia murmured and gave the jar a little shake, forcing the coin to rattle against the other metal trinkets inside. She screwed the lid on and quickly checked her e-mail. Harris had come through. He'd discovered the name of the New Bern prisoner guard's son.

"Raymond Hatcher." Olivia smiled in satisfaction. "I look forward to meeting you."

She sent Harris a short note of thanks, shut down her computer, and loaded Haviland into the Range Rover. It was time to review menus, see to paperwork, and have a cocktail. And not necessarily in that order.

Harris had also found out that Raymond Hatcher worked for a freight company in an industrial park outside of Grantsboro. Olivia waited until eleven thirty Monday morning before setting out for Hatcher's place of employment. She hoped to intercept him en route to his lunch break.

She hadn't called first. It was her experience that a few white lies, combined with an envelope of twenty-dollar bills, made even the most tight-lipped people transform into effusive chatterboxes. If Raymond wouldn't meet

172 · Ellery Adams

with her today, she'd find a time and place more condu-
cive to a lengthy chat.

Assuming that loading docks were not unlike fishing docks, Olivia bypassed the front entrance and drove
around to the back of the mammoth steel structure.
Dozens of tractor-trailers were backed up to deep bays,
and the industrious whir and bleeps of forklifts maneuvering around the loading areas reverberated against
the metal walls.

Olivia decided to leave Haviland in the car, so she
parked the Range Rover on the shady side of the building, opened the windows, and handed him one of his
favorite treats: dried tendons from grass-fed South African beef. His eyes glimmered as she placed three more
snacks on the console. "I know they're high in protein,
but take your time. I don't know how long I'll be."

Ignoring her, Haviland took his prize to the back,
sank onto his belly, set the tendon between his front
paws, and got to work. His white teeth flashed, and the
gleam in his eyes was that of a satisfied predator.

Shouldering her purse, Olivia walked into the nearest bay as though she frequented the business on a regular basis. She saw a middle-aged man with a kind face
scrutinizing a sheet of paper on a clipboard and headed
straight for him.

"Excuse me," she said, giving him her most daz-
zling smile. "Could you tell me where to find Raymond
Hatcher?"

"Sure thang, sweetheart." The man ogled her appre-
ciatively and then immediately caught himself. "Sorry.
We don't get fine-lookin' women such as yourself in here
every day." He gestured at a pair of vending machines
positioned near the back wall. "Ray's gettin' himself his

tenth Mountain Dew of the mornin'. See him? He's the big guy in the John Deere cap."

Olivia thanked him and, skirting around idling fork-lifts and veritable mountains of boxes, she came to stand behind Raymond Hatcher. Her first impression was of his height. She was nearly six feet, but he probably had another five or six inches on her. He wasn't lanky like many very tall people, but was as solid and heavily muscled as an NBA center. When he turned, she met his electric blue stare and momentarily felt at a loss for words. There was something familiar about his face, but she knew she'd never seen him before. His eyes alone were unforgettable, and one didn't pass by a man in his midsixties of Raymond's size without taking note.

"Hello," she finally managed to say. "Are you Raymond Hatcher?"

He nodded, his gaze intense but not unfriendly. He said nothing.

"Do you have a moment? I'd like to talk to you about Nick Plumley." She waited for the giant to react to the writer's name, but he only cocked his head to one side like a curious bird. "I'm here because I'll be ghostwriting the rest of the sequel to *The Barbed Wire Flower*," she lied.

Instead of answering, he popped the tab of his soda, raised it to his lips, and took several long swallows. "I can't talk now," he said after lowering the can to his side. He gave it a little shake and then absently squeezed the metal with his fingertips. "I don't have a break for another two hours. You'll have to wait until my shift's over."

"When would that be?" Olivia asked, trying not to let her focus waver; the subtle cracks of the deflating soda can filled the air.

Raymond glanced at his watch. "I came on at eleven, so I'll be here 'til eight."

"Okay, then why don't I buy you a beer? Are you familiar with a place called Fish Nets in Oyster Bay?"

He nodded. "I've been there a time or two."

"How's nine o'clock?"

One of the nearby forklift engines roared into life, startling Olivia. Raymond watched her jump to the side, and the shadow of a grin curved his mouth upward. "All right, but it's not the kind of place I expect you visit much. Are you sure you wanna go there?"

"Trust me, I've been to Fish Nets more times than I care to remember, but I happen to know the bartender. She'll take good care of us."

Raymond slipped a finger beneath the brim of his baseball cap and scratched his temple, his grin widening a fraction. "You can call me Ray."

"I'm Olivia," she said and held out her hand. He shook it carefully, nodded at her, and then walked away. Several men observed his progress and then turned their attention toward her, clearly interested in why this beautiful, sophisticated woman had paid their coworker a visit.

Olivia was accustomed to being the object of people's stares. They did not trouble her. What did trouble her was that she considered herself an astute judge of character. She believed she had a gift for reading people and that everyone had a tell. Raymond Hatcher was an exception, however. Olivia couldn't glean the slightest sense of his personality. She didn't like that. In fact, it made her nervous.

Inside the Range Rover, Haviland was obediently pacing himself and still had a full beef tendon left to eat. Olivia let him be. Turning on the car, she commanded her dashboard phone to dial Millay's number.

"You demonstrated a great deal of skill Saturday night," she told her friend. "I hope you're prepared for an encore performance."

Olivia paused to listen to the bartender's confident answer. "This one's different," she warned Millay. "We need to tread carefully."

Chapter 11

A pure hand needs no glove to cover it.

—NATHANIEL HAWTHORNE

Had Ray Hatcher shown up at the crowded bar of The Bayside Crab House, the patrons would have done a double take upon seeing his formidable figure. Then they'd have carved a path for him, staring at him out of the corner of their eyes as they drank exotic martinis or microbrews in chilled pint glasses.

In Fish Nets, Ray was just another guy. A few people cast mildly curious looks his way when he first walked in, but their attention quickly returned to their bottles of Bud, shots of whiskey, and games of darts or pool. Smoke hovered in the air like early-morning fog, and Hatcher's head cut a swath through the white wisps as he moved toward Olivia.

She noticed that one or two locals greeted Hatcher with a nod or a brief clap on the shoulder. This welcome gave Olivia cause to relax. If the hardened fisherman and laborers of Fish Nets knew Raymond Hatcher, then he posed less of a threat to her. Olivia's father had been one of these men, and as his child, she had a keen sense of the rhythm of their existence, of motoring to the deep waters well before dawn, of the backbreaking work beneath the unrelenting sun, of the thousand tiny cuts to the arms and hands from serrated fish scales. Every face in the bar was marked by the sea, the sun, and the struggle to make ends meet.

Olivia felt as comfortable among these locals as she did mingling with the wealthy and sophisticated diners at The Boot Top. In a sense, she was a child of both worlds, but her father's confederates would defend and protect her in a way that none of her grandmother's circle would. The upper-crust members of society that made up her grandmother's set had been self-serving and remarkably uncharitable. They only rallied around one another to avoid scandal or the loss of assets. Olivia shared her grandmother's love of the finer things, but she also felt a deep kinship with those whose lives depended on the fickle ocean. It was as though this community who breathed in the salty air and bathed in the cool water for countless years were set apart as a different species of human.

"Damn, you didn't tell me you were meeting with Sasquatch," Millay stated in admiration as Ray made his way to the empty barstool next to Olivia. "Good thing you left Haviland at The Boot Top. This could get ugly."

Ignoring Millay, whose hair was gelled into a cresting wave of black and silver down the center of her head, Olivia greeted Ray and asked him what he'd like to drink.

"You buyin'?" he asked, his mouth curving into the hint of a smile.

Olivia nodded. "That was part of the deal."

After requesting a whiskey and soda, Ray eased himself onto the stool, casting a nervous glance at his feet as the wood creaked and groaned in protest.

"It'll hold," Millay said, serving Ray his drink. "Trust me, these old stools have borne more weight than you're carrying. Guess it's a good thing we don't serve food."

Ray studied her. "You've got some wild hair. Reckon I like it." He then pivoted his massive trunk so that he faced Olivia. "Tell me about this book you're writing."

Olivia took a sip of beer and tried not to grimace. It had grown warm while she'd waited for Ray to arrive. "First, let me figure out how much you already know so I don't waste your time. Did Nick Plumley interview you or make arrangements to do so?"

"He called a time or two," Ray answered cryptically.

Undeterred, Olivia held his inscrutable gaze. "And?"

Ray's eyes slid away from hers and he took a slug of whiskey. "I went to his house. He wanted me to bring the pictures I have of the prison camp. See, my older brother Dave went to work with James most days when he was a kid. It was a long time ago, but I remember hearing all kinds of things about that place. Dave and I were real close, and he used to tell me about the men there when I was little, kind of like his own brand of bedtime stories, but I guess your writer friend wasn't as interested in them as he let on."

Olivia tried to conceal her eagerness. This man had photographs of Camp New Bern? And Plumley hadn't been interested? Suddenly, Olivia understood what had happened. "He wasn't willing to pay your price," she hazarded a guess.

Swallowing the rest of his whiskey in one gulp, Ray slammed his glass against the bar, sending russet-colored droplets across the battered wood. "Look, lady, before you go judging me, let me give you a little glimpse of my life. I'm sixty-six and I drive a forklift for a living. I'm still making mortgage payments on my piece-of-crap house, and what's left over from that at the end of the month is soaked up by the regular bills." Warming to his subject, he leaned toward Olivia, breathing whiskey in her face. "I've got nothin' saved for a rainy day, let alone my so-called retirement. At this rate, I'll die on that goddamn forklift. Forty years I've done that job. All I want is a break."

Scanning the room, Olivia wondered how many of the grizzled men and women felt as Ray Hatcher did. Life wasn't easy, but for some of the Fish Nets patrons, it had been especially tough.

In a place like this, most people wore their physical and emotional scars with pride, but Ray had passed beyond that point. He was weary of the struggle, and Olivia was aware that this could make him especially dangerous. If he had nothing to lose, he might very well take a serious gamble to get what he wanted. Clearly, what he desired most was money, and Nick Plumley had refused to pay.

"I'm not judging you," she assured Ray. "Information is a commodity. You possess photographs and personal experiences that no one else does. I can understand why you'd be unwilling to sell them cheaply." Furrowing her brows, she suddenly asked, "Why did you call him James? You didn't say 'my father.'"

"'Cause he wasn't. James Hatcher died before I was born."

Completely intrigued, Olivia put her palm on the bar, signaling for Millay to refill Ray's glass. "Would you entertain another offer? For both the photos and your memories?"

Ray made a point of thanking Millay for his drink and then shrugged. "I can tell you plenty of stories." He tapped his temple. "Those are safe in storage and I'll sell you as many as you want, but the pictures are with a college professor right now. He's kind of . . . renting them out. So if you want to pay to see them too, it's fine by me, but you'll have to wait."

"Is he at UNC?" Olivia asked.

"How'd you know that?" Ray's expression became instantly suspicious.

Olivia decided to be honest. "I stumbled across his name on the Internet while searching for yours. Professor Billinger, right?" It was obvious from Ray's frown that she was correct, "Look, I'd love to see the photos. I can pay you immediately for the right to examine them If it's okay with Professor Billinger, I'll just drive to his office in Chapel Hill and ask for a quick viewing. I'm sure he won't mind."

"He might, seeing as he's also writing a book."

Placing an envelope on the bar, partway between her bottle of beer and Ray's glass of whiskey, Olivia said, "I'll take my chances. Do I have your permission to contact Professor Billinger?"

Ray palmed the envelope, dropped it down to his lap, and hunched his shoulders so that he could quickly count the money without drawing attention to his actions. He seemed satisfied by the contents. "It'll do."

Olivia decided to take advantage of the moment. "Did Plumley share any details with you about his sequel?"

Ray regarded her curiously. "You'd know more about that than me."

"Please," she said. "His notes and laptop are missing. I'm working blind here."

While swirling the dregs of whiskey in his glass, Ray seemed to be deciding how much to tell her. "James Hatcher was killed when those Krauts escaped. Everyone's always asked me about that night, wondering what my brother Dave remembers, but Plumley told me he'd already written about it in his first book. Said he was more interested in what the prisoners were like before they decided to murder an innocent man. What life was like when things were peaceful at the camp. He had it in his head there was a local woman involved with one of the German scums that got away in '45. He was going to write about how they fell in love."

The note on the back of Heinrich Kamler's painting surfaced in Olivia's mind. "A local woman. Was her name Evelyn White?" she said.

Ray narrowed his eyes angrily. "Like I said, your writer didn't take me up on my offer, so I didn't answer any of his questions any more than I'm going to sit here and answer yours. This is payment for looking at the photos. That's it." He stood abruptly. "You know where to find me when you're ready to get down to business." He waved the envelope at her. "And it'll take more than this."

"Please, I don't mean to sound callous," Olivia said after a brief hesitation. "And I know you said that you were very close to Dave. But James, a man you'd never met, died before you were born. Why does this affect you so much?"

Olivia expected Hatcher to explode with rage, but he seemed to welcome the question. "Agnes Hatcher adopted me when I was only a few weeks old. She'd gone to the orphanage looking for a sweet little girl. A pretty thing to take her mind off her grief, but she picked me instead. She and Dave were the only family I've ever known. Times were real tough for the Hatcher clan after James was killed, but I don't remember much of that. All I know was that Kraut Kamler stabbed their husband and daddy in the back like a yellow-bellied coward. I watched that loss tear them up inside with every year that passed."

Olivia watched as Hatcher's fingernails dug into the bar and a deep, slow-burning rage surfaced in his eyes. She could see that Plumley had awakened sleeping demons by contacting this man. Hatcher had gone silent for a moment, but then he directed his ire at Olivia. "Because of Kamler, I never had a chance to have a father. And you people are almost as bad—you write your books and make money off of James Hatcher's murder. Money nobody in the Hatcher family ever sees! You're a bunch of leeches!"

Olivia shrank back in the face of his anger, yet she agreed with Raymond Hatcher. Nick Plumley had become rich and famous fictionalizing James Hatcher's violent death, while Ray hadn't received a single benefit except for an invitation to speak at the school's annual fund-raiser.

"You're right," she said softly. "I'll try to amend that. Is Dave still around?"

Hatcher shook his head. "His number came up in Korea. He was in the prime of his life. And he had nothing to leave me but his stories, and that's why I'm not going to give them away. What happened to his daddy haunted him every day of his life. It haunted my life.

That's why folks owe me for what I know. A price was already paid, you got it? Now it's *my* turn to get paid."

"I do understand. Thank you for agreeing to see me, for sharing this much. It can't have been easy," Olivia told Hatcher with as much sincerity as she could and then watched his towering form disappear through the doorway, where it merged into the night shadows.

Millay handed one of her customers a beer and then put her forearms on the bar, bending at the waist to get closer to Olivia. "I hope you didn't piss him off. That man could strangle you with his pinkie."

"A sobering thought." Olivia pushed her nearly full bottle of beer into Millay's hand. "He may have gotten angry enough at Nick Plumley to have done exactly that." She dug out her cell phone. "I'd better call Rawlings from outside. Thanks for your help."

Sliding a new beer down the bar, where it was expertly caught by a shrimper Olivia recognized from her weekly trips to the docks, Millay frowned in puzzlement. "Why thank me? I didn't do squat."

Olivia placed a twenty on the bar. "But you would have. You had my back. That matters to me more than you know."

Embarrassed, Millay began to wipe the bar with a frayed rag. "Somebody has to be your wingman when Haviland isn't around. It was smart of you to leave him with Michel and the kitchen staff instead of bringing him in here. I'm not sure if he would have responded well to Hatcher's body language. And I am not paid enough to mop up blood." Millay pointed a finger at Olivia. "Keep me in the loop, okay?"

On her way to the door, Olivia stopped to exchange small talk with a few of the fishermen she knew from either her childhood or as suppliers to her restaurants. Several offered condolences on the loss of her father, saying that he was a fortunate man to have died in his bed with his family gathered around when all of Oyster Bay believed he'd been claimed by drink and the sea more than forty years ago.

"Part of him did die that night," Olivia said to one of her father's former crewmembers as she stood beneath the exit sign, a nimbus of neon red illuminating her pale hair. "That storm took my father and gave him another life, another family. And because of that, I gained a brother. I guess we made a good trade, the ocean and I."

The man had met Hudson at the docks a few weeks before The Bayside Crab House had opened and now knew him as well as anyone. "You can tell he's Willie's boy from a mile off. Both of 'em got thunder in their eyes, but your brother has heart too. He'll stick by you when you need him most. Sometimes it's the quiet ones who have the most to say."

Olivia paused, one hand on the door. She was intrigued by the fisherman's words. Nodding at him in recognition of his wisdom, she stepped outside and was surprised by the feel of rain against her skin. Shallow puddles reflected the streetlights and electric store signs, and the sidewalks had emptied of people. Olivia walked unhurriedly to the Range Rover, relishing the warm rain and the mingling scents of moist pavement and ocean air. She felt both invigorated and poignantly lonely, and the moment she was inside the dry cabin of her car, she dialed Rawlings' number.

When he answered, she could hear the din of conversation in the background.

"Sorry to interrupt," she began, experiencing a pang

of disappointment. She'd wanted Rawlings to be alone, to be available to her need, but he clearly wasn't.

"Hold on," he commanded, and she could sense him distancing himself from the noise, seeking out a quiet, private place. After a few seconds he said, "I never thought I'd see Haviland without you."

Olivia started the car and turned her headlights on, shimmering raindrops refracting in the beams. "You're at The Boot Top?"

"It's Jeannie's birthday. This is where she wanted to come, and since it's the big five-oh, her husband said the sky was the limit. We're just finishing up dessert now."

Imagining Rawlings' kindhearted sister enjoying a slice of Michel's decadent hazelnut chocolate mousse cake, Olivia pushed down on the accelerator, rocketing the Range Rover through an intersection, water splashing from her tires onto the shiny, black road. "Can we meet for an after-dinner drink in the bar?"

"As long as we stick to coffee," Rawlings agreed. "I have more work to do tonight."

Olivia said, "I'll order coffee for you, but I need something with a little more kick."

The Boot Top's parking lot was far from full, but it was past nine on a Monday night, and most of the restaurant's patrons would have finished with their meals. There were others, however, like Jeannie and her family, who were still lingering over coffee and dessert.

Lately, Michel's cakes, tarts, and mousses had become even more seductive than usual, and he took great pride in his artistic presentation. His reputation was growing to such an extent that he refused to take any time off, and Olivia worried he might soon collapse from sheer exhaustion.

Entering by the front door, Olivia immediately sought out the hostess and gave her instructions to tell Jeannie's waiter to comp their entire meal. She then made her way to the bar, where Rawlings waited for her at one of the intimate side tables. A steaming coffee mug sat on a cocktail napkin in front of him and a tumbler of Chivas Regal waited for her.

"You're a saint," she told him and took a grateful sip before even bothering to sit down.

Rawlings watched her, his eyes glinting with curiosity. "What's on your mind?"

"I have another suspect for you," she said and, without further preamble, told the chief about her conversation with Raymond Hatcher. When she was done, Olivia concentrated on her cocktail, giving Rawlings the silence he needed to digest all she'd imparted.

After two or three very long minutes, the chief put his elbows on the side of his chair, made a temple with his fingers, and rested his chin on his fingertips. "We got the lab results back. The fibers found on Mr. Plumley's neck matched those on his robe. In other words, he was strangled by the sash of his own robe."

Olivia recalled the red welt striping the flesh of Nick Plumley's throat. She said nothing and waited for Rawlings to continue.

"I believe the killer wore latex gloves. Trace amounts of latex were found beneath Mr. Plumley's fingernails, along with bits of bread and cream cheese from his breakfast." The chief frowned. "But there's something odd about these results."

"Such as?"

Rawlings stood up and walked behind Olivia's chair.

He leaned over, close enough for her to smell coffee and chocolate cake, and put his forearm around her right shoulder. He then pressed his arm backward into the soft flesh of her throat.

"Pretend I wasn't being gentle," he whispered into her hair, his breath caressing her neck and sending a pulse of desire through her body. "What would you do?"

Olivia curled her hands and reached for the chief's ropy forearms. She locked her hands on to his flesh, attempting to free herself from his hold, when in truth, she longed for him to put his lips on the skin just below her jaw line. She wanted to turn her head and capture his mouth in hers, to lock her fingers in his thick hair, pushing the world and all of its interferences away for just a moment.

"See? You'd scratch and claw at my arm, desperate to breathe, doing anything in your power to break free." Rawlings resumed his seat across from Olivia. He averted his gaze, and she knew he'd felt her hunger for him, that it had shocked him with electricity, like water dripping onto a live wire.

Reaching for her glass, Olivia nodded. "You expected to find the killer's skin under Nick's nails."

"Yes. The nails obviously weren't cleaned, so I've begun to believe that Mr. Plumley also wore gloves."

Several thoughts vied for attention once the chief voiced this theory. Olivia remembered Shala Knowles and her fellow curators donning their white gloves to examine Harris's painting. She also envisioned Ray Hatcher showing up at Nick's house with the photographs the author was so desperate to examine. Plumley would have gladly put on a pair of latex gloves in exchange for the right to view images of Camp New Bern.

Rawlings had come to the same conclusion. "I need to pay a visit to Mr. Hatcher tonight. There are far too many suspects in this case, too many people who'd take a risk in the hope of walking away with a pile of money."

"Or for the chance at possessing an original work by Heimlich Kamler," Olivia pointed out. "There must have been half a dozen art aficionados in the curator's office. Who knows how many people they told about the painting? They knew my name and that I'd come to Raleigh from Oyster Bay. I would have been easy to find . . ." She trailed off, feeling foolish.

The chief dismissed the notion. "The murderer wanted Nick dead, not you. I don't know how the painting fits into the case or if it has any connection at all, but I need to find Hatcher before it gets any later."

He put his hand on her shoulder in passing. "Nice work, Olivia."

Without turning, she felt him leave. It was as if the room grew suddenly duller, the warmth on her skin where his breath and fingers had touched her was replaced by the cool exhalation of air-conditioning. Even the candle sputtered, sending fractured shadows onto the table where Rawlings' empty coffee cup sat.

At that moment his sister entered the bar, her cheeks flushed from an evening of celebration. "There you are!" she exclaimed merrily. "You shouldn't have paid for my birthday supper! We barely know each other."

Olivia smiled. "Fifty is a milestone. I couldn't resist the chance to do something to contribute to your party."

"And maybe impress my brother at the same time?" Jeannie winked impishly.

Holding her hands out in surrender, Olivia had to laugh. "You got me. I did have an ulterior motive."

Jeannie squeezed her on the arm. "Thank you all the same. We'd better be going so you all can close. I've never been the last person in a restaurant before, but it sure makes me feel young and adventurous. Good night!"

"Wait! Please." Olivia put out her right hand, hoping to impede the woman's departure.

The chief's sister drew close again. "Go on, I can see that you want to ask me something about Sawyer."

Olivia cast her gaze down. "I screwed up with him. He was willing to be with me, but . . . well . . . I pushed him away," she confessed miserably. "How can I prove that I'm ready now, that I know I made a mistake the morning I let him go?"

Jeannie took a long time answering. She seemed to be deciding whether Olivia Limoges was worthy of her brother. Finally, her eyes softened. "He was torn in two when Helen died, so he's not going to come knockin' on your door if you've already shut it in his face once. He's going to protect his heart now. You want to claim him?"

Uncomfortable in the face of such a direct question, Olivia clenched her jaw to hold in the uprising of feeling and nodded, her sea blue eyes glittering with intensity.

"Well, then. You're going to have to do something *big*. And I don't mean buy him a yacht or write his name across the sky. Something big is something that scares the life out of you, that makes you tremble in your shoes because it's chock-full of risk. You *show* Sawyer what you're letting me see and he'll never let you go again." She raised a finger in warning. "But don't you mess around with his heart, Olivia. I might be a plump, God-fearing wife and mother, but I'll tear you to pieces with my bare hands if you hurt him."

Olivia believed her. "I read you loud and clear. He's lucky to have such a devoted sister."

Jeannie shrugged, merriment instantly returning to her round cheeks. "Trust me, I wasn't always nice to him. He did some *terrible* things to my doll collection, and I held that against him for years." She smiled. "Word has it that you have a brother too."

"Hudson. He and his wife, Kim, and their daughter, Caitlyn, all live here now. And they just had a baby. A boy named Anders." Olivia felt a pang when she spoke his name. She had an inexplicable urge to get in the car and drive to Greenville, to see the infant's little face and to watch the steady rise and fall of his small chest. Instead, she silently vowed to call Kim first thing in the morning.

"Whatever it is, the child'll be just fine," Jeannie said, correctly sensing Olivia's anxiety. "Babies are tougher than they look." A movement near the hostess podium caught her attention. "There's my gang, waiting on me as usual." She patted Olivia's hand. "You take care."

Olivia watched as Jeannie's husband slid an arm around her waist and kissed her several times on the brow and then once on the lips. Their teenage children followed behind, looking both embarrassed and protected by their father's open display of affection.

When they'd gone, the emptiness of the restaurant resonated around Olivia. It was only when the waitstaff turned up the lights in the dining room and set about their closing tasks that Olivia was able to shake off her stupor and head through the swinging doors to greet Haviland.

In the kitchen, the sous-chefs weren't exchanging their usual insults and lighthearted banter. Instead, they were strangely silent. The dishwasher's banging and splashing reverberated against metal pans and mixing bowls, and no one looked up when she approached.

Olivia paused, glancing from her office door, which was closed, to the sous-chefs. They wouldn't meet her inquisitive gaze, but their hands betrayed their feelings, straying to twist water from a dishrag or to diligently polish an already gleaming knife blade.

Without bothering to knock, Olivia threw open the door to her office and let out an involuntary gasp.

There was Michel, one arm wrapped around a woman's back, his free hand stroking her wheat blond hair. Her face was buried in the chef's neck, and though Olivia couldn't quite hear the words she whispered, the raw desire behind them was clear enough, tainting the air with a heady, cloying perfume like that of a million jasmine blossoms opening at once.

Haviland bounded up from his position on the floor and gave Olivia a toothy smile. She reached for him and, at the same time, found her voice.

"Laurel Hobbs! What the hell is going on here?"

Chapter 12

~~~~~~

*Life is not significant details, illuminated
by a flash, fixed forever. Photographs are.*

—SUSAN SONTAG

Olivia twirled the Mercury dime on the tabletop, watching it reflect splinters of morning light onto the Formica. It winked like a buoy on the water until bumping into the edge of her coffee cup and then clattering to a stop. She picked up the dime and sent it spinning once again.

"Are we borin' you?" Dixie asked, indicating the half-empty diner with her hand. "See Mr. Jeffries? The cute little man at the *Evita* booth? He's been lookin' for an excuse to sing 'Mr. Mistoffelees' ever since I can remember. Should I tell him you'd like nothin' better than to hear your favorite song from *Cats*?"

"Not if you value your life," Olivia threatened and then sighed. "And I'm not bored, just impatient." She tapped on her cell phone, which sat on the center of the table alongside her coffee cup. "I'm waiting for two calls. One from Greenville and the other from Chapel

Hill. I was hoping to have been on the road by now, but my damned phone refuses to ring."

Dixie climbed into the booth opposite Olivia and stretched out her short legs on the surface of the red vinyl cushion. "Oh, that feels good. I've been skatin' my ass off since five thirty." She glanced at her purple Swatch. "This is late for you to be eatin' breakfast. And no laptop? What's goin' on with my favorite Egyptian strumpet?"

"Not a thing since she managed to seduce Ramses. I can't concentrate on Kamila. Nick Plumley's murder has taken over my thoughts. That and an incident that occurred at The Boot Top last night, but I absolutely *cannot* tell you about that, so don't even ask."

Dixie opened her mouth to speak when Olivia's phone vibrated, causing it to skid sideways. Olivia swept it up and examined the screen. "It's a text message with an attachment. I have no idea how to open this. I'm not thirteen, for crying out loud."

"Don't be such an old fart," Dixie chided and reached for the phone. "Come on, you know my arms are too stubby to grab that far, so give it here."

Olivia obeyed, and Dixie punched a few buttons and then read the message aloud. "'Anders is doin' fine. Caitlyn and I spend most of the day at the hospital and I've been able to hold my boy and even give him his first bath. Nurse Love is visitin' us today. She is an angel! Here's a pic of another angel. This is Anders sendin' love to his Aunt Olivia. oxox Kim.'" Dixie fluttered her fingertips over the phone and then her face broke into a bright smile. "Lord have mercy! If this isn't the most precious child I have *ever* seen!"

She placed the phone flat on the table and pushed it toward Olivia. A cherubic face rested in the middle of the screen, and Olivia pulled the Anders image closer. "He's filled out," she remarked proudly. "Look at those dimples. And his eyes . . . they're not dark like Hudson's. They're gray. Almost pewter. Beautiful." She felt a warmth spread through her chest, rushing up her neck to her cheeks. It was an odd feeling, this delight over receiving a photo of her half brother's child, but delight is what it was, pure and simple. In a small way, this child belonged to her. They were tied to each other by the bonds of blood and the finer, less tangible thread of experience. Olivia had been on the other side of the wall while the doctors had repaired Anders' heart, she had stood over his incubator when the surgery was over, and she had touched his tiny hand. With that touch, she had instantly committed herself to him.

"Look at you, 'Livia!" Dixie teased. "That boy's got you wrapped around his itty-bitty finger. I'm surprised you haven't hired a helicopter to fly him home to Oyster Bay."

Olivia pretended to mull over the idea. "Too noisy," she replied. "But there is the nursery to consider. I don't know if Hudson got the crib ready or has a supply of diapers and all the millions of gadgets one seems to need to raise a child these days. I should stop by the house and find out."

"Bring Laurel along," Dixie suggested. "She'll point out what's missin', and you two can do some damage with your Visa card. Shoot, I might move into Anders' room, especially if Grumpy won't stop wakin' me up at two in the morning . . ." She trailed off. "Hey, why'd a black cloud form over your head when I mentioned

Laurel? Does she have somethin' to do with what happened last night at The Boot Top?"

Haviland got up from his seat on the floor, stretched, and stuck his nose between Dixie's skates. He sniffed the wheels with great interest and then sat on his haunches, looking expectantly from one woman to the other.

"See? Even Captain wants you to spill." Dixie lowered her voice. "Fifty bucks says she's got the hots for Michel."

Olivia, who had just poured a small whirlpool of cream into her coffee, held her teaspoon in the air. "How did you know that?"

Dixie lifted her chin and looked smug. "Honey, I've got two good eyes in my head. Every time I run into that man at the docks or the grocery store or even at the farm stand south of town, he acts like he's lost in a dream. A man doesn't walk around wearin' a secret little smile on his face unless there's a woman involved." She shook her head. "I just never thought it would be Laurel. I know your French-fried chef has a thing for married women, but *Laurel*? She's a girl scout!"

"I don't think they're having an affair, so don't go spreading this around like a cold. Last night, I walked in on Michel comforting Laurel, and they looked, well . . ."

Dixie studied her friend. "Like they fit in each other's arms?"

Olivia nodded.

"And what about Mr. Pearly Whites? Do you think he knows his wife has her eye on another man?"

Even though the cream had already dissipated into the coffee, Olivia stirred the spoon around and around, staring into the light brown brew as though it held an answer. She raised the spoon, cutting through a swath of steam, and then placed it absently on a napkin. "Laurel believes that Steve has been cheating on her for months, maybe longer. The whole thing's a mess."

"What are you going to do?" Dixie asked with concern.

"Not a damn thing," Olivia answered in surprise. "I make it a point not to get involved in domestic squabbles."

Dixie undoubtedly had much to say on the subject but was forced to call an end to her impromptu break when Grumpy stuck his head out of the kitchen and bellowed, "Order up!"

Haviland took this as a sign that he should accompany the dwarf as she zipped off to the pickup window. Seeing as he was encouraged by Dixie's whispered promises of a plate of crunchy turkey bacon, Olivia let the poodle wander away.

Thankfully, her phone vibrated again, and this time, Olivia recognized the name and greeted the caller with uncharacteristic affability.

Professor Emmett Billinger was exuberant. "I phoned the second I finished listening to your voice mail this morning. I'd be glad to exchange information and to show you these extraordinary photographs. And you're willing to drive here? And to bring the painting?"

Olivia assured him that she was more than happy to spend a few hours in the car if it meant discovering a clue to Nick Plumley's murder. Harris's Heinrich Kamler watercolor had been safely stored in the vault of the Coastal Carolina Bank, and Olivia told the professor that she'd pick up the painting and be at his office by lunchtime.

"Splendid! I'll have sandwiches ready so we don't have to interrupt our time together searching for food."

Sensing that she was going to get along with this efficient academic, Olivia asked whether he had any objection to Haviland's presence.

"Not at all. I'm owned by a pair of rescued greyhounds," he replied cheerfully. "They go to daycare when I'm at work, but I'll have a suitable meal on hand for your companion."

Olivia left money on the table and peered into the kitchen while Dixie was busy delivering platters of Belgian waffles. On the other side of the swinging door, Olivia caught Grumpy tossing a piece of meat into the air directly above Haviland's quivering snout. With a flash of teeth and a lightning-quick snap of the jaw, the meat disappeared into the poodle's mouth.

"You're not going to make much of a profit giving away food like that," Olivia remarked with a grin.

Grumpy was a man of few facial expressions. He glanced at her and then cracked a pair of eggs onto the sizzling grill. "With the tips you give Dixie, I don't need to worry about it."

Casting her eyes around the orderly kitchen, Olivia paused for a moment to consider what it would be like to spend eight hours in the same space, day in and day out, with only an aged radio for company. "What's it like? The life of a master fry cook."

Many people would have taken offense at such a question, but Grumpy knew she meant no harm. "It's quiet," he answered stoically. "Before this, I didn't have much quiet. I'm no chef, but I make decent food, and folks can afford to eat here regular. I'm proud of that."

Grumpy slid the eggs on a plate, dumped two cups of crisp hash browns beside them, and piled four strips of bacon on top of the potatoes.

Olivia snapped her fingers at Haviland, and then, before turning to leave, she touched Grumpy briefly on the shoulder. "This diner is the heart of our town. And your food is far better than decent. Don't tell your wife, but I don't come here because of the décor."

A rare rumble of laughter followed her through the swinging kitchen door.

Olivia's drive to Chapel Hill was uneventful. On the way, she listened to an audiobook dramatizing the life of one of her favorite women, Eleanor of Aquitaine. It was easy to become lost in Eleanor's world of drafty castles, thwarted romance, and endless wars while traveling west on I-40, but when she neared Chapel Hill, she was too distracted by the traffic and a landscape populated predominantly by chain stores that she had to turn off the CD.

"Talk about suburban sprawl," she said to Haviland. "Last time I was here, none of these strip malls existed." She sighed. "Small-town America is disappearing before our eyes. I hope the area around the university is better preserved. I remember it as being so charming."

To her relief, Franklin Street was relatively unchanged. The college town was not as bustling as it would be when the students returned in August, but it was far from sleepy. Olivia knew that downtown Chapel Hill was a hotspot for both foodies and music lovers and felt a pang of remorse that she'd have to make do with sandwiches for lunch when she could be trying out one of the many unique cafes. Instead of enjoying summer rolls at Lime & Basil or vegetable fritters from Mama Dip's, she'd probably end up with cold turkey, processed cheese, and a leaf of limp lettuce squashed between two store-brought slices of bread.

Her anticipatory mood could not be deflated by thoughts of lunch, however. The university at Chapel Hill's tree-lined campus was simply too lovely, too replete with tasteful architecture and an aura of history to inspire any feelings other than optimism and a sense of purpose.

Finding parking near Hampton Hall was no easy feat, and Olivia flirted with the idea of occupying a faculty spot.

"I doubt they're all here today," she stated defensively to Haviland, who cocked his head to the side and sniffed to indicate his disapproval.

Billinger's office was on the second floor. The thick, wood door was ajar, and Billinger was at his desk. He was examining a document turned yellow with age but immediately glanced up when he heard Olivia's footsteps and the sound of Haviland's paws come to a halt at his threshold.

"You're ten minutes early," he said, rising to his feet. "Excellent."

Moving around his desk, he shook Olivia's hand firmly and then held out his palm for Haviland to smell. The poodle was clearly interested in the scent of other canines he detected on Billinger's skin and clothes but was too polite to sniff the professor's pant leg or shoe. Instead, he gave the man a welcoming smile and waited to be invited inside.

Emmett Billinger was handsome in a bookish way.

In his late forties, he was tall and slim like Olivia. Like her, his thin frame radiated good health and strength, and the flush on his cheeks indicated that he didn't spend all of his time indoors. His eyes were brown, as were the frames of his glasses and his tousled hair. Olivia liked his face, seeing in it a contrary mixture of boyish eagerness and the wisdom of an old soul.

The jacket of Billinger's seersucker suit was draped on the arm of a small sofa, and he'd rolled up the sleeves of his dress shirt, revealing gently freckled forearms. Olivia had never laid eyes on a man who looked sexy in a bowtie, but Emmett Billinger did.

"Are you hungry?" he asked politely, indicating a neatly laid table with a view out the only window.

Olivia shook her head, taking in the built-in bookcases, the wooden file cabinets, and the attractive design of the blue and maroon Oriental rug obscuring most of the industrial gray floor. "This is a wonderful office." She removed the canvas bag holding Harris's painting from her shoulder and laid it carefully on the sofa. "Would you like to clear a space on your desk?"

Billinger jumped to comply. He piled papers, file folders, and his laptop onto the bookshelves behind the desk and then stood back, waiting for her to set the painting on the clean surface.

Without speaking, she unwrapped the watercolor from its protective layers and stepped back, allowing Billinger the time and space he required to examine it.

Olivia settled on the sofa with Haviland at her feet and watched the professor. She liked how he sat very still and studied the winter scene, his eyes glimmering with unadulterated pleasure. He then slid on a pair of gloves, similar to those worn by the museum curators, and drew a jeweler's loop from a desk drawer. He looked at Heinrich Kamler's initials and then, a slow smile creeping across his face, turned the painting over.

"This is marvelous," he declared happily, meeting Olivia's eyes briefly before letting them fall on the handwriting again. "This inscription . . ." He pushed back his chair, grabbed a file folder, and hurried to take a seat next to her on the sofa. "It sheds light on a relationship that presented itself during the course of my research earlier in the year. I've seen a photograph of Kamler and Evelyn White and, earlier this year, heard stories about them from another guard's child. That child, who's now an elderly woman named Mabel, has been my primary source up until this point, but this is the first written evidence I've laid eyes on that suggests the extent to which Kamler cared for Miss White."

He handed Olivia a black-and-white photograph. "This has been digitally enhanced, but it shows Heinrich Kamler giving Evelyn White a painting lesson."

The image showed a dark-haired girl in a modest, light-colored dress, seated on a campstool in front of an easel. She held a paintbrush in her right hand and was facing a small canvas, but her eyes slid sideways and her mouth curved into a slight and secretive smile. Kamler was in profile, but it was clear from his chiseled features and locks of thick hair that he had been a good-looking man. He held a palette in one hand and was gesturing at the canvas with a wood-handled knife in the other. His expression was one of unmasked adoration.

"That's the knife that was used to kill the guard the night Kamler and Ziegler escaped." Billinger handed her another photo, this one a blowup of the knife in Kamler's hand.

But Olivia didn't take the photo. Her mouth hung agape in shock. "Ziegler? *That* was the second prisoner's name? The one who escaped with Kamler?"

"Yes. I thought you knew that already." Billinger's face clouded in confusion.

Accepting the photograph, Olivia explained, "Nick Plumley's real name is Ziegler. That's no coincidence."

Billinger nodded. "Absolutely not. Nick was Ziegler's son." He pointed at the photo, unaware that Olivia was still trying to absorb what he'd just said. "See this knife? There's an *H* burned into the handle. The piece is now in the North Carolina history museum. It's difficult for me to call it a weapon after seeing it in this scene with Kamler and Evelyn."

"They're both so young," Olivia whispered, temporarily distracted by the first photo of Evelyn and Heinrich Kamler. She'd need a moment to herself to fully consider the significance of Nick's parentage.

"Evelyn would have been sixteen and Kamler eighteen," Billinger agreed. "He was one of the youngest crew members on the U-352 sunk off the North Carolina coast. It's no wonder he and Evelyn hit it off. According to the woman I spoke with in the spring, Kamler already knew some English and, by the time of his escape, spoke it like a native North Carolinian, right down to our ever-so-subtle drawl. And Evelyn had always loved art, so it's easy to see why she fell for the talented German."

"But I'm astonished that her parents would approve of her being taught by the enemy. Wouldn't the Whites have been ostracized by giving their consent?"

Billinger was clearly delighted by the question. "In the beginning of the war, probably. But as the war dragged on, most of them became a part of the community. They went to baseball games and the cinema, worked the area farms, and traded with the townsfolk. All of these activities took place under guard, but toward the end of the war, several locals were being given language lessons by the prisoners. As long as Evelyn was chaperoned, no one viewed her art classes as a scandal."

Fascinated, Olivia took the rest of the photos Billinger held out. "Did you get all of these from Raymond Hatcher?"

Billinger shook his head. "Just those three on top. They're perfect for my research, though, because they show the prisoners interacting with the guards and other locals. Here's a prisoner trading handmade soap for some fresh fish." He moved closer to her, pointing enthusiastically at the next photograph. "Now we have two prisoners and three guards playing cards for peanuts. It wasn't uncommon for prisoners to work in the peanut farms or pick cotton or help out in the paper mill, and as you know, peanuts are a healthy and filling snack and were often more useful than money."

Olivia was amazed at the expressions of amicability between the prisoners and their keepers.

"In these next few photographs, the prisoners are wearing American uniforms or civilian clothing," Billinger explained. "These men had probably been in our country long enough to blend in. Even today, many people are startled to learn that Germans and Italians, Austrians and Poles, and French and Czechs were filling the manual labor jobs left empty after our men went overseas."

When Olivia came to a large image showing a group of prisoners posing for the camera with the frank, open stares of schoolchildren, she paused for a long while. These young men were as fresh-faced and wholesome as any group of American soldiers. They stood straight-backed and proud in the back row. In the front row, they knelt, one arm slung casually over a raised knee, as though they'd been interrupted in the middle of playing baseball or dancing with a pretty girl.

Olivia looked into their eyes, all rendered into dark pools by the black-and-white film, and wondered which of these men had returned to their homes, which had been shipped to another camp, and which had died before the armistice.

She felt the waste of war in her hands, and suddenly, the photographs felt very heavy. The images of these boys, both foreign and American, whose lives had been turned inside out by circumstances beyond their control, filled her with sorrow. A part of her felt foolish too. She lived so close to Camp New Bern and had never known about its existence or that prisoners from other countries had toiled to put food on the tables of her fellow North Carolinians.

"Very few of these guys were Nazis, you know," Billinger said, misreading her frown. "Many were coerced into joining the army. Threatened. Some wanted to defend their homeland even though they didn't support Hitler. Nothing about war is as black-and-white as these photographs."

His words echoed Olivia's feelings exactly. War, like a murder investigation, was a mess of emotion, conflicting stories, and useless violence. The pair fell silent for a moment. Haviland yawned and gazed up at them, his eyes conveying his interest in procuring a midday meal.

"Why don't you tell me how I can help while we

eat?" Billinger suggested, ruffling Haviland's ears. "I picked up some muffulettas from one of my favorite sandwich shops, and I have bottles of Perrier in my dorm fridge. Please." He pulled a chair up to the table by the window and held the back, waiting for Olivia to be seated. "I brought Haviland organic chicken breast. That all right?"

"Perfect," Olivia answered, warming to the professor more and more as the hour progressed. The sandwich was delicious. Her fear of being forced to swallow processed meat and cheese disappeared the moment she tasted salami, ham, mortadella, mozzarella, provolone, and a tangy olive spread piled between round slices of fresh Italian bread.

Billinger poured Perrier into two coffee mugs and clinked the rim of his cup against hers. "So what are you looking for, Olivia? What does Nick Plumley's death have to do with Kamler's painting or the New Bern camp?"

She swallowed a mouthful of sandwich. "As I said over the phone, Nick Plumley didn't just die; he was murdered. I can only assume that he changed his name from Ziegler to Plumley because he was ashamed to be the son of an escaped prisoner. Either that, or his father had adopted the surname Plumley in order to avoid capture. Whatever the reason, Nick's father must have given him a firsthand account of life in the camp, his and Kamler's escape, and how Kamler killed the prison guard, so why was Plumley searching for additional accounts?"

Picking a wayward sesame seed from his shirt, Billinger looked thoughtful. "Since listening to your voice mail, I've wondered about that as well. I'm writing a nonfiction book on the POW camps in North Carolina, and if there's one thing I've learned as a historian, it's that one cannot find the facts without also sifting through a heap of gossip and rumor. Sometimes, rumor leads to fact. I wonder if that might be the case with your murder investigation."

Olivia put down her sandwich. "Please explain."

"Mabel, the woman I mentioned, was also the child of a prison guard. Like our mutual friend Raymond Hatcher, Mabel was a terrific source for personal accounts of life at Camp New Bern from a young person's perspective. In fact, Mabel was a teenager then, so her memories are more detailed than the ones Mr. Hatcher recalls his older brother having told him. Mabel and Evelyn White were best friends."

This revelation caused Olivia to lean forward in her chair, anxious for the professor to keep talking.

Billinger took a sip of Perrier, as though he needed a moment to pluck up the courage to continue. "Mabel repeatedly told me that Evelyn and Heinrich Kamler were lovers. She also refused to accept that Kamler murdered Hatcher. According to Mabel, Kamler had a gentle and quiet nature. He was popular among the guards, the other prisoners, and the locals. More importantly, he was content, or so Mabel claims. She was adamant that Kamler had no desire to escape because he had no family left in Germany and he would never want to be parted from Evelyn. He planned to marry her when the war was over, naive as that may sound to you and me."

Rising to her feet, Olivia returned to Billinger's stack of photographs and picked up the one of Evelyn and Heinrich. His features were too distant to be perfectly clear, but even a blurred image couldn't suppress the easy attraction passing between him and Evelyn. "What if Kamler was innocent?" Olivia looked at Billinger. "He was never captured, right?"

"No."

"What if Kamler wanted to punish Plumley for branding him a murderer?"

Billinger rubbed his chin thoughtfully. "And becoming the thing he was falsely accused of being? And why now? *The Barbed Wire Flower* has been out for ages."

"Maybe Kamler didn't have access to Plumley until now," Olivia guessed. "Maybe he didn't know he was Ziegler's son. Maybe Ziegler was actually responsible for the guard's death."

With an indulgent grin, Billinger indicated the seat Olivia had abandoned. "All conjecture."

"And what of Evelyn?" Olivia asked, her eyes betraying her hope. "Is she still alive?"

"I'm afraid not," Billinger replied softly. "She passed away several years ago."

Olivia didn't return to her lunch. She was too restless to sit down. Something was gnawing at her, an elusive thought she couldn't grasp. It fell away like a handful of sand running between her fingers. She also knew she wasn't asking the right questions yet. "Plumley was looking for this painting. If I can find out why it mattered to him, I believe this murder investigation will crack wide open. Could we visit Mabel? I'd like to hear her talk about Evelyn and Heinrich."

Billinger hesitated. "She's in a nursing home in Hillsborough, a town north of here. It's only a twenty-minute drive, but it might be a waste of time. Mabel's mind is not what it once was. She's been steadily deteriorating into senility."

Wrapping up her sandwich to indicate her decision, Olivia stared, unseeing, at the butcher paper. "Did Mabel ever mention Ziegler?"

"Several times. He was a late arrival to the camp and a full-blooded Nazi. He and a small group of men kept themselves apart from the rest of the prisoners, and according to Mabel, Ziegler was also in love with Evelyn White."

Olivia walked around the professor's desk and looked down at the faint note written on the back of Kamler's painting. "This message can be read one of two ways. Either Heinrich is telling Evelyn that he's planning to escape and they can elope, or he's assuring her that the war is drawing to a close and that he will find a way to remain in the States and build a life for them both."

After wiping his hands on a napkin, Billinger put on his cotton gloves again and tenderly turned the painting over. "What do you see when you look at that cabin?"

"Sanctuary," Olivia answered immediately. She had had plenty of time to consider the emotions that the cozy structure evoked. "Security. Home. Welcome."

Billinger nodded. "This might very well be an image from Kamler's past, from his childhood. But it could also be his hope for the future. A simple life, a private life, a place where one could step away from the world and hide. A nest, so to speak."

"Evelyn would have been a legal adult by the end of the war," Olivia said, her eyes riveted on the bar of light streaming from the crack under the cabin's front door. "How was he planning to support her even if he could stay? As an artist? A farmhand?"

An idea struck Billinger. He clamped his hand around Olivia's forearm in an attempt to gain her full attention even though her eyes were already locked on his face. "The last time I went to visit her, Mabel was going on and on about Evelyn's treasures. It didn't make any sense at the time, but what if Evelyn had more paintings? What if there are *more* of these"—he gestured at the watercolor—"hidden in your friend's house?"

A knot of fear formed in Olivia's stomach. "Then Harris isn't safe. Kamler's works are worth a small fortune."

Wordlessly, the pair flew into motion. Olivia packed up the painting, and Billinger tossed the debris from their lunch into the trash bin. Grabbing his suit jacket, he hurriedly collected the photographs and dropped them into a large envelope.

"Bring the painting," he told Olivia. "Who knows what flood of memories might come flowing from Mabel's mind when she sees it."

Olivia shouldered the bag and pulled her cell phone from her purse. "I'm glad you're driving. I need to put a call in to Oyster Bay's police chief and have him put a detail on Harris's house."

"You know the chief of police?" Billinger seemed impressed.

Thinking of Rawlings' brown eyes flecked with green and gold, his tacky Hawaiian shirts, his penchant for chocolate milk, and his undeniable skill as an artist, Olivia murmured, "Not as well as I'd like, but I plan to do something about that very soon."

Chapter 13

Rawlings was a step ahead of Olivia regarding Harris's safety. He'd already established a rotation of drive-bys during the day and had offered overtime pay to any officers willing to sit in a squad car outside Harris's house during the night.

"I can't afford to do this much longer," Rawlings admitted. "Don't have the budget for it. If I can't break this case soon, Harris might be living with me."

Olivia would fund the cost of overtime herself if need be and told the chief as much. "Especially after dark. He's more vulnerable then."

"Except that he always has company," Rawlings said after a discreet pause. "It's one thing to incapacitate a single person in order to search the house for hidden artwork, but to take two people out requires more planning." Olivia heard a rustling at the other end of the phone as if the chief was sifting through sheaves of paperwork. "But the killer's had enough time to plan, and that puts me on edge. I feel like Mr. Plumley's murder only partially fulfilled his agenda and that he or she is ready to make a move. I believe that the countdown was initiated by that murder but is racing toward another act of violence."

Olivia had experienced the same prickling of unease, an unidentifiable sense of urgency that pushed at her like a wind at her back. Even now, on a wooded road north of Chapel Hill, Olivia felt the pressure building and intensifying like a wave preparing to crest. She tried not to fume at the ancient Chevy pickup in front of them, even though it forced them to drive below the speed limit.

Billinger was lost in his own thoughts, but Olivia found his presence comforting. She hadn't expected to have formed an immediate alliance with the professor, yet here he was, having put aside whatever plans he might have had for the rest of the afternoon, taking a chance on an old woman with an inconsistent mental state.

Mabel was in a wheelchair in the garden of The Sunrise Retirement Community. Olivia almost made a caustic remark about the nursing home's name, but held it back. She recognized a need to step into this insulated world with a positive attitude and could see that Billinger was well practiced in walking with soft footfalls and wearing a bright smile. He raised his hand and waved to a nurse watering a ceramic urn filled with red geraniums before approaching Mabel.

"Good to see you, Professor!" The nurse greeted him warmly. "Mabel's havin' a good day. She'll be right glad for some company."

The woman they'd come to visit was a tiny thing. Her

body was so slight that it seemed as though she couldn't hold herself upright without the support of the wheel-chair. Mabel had tufts of white cotton-candy hair and rheumy blue eyes, but when she heard Billinger's voice, she smiled and blinked away the fog of memory and held out a fragile hand, marked with age spots and swollen rivulets of blue veins, and reached for him.

Billinger squatted down and looked at Mabel with genuine affection, accepting her hand and gently placing his over the thin flesh. He wheeled her alongside a nearby bench and gestured for Olivia to join them.

The professor had told her that Mabel was only in her seventies, so Olivia was caught off guard by the woman's appearance. She wore all the marks of someone who'd struggled, kicking and clawing, through life. The years had shrunken her and bit away at her curves until she had the body of an undernourished child—all sharp angles and skin stretched tight across the bones. Her face was carved with deep wrinkles, like those on a walnut shell, but there were many fanning from the corner of her eyes, indicating that she'd born her troubles with a healthy dose of good humor.

"How lovely to meet a friend of Emmett's," Mabel said to Olivia in a voice as insubstantial as a leaf pushed about in the breeze. "He's such a dear." She gazed at Billinger fondly.

Instead of taking a seat next to the professor, Olivia stood directly in front of Mabel. "May I show you something?"

As the older woman nodded in assent, a stray shaft of sunlight broke through the protective boughs of the oak tree to the northwest and illuminated Mabel's face, erasing away the decades. For a fraction of a second,

Olivia saw how handsome this woman had been in her youth and that the ghost of this beauty coexisted with her brittle bones and mottled skin.

Olivia froze for a moment. Had her mother survived, would she be like Mabel? Would her radiance have shone through the sea blue eyes she shared with her daughter? Or would a lifetime spent growing old alongside an erratic man have robbed her of all her softness and grace, replacing them with furrows of worry and hard edges of regret?

Mabel turned her hands over, showing Olivia her palms and inviting her to come back to the present moment. Happy to obey, she unwrapped Kamler's painting and, keeping it anchored on a piece of cardboard, tenderly placed the watercolor on Mabel's lap.

The woman slipped on a pair of bifocals that had been hanging from her neck on a chain of finch yellow and gasped. "This is one of Henry's!" Then, assaulted by doubt. "Isn't it?"

Olivia and Billinger exchanged looks.

"Henry?" Billinger prompted in a patient voice.

Mabel covered her mouth as though she'd let loose a secret entrusted to her long ago by a dear friend. "I sometimes forget that Henry wasn't his real name, but Evie called him that instead of Heinrich. Almost from the beginning. To her, he was Henry." Mabel's eyes drank in the winter scene. It was almost a tangible thing, to see her slip away from the senior center's garden and travel back to Camp New Bern, to her girlhood, to Evelyn White.

Barely breathing, Olivia imagined she could follow Mabel through this wormhole of time, spying the pair of teenage girls in starched dresses and Mary Janes, schoolbooks clutched against their chests as they giggled at the sight of a group of cute boys hunched over glasses of cherry cola at the drugstore counter.

"Evie'd never been sweet on a boy before," Mabel said. "It was like she was waiting for that German boat to get sunk, waiting for those young men with their strange language and their strange uniforms to wash up onto the beach like a group of mermen. Henry was the best looking and the sweetest. He never acted like a prisoner. It was more like he'd come to visit distant relatives. The first time Evie and I went to take lunch to our daddies, she spotted Heinrich through the chain fence, and it was . . ." She trailed off, nostalgia tugging her lips into a grin.

Billinger tried to finish her thought. "Love at first sight?"

Mabel's finger rose, hovered over the cabin, trembling a little. "No. Evie was so pretty that her parents fretted over her. She was raised to be careful, modest, to not even talk to older men outside the family. But when their eyes met, Henry's and hers, it was as if they recognized each other. Something deep inside each of them reached out to the other. No power on this earth could've stopped it, no matter how foolish folks thought they were. I've never seen anything like it, and it was a long, long war."

Her finger came so close to touching the painted cabin that Olivia almost moved to interfere, but she merely held her breath and waited.

"The way they were when they were together . . . so easy, so sure. They were just like this little house—all light and laughter and warm rooms in the middle of a crazy, cold world that couldn't seem to comfort any of us, especially when the food started running out and then telegrams came and half the town dressed in black."

Olivia met Billinger's eyes. Mabel, who'd known both the players in this drama, had taken one look at the browns and yellows that Kamler had blended together to create the cabin and had immediately recognized it as a pledge from one lover to another.

"Then why did Henry leave Evelyn?" Olivia asked, reluctantly playing devil's advocate. "Why try to escape? Were they planning to elope?"

Mabel put her hand back on the armrest of her wheelchair and shook her head firmly. "She would have told me. Evie was . . . broken by what happened that night. On the last day I saw her, she swore on her Bible that Henry didn't want to escape, that he'd never kill that guard . . . Oh, I can't remember his name . . ." The realization that there was a gap in her memory disconcerted Mabel so greatly that she stopped speaking, only making soft scratching sounds in the back of her throat.

Billinger tried to coax Mabel back by asking after her family, but her eyes had grown misty again, her thoughts blanketed by a fog too thick to be shaken off by the professor's voice speaking the cherished names of children and grandchildren.

Gently, Olivia turned the painting over and placed it back on Mabel's lap. "I think Henry wrote this note to Evie." She read it aloud and watched for a reaction. Nothing.

"Mabel?" Billinger whispered and then shook his head at Olivia. "This is how it's been. She fades in and out."

The professor left the bench and strolled away to

exchange a few words with the nurse. Olivia lifted Kamler's watercolor from Mabel's lap, but the older woman didn't even seem to notice when the weight of it was no longer there.

Olivia repackaged the work of art, slipped it into the canvas tote, and sat back on the bench with a sigh. Thinking that Haviland would be delighted that their visit had been so short, she waited for Billinger to wrap up his conversation with the nurse.

Noises spilled out of the closest set of double doors, and a family of five stepped onto the sun-dappled patio. A little boy of five or six came running over the flagstones, his arms outstretched as he raced toward an elderly man leaning on a walker.

"Jimmy!" the man called in a cheery albeit tobacco-rough voice and smiled as the child hugged his skinny leg. His family encircled him, and the three adults began to chat as the two children tried to one-up each other in volume and enthusiasm. There was a baby too, held in the protective cradle of the mother's arm. Olivia assumed he was quite young, for his small limbs were encased in a blue cotton sleeper with feet, as if the parents feared the effects of the light on the fragile, new skin.

Using his right hand to steady himself on the walker, the grandfather reached out with his left to touch the baby's plump cheek. The mother pivoted the child so that his face was turned toward the old man. Their eyes met, the two males separated by a gulf of age, united by blood. The baby held still and then sucked in a great breath only to release it in an ear-splitting wail.

The mother laughed, embarrassed, and unobtrusively comforted her child. Next to Olivia, Mabel stirred in her chair, somehow awakened by the child's cry.

"Oh, Evie!" The older woman's eyes pooled with tears. "After they sent you away, things were never the same. I missed you so much. I still miss you . . ."

Olivia looked from the baby, who was quickly responding to his mother's kisses and hushed assurances that all was well, to Mabel's stricken face, her eyes focused on the infant. Billinger had turned when he caught the sound of Mabel's grief floating through the honeysuckle-scented air of the garden, but Olivia shook her head, silently warning him not to move.

"I'm sorry Evie was sent away," she whispered and laid a hand on Mabel's. "What happened to her child?"

The tears overflowed, ribbons of water wetting the older woman's cheeks. "She never came back. I never saw her again. My Evie . . ."

Mabel clammed up again, adrift in the painful memory of losing her best friend. Her lip trembled, but her tears quickly ran dry and her eyes fastened on an iridescent blue gazing ball in the garden bed opposite the bench.

Olivia could picture Mabel as a young woman, filled with hope that the war was coming to an end, rushing to the Whites' house to share some piece of news with Evelyn, only to find no one at home.

Bewildered and more than a little afraid by the sense of emptiness clinging to Evelyn's home, Mabel might have ridden her bike into town in search of information. The people she'd known for all of her nineteen years would be unable to meet her desperate eyes. Instead, they'd murmur something about the Whites having to move in haste because of a job offering or a sick relative or some other acceptable untruth.

Racing home to ask her mother, Mabel would be

forced to consider the real reason the Whites had left
town. For the last two months, Evie had been acting
strange. At first, Mable thought her friend had grown
pallid and despondent due to a broken heart. Heinrich was now gone and worse, he was a fugitive. Evie
hardly left her room, and each time Mabel went to visit,
she complained of being sick to her stomach and too
wounded by Henry's disappearance to face the judg-
mental stares of the townsfolk.

Naturally, Mabel would have tried to comfort her
friend. She'd hold Evie while she cried, pass her tissues,
and try to distract her with the latest gossip. But inside,
she'd begin to wonder. Had Evie gone too far with the
German boy? Could she truly have been that reckless?
That foolish?

Out of loyalty and fear, Mabel would have dismissed
the notion, for if Evie were pregnant, then her reputation
would be ruined forever. It was already stained by the
fact that she was besotted by a foreigner capable of stabbing a local man in the back, but the community would
end up forgiving her by blaming it on her youth and
naivete. They'd dole out a measure of this blame to her
parents as well for allowing Evie to receive art lessons
from a prisoner, regardless of his talent.

A shiver ran down Olivia's neck. She picked up
Mabel's hand and stroked it lightly, caught up in the
tide of heartache. A young couple in love, a childhood friendship, the White family's place in the community—all torn asunder by one event, the murder of
a guard on the night Heinrich Kamler and Nicklaus
Ziegler escaped.

If Heinrich were truly innocent, then he'd lived an
entire lifetime separated from the girl he'd dreamed of

marrying and the child his lover had born in secret in some town far from Oyster Bay.

"Damn it," Olivia murmured, tears pricking her eyes. Her throat tightened, and she could not stop herself from seeing right through the canvas tote back to the cabin on the hilltop, to the hope of home, knowing now that the traveler had never made it up the narrow path. The loved one within had waited and waited for the familiar footfall outside the door and no one had come.

The war ended, the prisoners were sent overseas, the Whites' house was sold and relocated and sold again. And the children of wartime, like Evelyn and Mabel and Ray Hatcher, grew older, bearing the weight of their memories like women carrying heavy jugs home from the well.

At some point, Billinger appeared and rejoined Olivia on the bench. The nurse came to collect Mabel, and Olivia was deeply sorry to release the older woman's hand. She bent over and placed a wisp of a kiss on Mabel's forehead before letting go. Mabel smiled, the pain evaporating from her features like a shadow chased off by a bright moon.

Billinger had the good grace to wait until they were in the car before asking, "What happened back there?"

"I believe Evelyn White might have had a baby out of wedlock. Her family left town abruptly, but I have no idea where they went or what became of the child." She turned to the professor in appeal. "Can you find out?"

He touched her arm. "I'll do my best. You have my word on it."

Olivia nodded. She instinctively knew that Billinger would work relentlessly to help her.

The afternoon was on the wane as she drove west toward the ocean, toward home, toward a killer.

*　*　*

When she stepped into the welcoming cool of her house, she noticed that her answering machine was blinking furiously. Rawlings had called an emergency meeting of the Bayside Book Writers for that evening. Olivia checked her watch. She had less than an hour until her friends would arrive at the lighthouse keeper's cottage and she desperately wanted to take a shower, to rinse off the fine dust of sadness that coated her body.

Slipping her feet from her shoes, she picked up the phone, dialed The Boot Top, and paced across the floor, relishing the feel of the tiles against her skin. Olivia politely interrupted the hostess as she began her honey-tongued greeting and asked that Michel pick up the kitchen phone. Moments later, his voice ricocheted down the line, a frantic blend of passion and protestations.

"Michel!" Olivia cut him off with a bark. "I do not care to discuss your infatuation with Laurel at the moment. I'm calling because she and the other writers are coming over tonight and I have nothing to offer them by way of an impromptu dinner. Can you help?"

Vowing that he'd see to it personally, Michel cried, "I love her, you know!" and slammed the phone down.

Olivia rolled her eyes to the ceiling, fed Haviland his supper, and then trudged up the stairs. She shrugged out of her clothes and into the warm embrace of the shower stream. After washing her hair, she ran conditioner through the short strands and waited the recommended thirty seconds before rinsing it out. The glass panels of her shower stall fogged over completely, and she could barely make out Haviland's black form as he sank onto the bath mat for an after-dinner repose.

Closing her eyes, she arched back into the rush of water, feeling the tension ebb from her shoulders, the images of Kamler's cabin and Mabel's stricken face receding.

Suddenly, she heard a sharp crash followed by a violent thump from the first floor. Haviland leapt to his feet and was off in a blur of black fur and angry barking. Olivia knew from the hostile tone that the poodle was genuinely alarmed. She turned the water off with a jerk, stuffed her arms into a robe, and raced to the landing.

Haviland was going wild in the kitchen. She could hear his enraged barks and snarls bouncing off the cabinets and terra cotta tiles. Without another second's hesitation, Olivia grabbed her Browning BPR rifle from the coat closet, loaded it, and raised it to eye level. If someone were foolish enough to be in the kitchen when she turned the corner, they'd come face-to-face with the yawn of a gun barrel and a woman who was fully prepared to fire her weapon.

But no one was there.

Olivia lowered the gun but did not set it down. Tucking the stock under her right armpit, she approached the jagged hole in the glass of her closed kitchen door. She rapidly shuffled her feet into the shoes she'd discarded earlier and whipped the door open, crunching shards of glass beneath her heels. A large brown stone sat overtly on the welcome mat, discarded haphazardly by the intruders in their haste to gain entry to her house.

Realizing what this meant, Olivia swung around, her eyes targeting the wide pine table upon which she'd laid the canvas tote bag containing the watercolor before heading upstairs to shower.

It was gone.

Chapter 14

*It is by going down into the abyss that we
recover the treasures of life.*

—JOSEPH CAMPBELL

Rawlings showed up out of uniform, wearing a
Hawaiian shirt upon which cobalt sharks swam
across a field of pale blue. His khaki shorts were covered
with paint splatters, but his eyes were all business. While
Officer Cook dusted for prints, Rawlings sat at Olivia's
kitchen table with an untouched cup of coffee, his fingers
smoothing the pine surface as he took her statement.

"What am I going to tell Harris?" Olivia whispered
miserably when they were done.

The chief covered the back of her hand with his
warm palm. "We'll get it back. The fact that it was stolen reinforces my belief that Mr. Plumley's death was
more about money and less about his profession."

"I don't know," Olivia said doubtfully. "The past is a
part of these crimes. It's possible that Heinrich Kamler
has come back to the area to seek his revenge against
Plumley for casting him as a murderer in *The Barbed
Wire Flower*." She told him of her visit to Chapel Hill.

When she was done, Rawlings grew thoughtful. He asked for a broom and a dustpan and then squatted down and began to slowly sweep every shard of glass onto the pan. After dumping the entire contents into an evidence bag, the chief pivoted the bag under the overhead light, creating glints of light like sunshine on a level sea.

Meanwhile, Officer Cook had finished dusting the doorknob for prints and had bagged the rock. "Good thing we've got you on file already, Ms. Limoges," he said with a wry grin.

Olivia nodded absently. She and Cook had come to an uneasy truce last year, but she still found the young man's often condescending and close-minded attitude grating. "I'm sure the thief used gloves." She looked at Rawlings. "If he's after money, then he'll try to sell this painting immediately. Where does one unload stolen artwork? This is a notch above the average pawn shop merchandise."

"He could approach a private collector." Rawlings passed Cook the bag of glass and opened the door for him. "See you back at the station in a few hours."

Once the junior officer had departed, leaving the chief without a means of transportation, Rawlings glanced at his watch and then gestured toward the flat ocean visible through the bank of windows in Olivia's living room. "Let's take a walk before the others get here."

Olivia hesitated. "I need to pick up our dinner from The Boot Top. I figured our meeting might run later than usual, so Michel is making something for us."

"Can Laurel stop for it?"

"Absolutely not!" Olivia declared hotly and then turned away from the chief's quizzical stare. "I'll send Millay a text message. I need the practice anyway."

Rawlings didn't answer. His gaze slid away from her face, and he moved toward the door leading to the raised deck. Haviland followed on the chief's heels, his black tail wagging in expectation.

Olivia labored over the message, her fingers slow to find the letters and punctuation, pocketed her phone, and eased open the sliding door. Haviland raced ahead, careening down the stairs and over the dunes toward the water.

"I envy him," Rawlings said with a slight smile. "Why do humans lose that joy as we age? If we were younger, we'd have been right behind him, tearing down that path, howling in anticipation. We wouldn't care if the sand was hot or the water too cold. We wouldn't have considered how we looked in our swimsuits or whether we had enough sunscreen on. We would've just charged right in like little gladiators."

He was right. Olivia had spent most of her childhood by the ocean's edge, and every morning she'd rushed breathlessly outside to greet it, to see what treasures awaited her in the sand, to rescue beached horseshoe crabs and share the remnants of her breakfast with the gulls. It had always been there, a loyal friend. Even when it churned angrily during a storm or carried a plague of jellyfish to the shore, it was beautiful. Enchanted.

"Caution comes with age," Olivia said. She had a strong urge to take his hand and race after Haviland, but she sensed the chief's thoughts had already turned back to the investigation.

However, he surprised her by coming to an abrupt stop, and then he kicked off his boat shoes and walked into the surf. She watched as he dug his toes into the wet sand and then tossed a stick for Haviland into the deeper water. He stood like this for a long time, his eyes locked on the silver blur of the horizon. Olivia sat on the warm sand and watched him while Haviland investigated an interesting scent near a crab hole.

Olivia thought of Heinrich's cabin and of a young girl giving birth to a child she probably wouldn't see again afterward. She thought of Anders and his homecoming, of telling Harris that his painting was gone, and of Jeannie's advice on how to win back Rawlings' trust.

The urge to walk into the water and wash all these images away was powerful, but the sound of car tires crunching gravel on the road leading to the lighthouse keeper's cabin pulled her to her feet. Rawlings turned as well, gathering his shoes and meeting Olivia's gaze.

"The time for caution is over," he told her firmly. For a moment, she thought he was referring to their relationship. Her heartbeat doubled its pace, and she tried to express her readiness to put any and all reservations aside by nodding enthusiastically. Satisfied by her response, the chief began to walk toward the dunes. "We're going to set out bait for this killer, and when he leaves the safety of the shadows, we're going to catch him."

Around the front of the cottage, Laurel was helping to unload covered trays from Millay's car. Together, the four of them entered the cottage and set the food on the countertop. Millay grabbed a beer from the refrigerator and handed it to Rawlings.

He shook his head. "I'm afraid I'm on the clock."

"Nice uniform," she said with a smile and then offered the beer to Olivia. "You want this or should I fix you a real drink?"

Olivia accepted the beer. "This'll do, thanks."

Millay's brows shot up, her silver piercings glinting. "Whoa. What's going on?"

Laurel grabbed Millay's beer from her hand and retreated to the sofa. "Before you answer that, Olivia, *I* have something to tell all of you . . ." She paused to drink and then rested the bottle on the top of her knee. "Never mind, I'll wait until Harris is here."

"The chief has a plan to net Plumley's killer," Olivia replied to Millay as though Laurel hadn't spoken.

Rawlings nodded. "First, I need to get you up to speed on alibis. Raymond Hatcher was at work the morning Mr. Plumley was killed, but he took a break for an hour. He claims to have driven off-site to get a McMuffin, but the McDonald's employee who worked the drive-through doesn't remember him and the security video is taped over every twenty-four hours. So he's still on our suspect list."

"Along with Cora and Boyd?" Millay asked.

"Yes." Something flickered in the chief's eyes, and Olivia knew he had solved one of the many riddles of the investigation. "Three months after Cora and Nick Plumley divorced, Cora discovered that she was pregnant with Nick's child." A mild flush appeared on Rawlings' cheeks. "Apparently, they had good-bye sex after the papers were signed. She learned late in the pregnancy that her child would most likely be born with Down's syndrome."

Laurel sucked in her breath but didn't speak.

"Cora never told Nick about their son. He didn't know she was pregnant or that she gave the baby up for adoption. She was living in Asheville when the child was born."

"What happened to the baby?" Laurel wanted to know.

Rawlings gave her a reassuring smile. "He was adopted by a loving family and is still with them today."

Millay's face clouded with anger. "Then Nick's insurance money should go to those people and to his *son*! What kind of person doesn't even tell a man that he's a father? She totally robbed him of any say in that kid's future!"

The chief nodded in agreement. "That's true, but the boy, Colby, is not legally tied to Nick, so he stands no chance of receiving any benefits from Mr. Plumley's life insurance."

Olivia shot Rawlings a quick glance. "So the Vickers may still get their hands on Nick's money?"

"I believe they're desperately counting on a payout," he said.

"Add to that the fact that their alibi was as weak as watered-down whiskey," Millay remarked. "But they're not sitting in a cozy, post-nuptial jail cell, are they?"

"We're not on TV," Rawlings replied curtly. "The police can't hold people without evidence. We have theories, but for now, that's all they are. That's why I need to push things along. I've spent the last few nights creating a Heinrich Kamler reproduction. Watercolor isn't my medium, but it's good enough to fool a novice. However, to make the bait irresistible, I'll need your help, Laurel."

She shrank back into the sofa, instantly on guard. "What can *I* do?"

"Get an article on the front page of the paper announcing that two paintings by a famous German

POW have been discovered in the home of Harris Williams. Exaggerate the value of the second painting and don't mention that the first one's gone missing."

Millay jerked upright. "Missing? What happened?" She shot looks of accusation back and forth between Olivia and Rawlings.

"It's my fault," Olivia quickly admitted. "Harris entrusted me with the painting and I was careless."

Setting aside her beer, she told the other women about her day. As she spoke of the unrequited love between Henry and Evie, Laurel began to weep. Millay shot her friend and fellow writer a perplexed glance, and Olivia felt a surge of sympathy for Laurel. The story had struck a nerve in her too, and she knew that Laurel was in pain. The hurt united all of them—a German boy, a haunted young woman from a newspaper photograph, Olivia, and Laurel.

When Olivia finished by describing how the painting had been stolen, Millay jumped to her feet, her body coiled like a spring. "We've got to *do* something!" She looked around wildly, her hands curled into white-knuckled fists. "Where is Harris anyway? It's *his* painting, *his* house!" She pointed at Rawlings. "Do you plan to use him as bait without even discussing it with him? Why are we wasting our time talking about all this World War Two bullshit when Harris isn't even *here*?"

The level of Millay's ire stunned Olivia, but Rawlings saw it for what it was. Fear. "I'm worried about him too," he told her quietly. "I'm going to put a call in to the unit watching his place."

The three women watched Rawlings, exchanging nervous glances. The chief's voice took on an edge of sharpness.

"You saw Mr. Williams drive by in his car? You're certain? Did you see his face?"

A pause. A tightening of Rawlings' jaw. "What time was this?"

Three pairs of eyes fastened on the chief as he checked his watch. "Get back to Oleander Drive right now. Don't go inside until I get there."

The women's anxiety transformed into something more powerful, spreading tentacles of dread around the cottage. Olivia slapped her thigh and Haviland sprang to his feet. He raised his black nose, sensing that something had alarmed his mistress. Turning his head in search of a threat, he found nothing. He cocked his head inquisitively and waited for her command.

"Did they see Harris leave?" Olivia asked Rawlings.

"They saw someone in a baseball hat driving Harris's car. He waved to them as he drove by, and the movement obscured his face. Believing that he was safely on his way to meet me, the officers decided to take a dinner break. They're sitting in front of Pizza Bay waiting on a pair of meatball subs." The chief pointed at Millay. "Would you lend me your car?"

Millay had her phone to her ear. She shook her head. "Voice mail. Both numbers." She pulled her keys from the front pocket of her denim miniskirt. "What are we waiting for? Let's go!"

"I'll drive," Rawlings ordered and opened the cottage's front door. He then blocked the exit and faced the women. "I'd tell you to stay here, but I know you'll just follow in another car and I'd rather have you with me. When we get to the house, you will all do *exactly* as I say. Is that understood?" He included Olivia in his authoritative stare.

"Should I bring my gun?" she asked in all seriousness.

Rawlings scowled. "Just get in the car."

Olivia sat in the back. Haviland was squeezed beside her, his eyes aglow with curiosity, his body tensed for action. Millay was on the other side, her fingers flying over the tiny letter keys on her phone's touch screen. When she received no response, she called 411 and asked for a listing for Estelle's number.

"Estelle? This is Millay. Is Harris with you?"

Pushing Haviland to a seated position so she could watch her friend, Olivia watched Millay's shoulder tighten as her fingers gripped her phone like a hawk's talon closing over the torso of a mouse. "Actually, it *is* my business. He's supposed to be at our writers' meeting but he hasn't shown. Is he with you or not?"

Olivia could see that Millay was trying to hold her temper in check as Estelle dished out some coy response. "Could you *please* tell me when you last spoke with him?"

Millay had carefully masked her dislike and infused her voice with a calculated blend of courtesy, deference, and concern. Then she frowned. "I thought you volunteered at the senior center on Tuesday and Saturday afternoons. Or was that just a story to impress Harris?" She didn't bother concealing her disgust. "He's too good a guy to see the real you, girlfriend, but eventually, your mask will slip and he'll get a glimpse of your true self and run. Don't be buying *Brides* magazine just yet, princess." Millay snapped the phone shut and shoved it back into her skirt pocket.

"She hasn't seen him?" Olivia asked.

Millay twisted a lock of hair around her index finger.

"Not since this morning. I think they've had a little spat. Little Miss Sunshine didn't sound very chipper."

Laurel pivoted in the front seat. "Why do you dislike her so much?"

"Estelle knows nothing about Harris. All she cares about is his nice job and his nice house and that they'd have cute babies together," Millay said. "She has no idea that his favorite author is Frank Herbert or that he makes the world's most awesome potato skins or that he's seen every episode of the original *Star Trek* shows at least five times. She doesn't know him." Millay took a shallow breath. "Can't you drive a little faster, Chief?"

Haviland put his forepaws and head on Millay's lap, and she sank both hands into his fur. Olivia could see that her fingers were trembling.

Lights were on in the living room of Harris's bungalow. Yellow stripes escaped through the spaces in the closed blinds and fell onto the front porch. There were no cars in the driveway and the chief's men had not yet returned, but the house did not feel empty. Hushed, but not empty.

Rawlings threw the car into park, turned off the engine, and sprang out of the driver's seat. He moved soundlessly up the front steps, crouching low, every cell in his body on alert.

The women watched breathlessly. None of them had seen the chief in this state of sharp readiness, prowling on the balls of his feet like a big cat, one hand curled over his holster.

Olivia inched forward in her seat as the chief knelt

down to peer through a crack in the blinds. She could tell by the way his hand tightened over his holster that he was alarmed by what he saw.

As though he felt her eyes on him, Rawlings pivoted and signaled for them to stay put. He then disappeared around the corner of the house.

"I don't like this," Laurel said in a small voice.

Millay looked at Olivia. "Someone's in there. If it had just been Harris, the chief would have gone inside."

"I think you're right." She had seen the tension flood into Rawlings' shoulders. There was danger within the bungalow and she needed to know what it was. She needed to be certain that Rawlings would not face it alone. By the time his backup arrived, it could be too late.

"I'm going to look in the window." Touching Haviland briefly on the neck to assure him that she'd only be a minute, Olivia slid from the car and closed the door with a gentle click. The air was filled with the sawing of cicadas, the hungry buzz of mosquitoes, and the scent of rain. A breeze tickled the back of Olivia's neck, carrying a taste of the coolness of the thunderstorm, and the sensation helped sharpen her mind. She felt the blood rushing through her body, her heartbeat drumming with such force that surely the bats flitting about the treetops could hear her approach.

Following the chief's lead, Olivia sank low and put her face close to the glass. She tucked her chin and looked into Harris's living room.

There was Harris, tied to one of his kitchen chairs. His upper body had been secured with rope, and his wrists and ankles were fastened with duct tape. Face flushing a bright red, he was speaking to someone, his mouth moving rapidly. Olivia could see the sweat staining his shirt and could almost smell his fear. She moved carefully, hoping to catch a view of his assailants, but they were out of range.

Someone began to shout. It was a woman's voice, demanding, crackling with anger and desperation. Then, the lower timbre of a man's voice. Olivia couldn't hear the words distinctly. The man seemed to have more control over himself than the woman, but there was an edge to his speech, as though he was fully aware that their time was growing short.

Olivia saw Harris's eyes widen. He shook his head fiercely, and she didn't need to be inside the room to know that he was trying to convince the man and woman of something—that his life could depend on his ability to do so.

These observations took place in a matter of seconds, but to Olivia they stretched out, like a strip of sand curving far into the distance. Everything seemed to slow. The air was charged, filled with the dense electricity and breathlessness of the moment preceding a lightning strike.

Instinct told Olivia that Harris was out of time. The woman was yelling again, and then she suddenly came into view, charging into the living room with an enraged howl.

It was Cora Vickers.

She had a revolver in her hand, and as Olivia watched, she straightened her gun arm and brought her free hand up to steady her grip. Her right thumb pulled the hammer back, and an icy resolve surfaced on her features. This was no idle threat. Cora was not getting the answers she wanted and was prepared to silence Harris for good.

The swirling thoughts in Olivia's mind stilled, converging into one. She had to act before Cora's ire exploded, giving her the push she needed to pull the trigger.

Rushing to the front door, Olivia banged on the wood with both fists. She could hear Haviland's agitated barking inside the car but did not turn around. Her intention was to distract Cora, giving Rawlings a chance to gain entry and draw his own weapon. She had no idea where Boyd was and whether he was armed, but there was no time to come up with a more complex plan.

"I should have brought my Browning," she muttered and returned to her place at the window. Cora was no longer in sight, but Harris had turned his head to the side, his terrified eyes meeting hers. He shook his head in warning and then raised two fingers behind his back. Olivia didn't know what he meant. Had Boyd and Cora separated or were they coming her way together?

She quickly climbed over the porch rail and crouched down between the azalea bushes, listening hard. There were no more voices, just the creaks and moans of boards underfoot, barely perceptible beneath the drone of insects.

"Where are you, Rawlings?" Olivia whispered. And then, before she knew what was happening, Millay was at her side.

"Don't bother telling me to get back in the car because I won't," she hissed fiercely. "What's happening in there?"

Olivia began to creep around the corner as Rawlings had done a few moments ago. "Boyd and Cora Vickers have Harris tied to a chair. They must believe his house contains more Heinrich Kamler paintings. And Cora has a gun."

Most women would have let out a whimper or gone

wide-eyed in fear. Not Millay. She clenched her jaw and nodded. Olivia recognized that her friend would not cower before danger, nor would she back off, leaving Harris alone in a house with the couple that had likely murdered Nick Plumley.

Suddenly, like a cannon boom, Chief Rawlings shouted at someone inside. "DROP YOUR WEAPON!" he commanded.

Olivia and Millay ran to the kitchen door and eased it open. Millay reached into her boot and drew forth a switchblade. She crept into the living room and, without a trace of caution, rushed to Harris and began cutting through the duct tape and rope binding him to the chair.

Harris tore the rope from his chest and swung around to say something to Millay, reaching out his hand to shove the chair between them aside, but he never got the chance. Cora burst into the room, her gun aimed straight at Millay's heart.

"Nick said that Evelyn's two treasures were HERE!" She cried wildly, her eyes glittering. "In Oyster Bay! Tell me where the other painting is or she dies! *NOW!*"

And then Rawlings was in the doorway, his gun trained on Cora. She ignored him. Her eyes held a cold, predatory glimmer. Nothing existed for her other than the painting she believed was hidden somewhere in that house.

"Don't do it, Cora!" Boyd shouted from upstairs. "Just pick one of them to take with us and let's go! *There's nothing here!*"

Cora didn't respond. Boyd continued to repeat himself from the stairway until his wife's eyes lost a fraction of their mad light and she gestured at Millay with the revolver. "You're coming with us." Cora darted a sideways glance at Rawlings and spoke in chilly calm. "If you or your men follow us, I *will* shoot her. I've got nothing to lose now."

"Sure you do," Rawlings answered conversationally as he lowered his gun. "You've got a Heinrich Kamler original. And maybe some cash and an unpublished manuscript from a bestselling author. That's got to be worth something to someone, right?"

"Shut up, cop." Cora gesticulated at Millay again, but Harris stepped in front of her.

"If you want a hostage, you're going to have to take me."

"Look at the little hero," Cora sneered. "You don't know what the hell you're talking about, *Chief.* Yeah, we've got a painting that'll be impossible to sell, but it should've been ours anyway. Nick screwed me out of the money he owed me, and he was supposed to get the damned thing himself and give it to me, but then he went and got himself killed. We didn't do the deed and we don't have his damned book. We just want what we're owed, got it?"

Rawlings nodded in understanding. "You had a hold over Nick. You chose to honeymoon in Beaufort because your ex-husband lived there and it was time for him to give you a regularly scheduled payment, wasn't it? But he didn't deliver."

"No, he didn't 'deliver,'" Cora mocked the chief. "But he would have eventually. He's no good to us dead. His measly life insurance payout isn't going to last us long. We need our regular payments. We've got plans. Big ones. But stupid Nick screwed everything up." She was practically snarling. "Okay, that's enough chitchat. Kick your gun to Boyd, Chief, and get the hell out of our way."

"Sure," Rawlings said agreeably and gave his weapon

a gentle shove with his shoe. Boyd, who had appeared at the foot of the stairs, picked it up and, after sending Cora a brief, nervous look, held the gun inexpertly in a wobbly grip. Olivia sensed that he wouldn't even know to remove the safety before firing and that Rawlings could take him down in a matter of seconds if someone could neutralize the threat posed by Cora.

Olivia was too far from the armed woman to be of any use. Her only option was to throw something at her, but Harris didn't have a heavy bookend or paperweight or glass vase handy. His table surfaces were knickknack free, and Olivia doubted Cora would stand passively by as Olivia unplugged a lamp to use as a missile.

Once again, time seemed to slow, the seconds extending and lengthening until Olivia had the sensation of being underwater. Sounds grew muted. The insect murmur died away, and even Haviland's barking inside the car faded. And then, noise exploded like the roar of a hurricane gale.

It began with Boyd shouting a warning to his wife that he'd spotted a cop outside the window. Rawlings tried to keep Cora calm by assuring her that the officers were the same pair sent to watch the house. He hastily explained that his men must have realized something was amiss and that she and Boyd would be better off setting the civilians free and accepting him as their sole hostage.

"This is only going to escalate if you involve anyone else in this room," Rawlings told her, sounding more like a nagging aunt than the chief of police.

Cora's eyes were charged with a frenzied light. They were open so wide that the whites showed, giving her the appearance of a spooked horse.

Without warning, she lurched forward, intent on grabbing hold of Millay, but Harris put out his hand to stop her, as though his long elegant fingers could stop a bullet.

His abrupt movement caused Cora to jerk, and she pulled back on the trigger. At the same time a woman, Laurel or Millay, Olivia couldn't tell which, cried out with a shrill "NOOOOO!" The desperate scream sounded like a cave echo, distorted and too loud in the murky, underwater world that had once been Harris's living room.

What freed her inert limbs was the impact of the bullet hitting Harris. She only saw it from behind—the shiver of the muscles in his back as the metal seared into them. And then, a fraction of a second later, the forward fold of his shoulders; an innate, defensive gesture by his shocked and wounded body.

Another scream. Harris tottered and his knees began to buckle.

Olivia moved. She grabbed his left arm and fell with him, inviting his weight to come down hard on her, cushioning his limp form with her flesh.

Cradling his head in her arms, she squirmed out from under him and saw the blood blooming through his gray T-shirt like a poppy opening its petals to the sun. A cacophony of sound erupted above her head, but she took no notice.

Part of her mind registered the fact that the other officers had entered the house. Multiple voices exchanged shouts and threats. A woman shrieked. There was a crash of glass shattering against the tiles in the kitchen.

For Olivia, there was only the blood and Harris's slack, ashen face. She didn't remember stripping off her shirt, but there it was in her hand, pressed against the wound in Harris's chest. The bullet had entered below the ridge of his collarbone and Olivia had no idea what damage it had done. All she knew was that there was too much blood pumping from his body, a spring of fresh crimson staining her pale blue shirt a deep and frightening indigo.

At some point, she couldn't say how long, a pair of gloved hands eased her own away from her friend's chest. A soothing voice complimented her actions and then she was separated from Harris. Two paramedics, a bag of medical equipment, a breathing mask, and a gurney appeared. Olivia looked down at her red hands as though they belonged to another person.

Laurel coaxed her into the kitchen. She filled the sink with warm water and soap and used a dishtowel to scrub Olivia's hands. She did not speak but cried softly as she washed her friend's fingers and palms with infinite tenderness and then dried them with paper towels, her tears speckling the countertop.

Olivia gazed from her pink, clean hands to the freckled skin of her chest. She touched her bare flesh to the right of her bra strap, seeing the hole in Harris's chest. Laurel left the room and came back moments later with one of his T-shirts. Olivia slipped it on, and the two women stared at his company logo until the thud of the ambulance doors closing startled them into movement.

Outside, the dark yard was awash in flashing lights. Uniformed men and women milled about police cruisers, white noise emitting from their radios. They parted and fell silent when the gurney passed.

Olivia looked down and saw that she was holding Laurel's hand.

Haviland barked again, plaintively, and the yearning in his call brought Olivia back to life. She pulled Laurel to Millay's car as the ambulance rumbled down the driveway, the wail of its siren cutting through the humid night air, its red and white lights illuminating the pines lining the road.

Olivia hurried to turn the key in the ignition, hoping to close the distance between their car and the ambulance, needing to catch up to the pulses of light before the shadows returned to claim their territory.

Chapter 15

He wishes that he, too, had a wound, a red
badge of courage.
—STEPHEN CRANE

As if to make up for its sluggish pace at Harris's house, time rocketed forward, giving Olivia only a dizzying impression of hospital hallways and the scent of ammonia and an animalistic blend of sickness and fear. She ended up in a waiting room with blue chairs and beige walls. The area was so bland that the enormous vase of Matisse-bold daylilies on the counter of the nurses' station seemed jarringly bright.

At some point, Harris's parents arrived—a nice-looking, tidy couple in cotton shirts and khaki pants. They gripped each other as Rawlings explained what had happened.

Estelle showed up soon after, crying theatrically and cornering everyone in scrubs to demand an update on her boyfriend's condition. Millay paced outside the swinging doors of the OR like a caged leopard. Laurel pushed cups of vending machine coffee into people's hands. They all waited, glass-eyed, as the television relayed the day's news and hospital personnel passed by with carts of food, medicine, or clean linen.

No one said a word to Olivia about Haviland's presence. Perhaps because she sat so upright and so still, her gaze fixed on the too-bold arrangement of lilies, they believed she was visually impaired.

To escape the madness of waiting, of not knowing, Olivia had been thinking deeply about art. Influenced by the flowers, she visualized all the Matisse paintings she could call to mind. She repeated the exercise with Georgia O'Keefe. Then, trying to imagine what kinds of paintings would fit best on the waiting room's walls, she sifted through a mental gallery of Rembrandt and Dürer and Caravaggio, thinking that their use of chiaroscuro was more suitable for the oppressive atmosphere than the lackluster botanicals lined up above Estelle's head.

A doctor in Carolina blue scrubs pushed open the doors to the OR, and the images of art vanished from Olivia's mind like a snuffed candle flame. The physician scanned the room with quick, intelligent eyes and picked out Mr. and Mrs. Williams. He pushed his paper mask below his chin, and the smile of assurance he bestowed on the frightened parents caught everyone's attention.

Estelle sprang to her feet, peppering the man with questions until he put a hand on her shoulder and waited for her to calm down. Keeping his focus on Harris's parents, he spoke in a deep, confident tone, and though Olivia couldn't hear the specifics, she caught enough phrases such as "avoided major organs," and "bullet intact," and "in stable condition," to know that Harris was out of danger.

When Estelle demanded to see him, the doctor told her that the patient had had significant blood loss and he'd need to rest for now. The result of his gentle refusal was that Estelle burst into a fresh bout of tears. Looking pained, the doctor removed the paper cap from his head and scrunched it into a ball between his hands. "The moment he woke up, Harris asked to see Millay. Are you Millay?"

Estelle's pretty mouth curled into an angry sneer. "No. *I'm* his girlfriend. You must have misunderstood. Harris mumbles *all* the time. I'm always telling him to speak clearly, like *I* do on the phone. That's an important part of my job, you know." She sniffed and then dabbed at her eyes. "People notice you if you enunciate."

The surgeon sent Harris's parents a glance of befuddlement, but they were staring at Estelle with distaste. Olivia wondered if Estelle was even aware that it was unwise to insult their only child, especially when Harris had come so close to losing his life.

Millay, who had stopped pacing during this exchange, touched the surgeon lightly on the arm. "I'm the one he's asking for," she said softly, joy shining from her face like a lighthouse beacon. She then looked directly at Estelle, and Olivia was surprised to see sympathy in her friend's dark eyes. "Harris doesn't mumble. And unlike most people, he only talks when he's got something to say. You should have listened more closely. I bet you missed out on some good stuff." She paused. "I know I have."

The surgeon promised to return for Harris's parents as soon as it was clear he was up to having more visitors and led Millay away, cautioning her that she'd only have a few minutes with the patient.

"Don't worry, Doc. I'll make them count," they heard her say before they rounded a corner and were gone.

* * *

Olivia only hung around long enough to see Millay reemerge from the recovery area ten minutes later. Her skin, which had previously appeared jaundiced with shock and worry beneath the waiting room's harsh fluorescents, now glowed with relief and something else Olivia couldn't identify. Gratitude? Devotion?

Her friend shot her a brief, encouraging smile before heading straight for Harris's parents. Millay put her hand on his mother's arm and began to talk quickly and calmly. As Olivia watched, air seemed to rush from Mrs. Williams' lungs and the tight cords of fear that had pushed her shoulders together relaxed. Murmuring her thanks, she and her husband went off to the nurses' station to beg for a few moments with their son.

Estelle had fallen mercifully silent, clutching her can of diet soda and watching Millay with venomous eyes.

Having no wish to be around when the girl's dramatics began again, Olivia touched Haviland on the collar and crossed the room to where Laurel sat. "We probably won't be able to visit Harris until tomorrow, so why don't I call us a cab?"

Rawlings, who had left the waiting area to phone into the station, returned. His purposeful gait told her that his subordinates had given him good news and that he was impatient to join them. Once Millay informed him of Harris's condition, it was clear that the chief wouldn't hang around any longer.

"I'd like to get statements from everyone tonight. An officer will drop you ladies at home afterward."

Millay shook her head. "I'm not leaving."

Estelle slowly rose from her seat, chin held high like

a queen, and said, "You don't have to stay. *I'll* make sure they treat Harris right. *I'm* his girlfriend, remember?"

Olivia expected Millay to snap at her rival, but she didn't. "Okay," she agreed placidly. "You hold down the fort and I'll be back as soon as I'm done helping the cops tie Cora up in a supertight bow." Her lips thinned in anger and her voice grew cold as she turned to Rawlings. "I don't want anything to get in the way of her being shipped to the roughest, dirtiest women's prison in the state. I hope her cell mate has some major anger-management issues."

Rawlings slipped an arm around the girl's tiny waist and gave her a fatherly squeeze. "Rest assured, Millay. Mr. and Mrs. Vickers won't look back on their early days of marriage very fondly."

"And since those are the best ones, they don't have much to look forward to," Laurel mumbled but then hastily brightened. "But Harris is going to be all right and Oyster Bay is safe again. That's what really matters."

Olivia was momentarily stunned by Laurel's behavior but grinned and gave her a friendly nudge, buoyant with relief that she and her friends and her town could sleep soundly tonight. Not one of the Bayside Book Writers believed Cora's claim that she hadn't killed Nick. The woman had already been caught lying, but Rawlings would gently ease the truth from her. Olivia was certain of it. "Once again, you're going to have the lead article in the paper," she told Laurel. "Maybe you should consider writing a true-crime novel."

Laurel shook her head. "No way. I'm half done with my women's fiction novel, and *I* need to see how The Wife ends up."

"Me too," Olivia said quietly, looking her friend in

the eye. "But wherever that is, she won't be alone. She's got us."

Late the next morning, Olivia stopped by the station with bagels and coffee only to be informed by Officer Cook that Rawlings was on his way to Beaufort.

"Gathering evidence?" she asked conversationally, but the look on Cook's face was troubled.

She handed him the box of bagels along with a bag containing pints of flavored cream cheeses. "Is something wrong?"

He gave the hint of a shrug and set the food offerings on a desk. Prying open the cardboard carrier filled with bagels, he gave them an appreciative sniff. "There's been a little complication, but the chief'll sort it out."

Olivia knew the men and women of the Oyster Bay Police Department had complete faith in Rawlings, but there was a pause in Cook's voice that told her the case against the Vickers was not quite open and shut.

"That witch shot my friend," she said in a taut voice. "Please tell me she won't get off on some technicality."

Cook blinked in surprise. "No, ma'am, we've got the both of them on multiple charges, just not the one the media's gonna care about."

"Nick Plumley's murder?"

Having already confided more than he'd intended, Cook murmured something about bringing the bagels to the kitchen and hustled off.

After calling Kim and receiving a lengthy update on both Caitlyn and Anders, Olivia took Haviland to the park and then tried to work on her novel, but even the comfortable din of Grumpy's lunchtime crowd couldn't encourage her muse. Finally, she snapped her laptop closed and decided to whittle down the mound of paperwork awaiting her at The Boot Top.

At two o'clock, the restaurant was quiet. One of the sous-chefs was taking inventory, and he greeted her with a distracted wave of the hand before disappearing into the walk-in refrigerator. Olivia fixed herself a coffee, gave Haviland a bone, and settled down at her desk. She read e-mails, placed orders, and reviewed next week's menu until the kitchen began to fill with the sounds of preparation.

"Is it safe to enter your lair?" Michel asked after knocking lightly on the open door.

Olivia turned down the volume of her computer speakers, and Beethoven's Piano Trio in C minor faded to a whisper. "That depends. What's going on between you and Laurel?"

"Nothing shady," he answered with a note of disappointment. "She's an honorable woman. That bastard she married has no idea what a gem he had."

Olivia raised her brows. "Had? Laurel's going to leave Steve?"

Michel fidgeted with his watchband. "I don't know. All she'll tell me for certain is that he began treating her like dirt when she went back to work. Laurel thinks he's having an affair. I know that a woman's instincts are only truly understood by other females and the Almighty." He glanced heavenward, shaking his head in awe. "But I have learned to respect them."

Scowling, Olivia put down her pen. "But she hasn't confronted him, has she? Whenever things get unpleasant at home, she runs into your open arms instead. This Shakespearean crap is what *you* thrive on, Michel.

Laurel isn't like you. She has two little boys and, I hate to tell you this, but she's still in love with her husband. You're going to get hurt, Michel. You always do." She reached for his hand. "The difference is that this time, the woman whose heart you're playing with is my friend." Olivia exhaled wearily. "This has to stop before Laurel does something she regrets."

"*Mon Dieu*, how I wish she would!" Michel exclaimed and flounced from the office.

"Is it cocktail time yet?" Olivia wondered aloud and then dialed the chief's cell phone number. "You're probably exhausted," she said when he picked up. "But would you like to meet me for a drink?"

Rawlings hesitated. "Do you want my company or are you just fishing for updates on the case?"

"Both," Olivia replied honestly. "Though I'd be glad to see you even if you refused to talk about anything but the weather."

"Liar." Rawlings laughed. "But I accept. Your bar or mine?"

"Gabe will pour more liberally than any other bartender in town," was her answer. "Will you be off the clock or should he stock the bar with chocolate syrup?"

"I'll have what you're having," the chief said and told her to expect him in an hour or so.

After making two more calls, one to Harris and the second to Hudson, Olivia took the cosmetic bag she kept in her desk drawer into the ladies' room. As she combed through her white blond hair until it gleamed in the soft light of the wall sconces flanking the mirror and refreshed her lipstick, she thought of what a relief it was to know that Anders would be coming home in a week's time to a more peaceful town. Tomorrow afternoon Laurel would take Olivia shopping for the best baby gear money could buy.

How she wished Rawlings would tell her that the case was closed, leaving Olivia to concentrate on her family members and her new business. More importantly, she could finally prove to Rawlings that she was ready to have a relationship with him. She dabbed fragrant droplets of Shalimar onto the nape of her neck and the inside of both wrists, suddenly struck by the realization that whether the murderer was apprehended or not had little to do with her desire to be with Rawlings. She needn't conceal her feelings for him because the case was still open.

Seeing the glimmer of expectation in her eyes, Olivia gave her reflection a self-conscious grin and then headed to the bar.

Gabe began making her drink immediately. When Rawlings walked in, the barkeep welcomed the chief and gestured at the rows of shining bottles lined up behind the bar. "What's your pleasure, Chief?"

"Same as the lady, please." Rawlings ran the fingers of his right hand through his hair and sighed. "You'd better give me three fingers instead of two, Gabe. It's been that kind of day."

Olivia and Rawlings took their drinks and withdrew to one of the bar's intimate tables and clinked glasses.

"I feel better already," Rawlings said before taking a sip. "Just seeing you."

"That shows just how tired you are," she teased. "Harris is doing well, by the way. Millay's been texting me with regular reports, and I talked to him about an hour ago. He sounds almost happy to have been shot."

With a wry grin, Rawlings said, "Hey, if it gets you the girl . . ."

Their eyes met and they both smiled over the rims of their glasses. A waitress materialized and put down a plate of bruschetta with fresh basil and diced tomatoes as well as a small platter containing a round of baked Brie encircled by olives. Rawlings stared at the food but didn't reach for any of it.

"The Vickers did not kill Nick Plumley," he said solemnly. "The woman who owns their rental cottage inadvertently provided them with an alibi for the morning in question. Their credit card was declined the day before and she'd spoken to them about an alternate means of payment. They promised to have cash for her by the end of their wedding day on Wednesday but failed to give her any. By Thursday, she was concerned that the couple would try to skip out without taking care of their bill." He sliced through the soft Brie with a cheese knife. "We're not talking about small change here either. The landlady had taken care of all the arrangements for their marriage ceremony. Between the food, the photographer, and the rental house, they owe her a few thousand."

Olivia whistled. "So she went knocking on the door of their honeymoon suite the morning after they got married. Whoa."

Rawlings colored. "She stopped by several times but no one ever answered. Finally, she just let herself in and found Mr. and Mrs. Vickers in a rather, ah, compromising position. Mr. Vickers yelled at her to get lost and she was flustered enough to do just that." He took a bite of bruschetta and rolled his eyes in delight. "Delicious."

"The poor woman," Olivia said with a laugh. "Not only is she out a few grand but she got an eyeful too."

Nodding, the chief's good humor quickly evaporated.

"She was hoping that by telling me about the incident I could help recover her losses, but she ended up aiding the Vickers. They now have a solid alibi for the morning of Mr. Plumley's murder."

"But they *are* guilty of shooting Harris and of breaking and entering into more than one home. They stole the painting from my kitchen, right?"

"The Vickers have confessed to those crimes, yes. Thankfully, the painting was unharmed. I've got it in my office."

Olivia hadn't realized she was holding her breath until she let it go. "I was so worried about Harris that I forgot all about the watercolor."

"As you should, considering all that's happened." Rawlings fell silent for a moment. He placed food on a small plate and handed it to Olivia and then fixed one for himself. They ate quietly for a little while, enjoying the creamy cheese, the crisp bread seasoned with garlic and olive oil, and each other's company. "Mrs. Vickers told me something else," the chief said sotto voce. "Something I'm only going to share with you because I trust you."

Olivia could hear the unspoken directive. Rawlings was ordering her not to tell anyone else. She nodded in understanding.

"Mrs. Vickers confessed to having blackmailed her ex-husband for years. According to her, Mr. Plumley once told me that he was responsible for the death of an old woman. Other than his father, this woman was his primary source for *The Barbed Wire Flower*."

Leaning forward in her chair, Olivia opened her mouth to ask a question but Rawlings held up a finger. "I know what you want to ask, but listen to the whole story first. Mrs. Vickers alleges that Mr. Plumley made this confession after drinking a great deal of vodka. It was the same night they conceived their son, in fact. The two parted ways and then Mrs. Vickers had her own secret to carry."

He paused and Olivia wondered if he too was picturing Cora touching her swollen belly, her face slack with shock as her obstetrician gave her the hard news that her son had Down's syndrome.

"So they lived separate lives until Mr. Plumley's novel was released and immediately hit the bestseller list," Rawlings continued. "At that point, his ex-wife paid him a visit and demanded money. They struck a deal. She would remain silent about what happened to his source in return for quarterly payments in cash."

Olivia couldn't contain herself. "Was the woman Evelyn White? Did Plumley *kill* her?"

"Mrs. Vickers claims that Mr. Plumley let Ms. White read an early draft of *A Barbed Wire Flower*. This was years before the book was actually published. Ms. White never knew that Plumley's real name was Ziegler, and she told him over and over that it was Nicklaus Ziegler who murdered James Hatcher, the Camp New Bern guard, not Heinrich Kamler."

Groaning, Olivia picked up her glass. "But Plumley ignored her and portrayed Kamler as the killer, just like the papers did in 1945."

"Yes, and Ms. White became very upset. She'd only agreed to tell him her story on the condition that he'd rewrite that event the way *she* believed it to have happened." Rawlings noted Olivia's empty tumbler and gently took it from her hand. "Even though Mr. Plumley's book was a work of fiction, Ms. White had hoped that it would help right the wrong done to Kamler's reputation." He sighed. "I'd better get you a refill before I continue. Be right back."

Rawlings headed for the bar, but Olivia sat frozen in her chair. Once again, she was overwhelmed by the losses Evelyn and Heinrich had experienced. Plumley had had the chance to assuage a small bit of Evelyn's pain, but he couldn't do it.

After listening to Evelyn White's stories, Plumley must have suspected that he was the son of the real murderer. Evelyn didn't know this, of course, because he wasn't going by the name of Ziegler. This left Nick the freedom to continue burying the truth, filling his novel with the same lie the newspapers had printed, and profiting from the deceit.

Worst of all, the bastard had betrayed Evelyn. She'd given up her child, lived a lifetime apart from the man she loved, and then, in what was probably her last chance to seek a measure of redemption for her Henry, had been denied that small opportunity.

"So were both the Zieglers murderers? Father and son?" Olivia demanded angrily when Rawlings returned with their drinks. "And cowards? Stabbing a man in the back and killing an old lady!"

Rawlings squatted at her side, his eyes softening. "I knew this would upset you. You felt a connection to Ms. White."

It wasn't a question. Olivia said, "Tell me how she died."

"I will, but remember that this is all hearsay," the chief reminded her gently.

"Tell me," she insisted.

He took a swallow of Chivas Regal. "When Ms. White

read the escape scene in the draft of *The Barbed Wire Flower*, she grew hysterical. Mr. Plumley panicked, fearing that Ms. White's nurse would come running and would find out that he'd broken his promise. He was afraid that Evelyn would tell her story to others, to the nurse perhaps. According to his ex-wife, Mr. Plumley silenced Evelyn White by smothering her with a pillow."

Olivia closed her eyes, trying to keep her features under control. It was too easy for her to visualize Nick Plumley grabbing the pillow from under Evelyn's head and pressing it against the old woman's face. She could see Evelyn's limbs jerking below the bedsheets, her thin nails clasping at the arms that were robbing her of breath, of life.

"Why would he give her a copy?" Olivia managed to ask after several long moments of silence.

Rawlings threw out his arms in a helpless gesture. "Mrs. Vickers claims that Nick had come to view Ms. White as a sort of mother figure. He desperately wanted her approval and had convinced himself that she'd be so dazzled by his skill as a writer that she'd overlook the details of the escape scene. Perhaps he was convinced by his own fiction."

Disgusted, Olivia pushed the ice around in her glass with the tip of her finger. Suddenly, she was struck by a thought. "Did Cora talk about this to anyone else?"

"She said that only her new husband knew what Mr. Plumley had done. She promised Boyd that he'd be able to open his own gym one day with the payments they received from Mr. Plumley. When they stole the painting from your house, they planned to sell it and use the funds to pay off their credit cards and secure a loan. Between the painting and the life insurance payout, they could finally climb out of debt." Getting up slowly, Rawlings went back to his seat.

"Cora knew that Nick had come to Oyster Bay in search of that painting. Evelyn must have told him about it, but why did he want it so desperately? Was he afraid that Kamler had written something about his father on the back instead of a love letter to Evelyn?"

Rawlings rubbed his chin. "Perhaps he simply wanted to possess one of her treasures. They must have spent a great deal of time together and she obviously told him things she'd never told anyone else."

"That's it!" Olivia's eyes flashed. "Evelyn told him that her greatest *treasures* were in Oyster Bay. Trea-sure*s*. Plural. The painting was one of them, but the second was not made of canvas and paint, but of flesh and blood. I think Evelyn knew exactly who adopted the child fathered by Heinrich Kamler. That child's been right here the whole time."

"Her son. The living reminder of the man she loved." The glimmer in Olivia's deep-sea eyes was reflected in the chief's excited hazel gaze. "He'd be in his midsix-ties, just like our suspect, Mr. Hatcher."

"Exactly," Olivia said, barely above a whisper. "Ray-mond Hatcher was *raised* by Agnes Hatcher. Dave was his *adopted* brother. Ray was brought into the Hatcher home from an orphanage months after James Hatcher was killed. Ray claimed to have never known the iden-tity of his biological parents. So if Raymond Hatcher is Evelyn's son, then he has two motives: money and revenge. Nick Plumley tarnished his father's name and benefited financially from his mother's story. Hatcher is big and strong. He could have easily strangled Plumley."

The chief's face grew stony. "Could have, Olivia.

Don't form a lynch mob just yet." He pulled his cell phone from his pocket and made a call. "This long day is about to become a long night. I've got to order some coffee."

Olivia waved for him to stay put. "You have some time before your men bring him in. Please, let me order you something for dinner. If you're going to be up for hours, you'll need food."

Rawlings smiled at her, and she felt the warmth of it spread through her body. "Actually, if you could make me two dinners to-go, I'll share a meal with Mr. Hatcher. It's amazing what folks will say over a piece of steak and a bottle of beer."

"That's quite an unusual interview technique," Olivia quipped with a raised brow. "But then again, you never fail to surprise me."

The smile grew wider and warmer still. "Is that why you find me so irresistible?"

Olivia was fully aware that the chief was teasing her, but she walked to his side and looked at him, hoping the intensity of her desire would leap from her eyes into his like a jumping spark.

"That's one of the reasons." Her voice was deep and low, filled with the caress she longed to bestow upon him here, in front of everyone, if only she had the courage. "When this is all over, I'd like to discover more."

Chapter 16

The eyes indicate the antiquity of the soul.

—RALPH WALDO EMERSON

Thursday passed with Olivia attending to a vast array of tasks at both restaurants. She and Laurel also went on a whirlwind shopping excursion to prepare for the homecoming of her young nephew.

To keep her mind off the fact that she hadn't heard a word from Rawlings since he'd left The Boot Top to interview Raymond Hatcher, Olivia threw herself into work, scouring the docks for the freshest seafood, tweaking menus with Hudson and Michel, and answering hundreds of e-mails from customers, suppliers, and food critics.

When the inbox on her desk was barren, she and Laurel drove to the closest megamall, talking about everything under the sun other than Laurel's marital problems. Her articles on Cora and Boyd Vickers and the love story between Evelyn White and Heinrich Kamler had been picked up by several of the big-name papers. As a result, she'd had job offers from across the country, which she'd used as leverage to gain more flexible work hours and a higher salary.

"I'll be able to bring the boys to their preschool and pick them up again. And when I can't be there, I can afford to hire this wonderful retired schoolteacher who lives in our neighborhood," Laurel told Olivia with a smile. "I'm getting the best of both worlds. I get to be around for my kids and have the job of my dreams."

"I don't know how you do it all," Olivia told her friend. "You're so busy. How will you find the time to work on your book?"

Laurel shrugged. "I write after I put the boys to bed. I'm tired, but I pour myself some wine and sit down at the computer with Michael Bublé or Harry Connick and type away for an hour or two every night." She twisted a strand of wheat blond hair around her forefinger. "It's not like Steve and I are sharing a bottle of merlot in the kitchen and swapping stories about our day. We're not even watching TV together. For the past few months, I've barely seen him. He comes home after I'm already in bed, smelling like beer and cigarettes."

"Have you asked him where he's been?"

"I'm afraid of the answer," Laurel said after a pregnant pause. "As long as we're in this limbo, we're still a family."

Olivia cast her a sidelong glance. "And how does Michel fit in this familial arrangement?"

Laurel colored. "He's just a good friend."

"You know he wants to be more than that."

"I told him that I can't," she said firmly. "Not while I'm still married. I'm not that kind of woman."

Olivia wasn't sure what else there was to say. Only Laurel could determine when she was ready to address the problems with her marriage, and Olivia knew nothing about the intricacies of the institution. It had taken her most of her adult life to meet a man worth taking a risk for, and yet, she had no idea how to follow Jeannie's advice and do something big to show Sawyer Rawlings that she had no reservations left when it came to starting a relationship with him.

Laurel perked up the moment she entered the children's boutique. Moving through the store with utmost assurance, she filled a cart with bedding, clothes, diapers, bathing equipment, and toys. She then chose the nursery furniture, insisting upon same-day delivery. When the woman running the customer service desk spluttered an excuse, pointing at the schedule on her computer, Olivia gestured at the pair of loaded shopping carts and said, "We could leave these here and go to another store if that's what you'd prefer."

"No, no!" the woman hastily capitulated. "I'm sure we can work something out."

"I wish I had the guts to do that," Laurel said after their purchases had been totaled.

Olivia grinned. "I wouldn't have been so forceful, but the schedule page she showed us was for *last* week. I don't like being lied to, I don't like laziness, and I don't like people treating me like I'm a nitwit."

"No wonder Michel respects you so much," Laurel said with a laugh. "He refers to you as Madame General to the staff, you know."

"I think that has a nice ring to it," Olivia replied breezily.

After shopping, the two women and Haviland ate lunch at a dog-friendly outdoor café and then Olivia dropped Laurel off and drove across town to meet

Hudson at his house. Hudson gave her a quick tour of his home and then they sat on the stoop and drank iced coffee. It wasn't long before the deliverymen from the children's boutique arrived and set up the nursery furniture. Olivia tipped them handsomely and then she and Hudson hung curtains and framed prints and washed a load of baby clothes, blankets, and burp cloths. They put board books and soft toys on the shelves and plugged in a crescent moon nightlight.

When they were done, Hudson stood in the doorway and gazed around the room. Laurel had chosen a sailboat theme for the crib sheets, bumper, and quilt. A mobile of bright boats bobbed from the ceiling, and a lamp shaped like a blue whale threw a scattering of stars against the wall above the changing table. A rug made of squares of primary colors and the framed prints of swimming fish lent the small space a cozy, cheerful atmosphere.

Olivia couldn't even imagine what it would be like to have such a tiny, helpless being sleeping in this room. She pictured her nephew, his beautiful gray eyes gazing up at the boat mobile, hands curled into fists as he gurgled and cooed at the small aquarium attached to one of the crib rails. Would he cry as he watched the plastic octopus swimming by? Would the lullabies or bubbling noises soothe him to sleep during the early hours of the morning or stimulate him so that he woke up the entire household? Would Anders dream?

"Kim's going to pass right out when she sees this," Hudson said, his eyes smiling. "I planned to buy a used crib and a pack of diapers and let it go at that. This room looks like it could be on TV."

Knowing this was high praise, Olivia nodded in

agreement and then removed a gift-wrapped package from a shopping bag. "May I put this in Caitlyn's room? I didn't think it was fair to lavish things on my nephew while ignoring my niece."

"Sure." He examined the rectangular shape. "What is it anyhow?"

"An art set. It's a little advanced for her age, but the girl has real talent. You should have seen the drawings she did the night you and Kim came to The Boot Top to finesse the menu for the crab house." Olivia held up the present, which was wrapped in pink paper covered by silver and purple butterflies. "This has everything a budding artist needs. Colored pencils, pastels, charcoal, paints, brushes, and tons of paper."

Hudson put his heavy arm around Olivia. He didn't say a word, but she could feel his gratitude in the gentle squeeze he gave her shoulders. He then gave Haviland a scratch on the neck and glanced at his watch.

"Time for work," he declared, not bothering to conceal his eagerness to head for the restaurant.

Olivia followed him outside. "You're going to take a day off when Anders comes home, aren't you?"

Looking horrified at the prospect, Hudson shook his head. "Not a chance. I plan to be at the restaurant as much as possible. You've never lived with a newborn. All they do is eat, sleep, poop, and cry. By the time Caitlyn starts school, things'll be better, but until then, this is gonna be the summer of no sleep. Don't be surprised if you find me stretched out on the floor in the office."

Olivia thought of Laurel, of how she juggled her career and motherhood without much support from her husband.

"Aren't you modern-daddy types supposed to be

hands-on? Changing diapers and getting up with the baby in the middle of the night?"

Hudson snorted. "I'd just make a mess of things. Kim's real good with the kids. I don't know how to do things like she does." He paused, his gaze going distant. "I used to watch her with Caitlyn when she didn't know I was looking. I'd wonder how she could tell exactly what that kid needed. She knew when to burp her, when to change her, when to sing to her. Seeing Kim like that . . . it was like spying on a stranger."

Olivia let a moment of quiet settle between them. "I can't tell if that's a good thing or a bad thing."

"It's good, I guess. It was just different, that's all."

He shifted uncomfortably, and Olivia recognized that her brother had had enough sibling intimacy for the moment. However, she was in a lighthearted mood from working in Anders' room, so she laughed and chucked Hudson on the arm. "I don't like change either. Unless I'm revitalizing an old building or starting up a new restaurant, I'd rather stick with the status quo forever. But look at us, Hudson. The time is flying by. We've got to be able to keep pace with it, stare it in the eye, and say, 'Bring on the change. I'm ready.'"

Hudson gave her a strange look. "Are we still talking about me here?"

Olivia felt a tinge of heat prickle the skin of her cheeks. "Maybe not."

By Friday, Rawlings still hadn't returned Olivia's calls. He sent the Bayside Book Writers an e-mail saying that he'd try to make their next meeting but that he hadn't had an opportunity to critique Millay's chapter. Olivia had switched weeks with Millay because she didn't know what to do with Kamila now that her character had slept with Ramses. It wasn't the first time Olivia had faced writer's block, but this one seemed more formidable than previous ones. She sensed there was a parallel between her own stymied romance and her inability to plot the next passage of Kamila's life.

"How can I decide what happens next?" she'd complained to the blank document on her computer screen, glowing poltergeist white in the evening light. "I can't even map out the next scene in *my* life, damn it."

Now, as she waited for Kim to call to say that she and Anders and Caitlyn were home, Olivia turned her attention to Millay's chapter. She was looking forward to seeing what new adventure Millay's heroine, Tessa, had embarked upon.

A Gryphon Warrior, Tessa had been chosen to defend her land against a scourge of frightening mythological creatures. Up to this point, the narrative had focused mainly on Tessa and her Gryphon. The two were bonded like the dragons and their riders from the Anne McCaffrey books, and Tessa had recently discovered the secret name of her Gryphon. By calling his name, she'd awakened her own magical abilities, but with no training in magic, she was now vulnerable to attack as she headed to the furthermost outpost of her people.

Olivia leaned back in her chair and began to read.

Tessa held on to Variynt's thick mane as he dove between the sharp spires of rock. The Needle Mountains were a menacing cluster of towering stones, so tall that they blotted out the sun and obscured the horizon. Flying between their narrow, clawlike spires was dangerous at best, and in a thunderstorm with the wind currents shifting every few seconds, it was close to madness.

The Gryphon blinked drops of cold rain from his amber eyes and veered away from a jagged outcrop of rock. Tessa flew with her head tucked against Variynt's neck, but the biting rain battered the flesh on her hands and face. Finally, the icy downpour abated and the mountains gave way to a stretch of dark wood. It happened without warning. In the space of a heartbeat, Tessa looked up and the rocks were gone.

We're going to make it, she thought and knew that Variynt had heard her relief. She and her Gryphon were bonded telepathically. Tessa also experienced his pain as if it were her own and had been told by the priests that if her Gryphon died, she would follow him to the White Plains, the place where Gryphon Warriors rested after exhausting lives of battle and strife.

Suddenly, a trio of nets was discharged from the canopy of trees, pinning Variynt's wings to his sides. He cried out in rage and crashed through the foliage, the branches piercing his skin like razors, Tessa screaming with agony.

Just when she thought they'd collide with the hard ground, their bones snapping like kindling in the fire, the nets jerked upward, and they swayed back and forth, hovering over a clearing.

Tessa fought to regain her breath. The sound of her heartbeat roared inside her head, and Variynt was flooding her with a mixture of anger and distress.

Voices speaking in a foreign, raspy tongue surrounded them, and Tessa struggled to pull the blade from her bootstrap. She never got the chance, for the netting was rapidly removed and several men grabbed her, pinning her down. Though she cursed and spat, her hands were lashed behind her back and then she was yanked to her feet as though she weighed less than a pile of Variynt's feathers.

Before her stood a cloaked man. He slid the hood from his head, and Tessa held back a gasp. Both of his cheeks were tattooed with dragon scales.

He was a Wyvern Warrior, Tessa's mortal enemy. The race Tessa's people had warred against since the dawn of time. He was also the most beautiful man she had ever seen.

And he was smiling at her.

Olivia went back to the beginning of the chapter and made a few notes in the margins. In her opinion, Millay had a tendency to take her metaphors too far. She knew that Millay was a huge admirer of Dean Koontz's style but didn't feel that her metaphors were as successful, or original, as Mr. Koontz's.

Overall, Olivia enjoyed every installment of Tessa's journey, but something about the last line made her forget all about mythological beasts. Instead, her thoughts turned to Rawlings. Why wasn't he returning her calls?

Her iMac binged, indicating the receipt of a new e-mail. Olivia minimized Millay's chapter and noticed the sender was Professor Billinger. He'd sent her an enormous attachment, and she could only hope that he'd discovered something useful. The moment she read his message, she knew that he had.

Dear Olivia,

I hope this note finds you well. Excuse the clichés, but I have been burning the candle at both ends in search of more information on the ill-fated lovers. After exhausting the documents at the North Carolina Museum of History, I traveled to DC and began hunting there.

I won't bore you with the details, but within the seemingly endless archives of the Library of Congress, I found a treasure trove of documents and photographs on the prison camps of North Carolina. There were dozens of photographs from Camp New Bern, including the one I've attached featuring our mutual friend, Heinrich Kamler. Unlike the photo you saw in my office, this one shows his face quite clearly, and as you can see, Kamler stands apart from the rest of the prisoners.

I've also attached images of his watercolor rendition of the camp and some shots of the men taking exercise and engaged in other daily tasks. I still have many letters and military reports to wade through and will be in touch if I stumble across anything that could be of use to you.

Please let me know if you've made any fresh discoveries. I believe we make an excellent research team.

Affectionately yours,
Emmett Billinger

Olivia scrolled down, her finger hovering over the mouse as her eyes drank in the black-and-white photograph showing a group of uniformed prisoners standing on a row of wooden bleachers. A baseball game was in progress, and the spectators were facing the camera, relaxed and grinning.

The caption indicated that Heinrich Kamler was the last man in the second row, and Olivia immediately understood what Billinger had meant by his comment that Kamler stood apart from the others. He was a head taller than the rest of the men and had a lean, wiry body and the kind of chiseled, handsome face that would be at home on a movie screen. His eyes gazed into middle distance, but the unmistakable look of longing struck Olivia to the quick. She had seen the same expression in those very eyes. Recently.

Her mouth went dry.

She stared at the square jaw, the smooth brow, and the straight, proud nose and wanted to put her head back and cry out in misery. Instead, she hit the print button, pacing back and forth in front of the printer as it strung the pixels together into an image. An image that would shake the entire community.

Haviland watched her with anxious eyes, but Olivia was too lost in the picture emerging from the printer to pay him any heed.

The machine completed its task and the image fell neatly into a tray. Olivia snatched it up and carried it to the window. There was no denying it. The eyes gave him away.

Olivia leaned against the glass, pressing her right cheek against its cool surface as she glanced out at the ocean for a long time, desperately needing to be soothed by the dips and swells of blue.

It failed to comfort her.

She turned her stunned gaze on the interior of her

house, her eyes staring at the well-known patterns of tile and wood flooring and carpet. It was as if she didn't know where she was. Her surroundings, her town, and the people in it seemed to have turned inside out, and all that she knew had become cold and strange.

And no matter how much she wanted to, she could not avoid knowing what she now knew. There was no way to deny the truth that burned her lungs and brought hot tears to her eyes.

Olivia knew the identity of Heinrich Kamler. She'd known him for years and cared for him deeply.

The doorbell rang. Olivia leapt backward like a startled doe.

Haviland began to bark and raced into the kitchen. Olivia followed him slowly, like a sleepwalker. When she opened the door to Rawlings, she could not speak. She merely shook her head, again and again, clutching the photograph of Heinrich Kamler in her hand.

"Shhhhh," the chief hushed her and gently pried the paper from beneath her fingers. He studied the image in silence and then touched her cheek. "Olivia, I'm sorry that it has to end this way. Raymond Hatcher is innocent of Nick Plumley's murder. Heinrich Kamler is the killer."

Mutely, Olivia averted her gaze, but Rawlings put a hand under her chin and forced her to look at him. "I came to tell you before I picked him up. It's against every rule and regulation, and I'm half disgusted with myself for being here, but I knew this would hurt you. I didn't want you to find out from anyone but me, but I can see that I'm already too late. I suppose your professor friend sent you this?"

Olivia didn't even hear the question. She dug her

fingertips into the fabric of the chief's uniform sleeve and squeezed him hard. "Let me be the one," she begged, her voice hoarse and pitiful. "Let me go to him first."

Rawlings dropped his eyes. "I can't allow that. You'd have him on the next plane, the next boat, anything to save him."

"Even if I offered, he wouldn't run," she whispered. "He didn't want to before. Ziegler forced him to. Please, Sawyer. I want him to have a friend there when you come for him. He's been on his own for so long."

The muscles in the chief's jaw pulsed as he waged an internal battle over what was more important, following procedure and ensuring an airtight case or allowing another human being a moment of grace. In the end, he decided that Heinrich Kamler was worthy of a little compassion.

"You have an hour," he stated sternly. "And I'm trusting you, Olivia."

Too overwhelmed by emotion to respond, Olivia wiped the tears from her cheeks and gestured for Haviland to accompany her to the car. She backed out of the driveway, leaving sprays of dust and sand in her wake.

Never had she imagined that the end of the investigation would lead to the door of a friend. She'd always assumed that the killer would be some cruel and twisted stranger, a vengeful, spiteful, or greedy man with a black heart. But this one was funny, kind, and hardworking. He was one of them. He belonged to them.

Olivia sped through town, oblivious of everything around her. Five miles beyond the business district, she turned onto a narrow lane sloping down to the harbor. A small house with brown shingles sat perched on a gentle rise above the water. A worn path led to a small dock where a one-man fishing skiff was tethered, leisurely bobbing in the mild current.

The sight of the tiny vessel nearly made Olivia stumble, but she managed to make it to the front door.

There was no need to knock. Heinrich Kamler had seen her coming and had opened the door to welcome her inside.

"I'm glad it's you, 'Livia," he said in a voice heavy with sorrow. "Of all the people in this town, I'd have chosen you to know the truth."

Olivia nodded, angry that she could not control the tears that rushed down her face.

"There, there," the man said and reached for her. "I reckon we've got time for a glass of sun tea before the chief comes for me."

She went to him, putting both arms around his back, taking in the frailty of his body. She traced the vertebrae of his spine and could feel his ribs through his thin, aged skin. Yet in her mind, she saw him as Evelyn White had seen him, a young man in the prime of life. A young man doomed by a lie.

The only comfort she had to offer was this embrace.

Olivia held him close. Haviland licked their hands and whined anxiously, as she whispered his name over and over again. "Wheeler . . . Wheeler . . ."

Chapter 17

Your children are not your children.
They are the sons and daughters of Life's
longing for itself.
—KAHLIL GIBRAN

Wheeler led Olivia into his tidy kitchen. The room was Spartan, lacking the bric-a-brac, photographs, and souvenirs displayed by most people who'd lived for eight decades. Every surface was clean, and the scent of oranges and vinegar hung in the air.

Three storage containers, a knife block, and a cutting board were lined up with mathematical precision on the countertop. Wheeler placed a lemon and a lime onto the board, cut the fruit into nearly transparent slices, and stuffed them on the bottom of a glass tumbler. He then smothered them with ice cubes, poured in his homemade sun tea, and beckoned Olivia to join him out on the small deck.

They settled on a pair of chairs overlooking the harbor, and Olivia waited for Wheeler to speak, sipping the tea as though this was a relaxed social call, as if there wasn't a phantom hourglass present, its grains of sand already falling.

Wheeler sat for a few minutes, watching a sailboat pass beyond a pair of marker buoys. As the vessel headed for the open sea, he said, "Ziegler's boy was the spittin' image of his daddy. When he came into my place for breakfast, I thought I was seein' a ghost. A ghost with glasses and better manners, sure enough, but I saw through his mask. That writer thought he was above the rules, that he was better than the rest of us, just like his daddy did. When men like that think no one's watchin', their eyes go cold. They both had those ice-cold eyes."

"What happened the night Ziegler escaped?" Olivia asked. She wasn't ready to hear about Plumley's death.

In the tired afternoon light, the harbor seemed lethargic and calm, a contradiction to the turbulence and sorrow that ran through Wheeler's past like floodwaters.

"You gotta understand somethin'," Wheeler said. "Ziegler was a Nazi. He was brainwashed through and through, and he looked at the rest of us like we weren't worth the pot he pissed in. He reckoned we were traitors, workin' with the Americans the way we did. Watchin' their movies and learnin' baseball."

"Why were you on that U-Boat in the first place?"

Wheeler shrugged. "I wanted to see the world. My folks were farmers and I would've done anythin' to get away from that life. I didn't wanna get stuck, see? I was so young . . . I thought it was gonna be such a thrill to travel underwater, silent as a shark, and surface to find a white beach filled with beautiful women." He laughed. "Lots of boys got in that war outta boredom. What fools we were."

"But Ziegler was a true Nazi," Olivia stated.

"Would have killed us all if he could, his yellow-bellied countrymen, but what he wanted most was Evelyn." Wheeler winced, as if the act of speaking her name caused him physical pain. "That devil stole my knife and stabbed a good, hardworkin' man in the back. Poor guy never saw it comin'. We coulda walked outta there anytime without hurtin' a soul, but Ziegler wanted blood. He'd wanted it since the war started. Craved it, even. I followed him that night 'cause I saw his eyes at suppertime. There was murder in those icy blues. It was shinin' out like the ghost lights you see in the fog every now and again."

Olivia knew about those lights. She'd seen them the night her father had disappeared, while she'd waited, shivering and alone in a small dingy, to be rescued. More than once, she'd spotted a glow and expected the prow of a ship to slice through the curtains of fog, but the luminescence had faded as quickly as it had appeared. Many a fisherman had gone temporarily mad in the deep waters, having gone adrift far off the coast because of a storm or mechanical problems. These grizzled seamen talked of hearing strange noises and seeing an unearthly light, unable to completely believe that the soft twinkles were the product of hallucinations brought on by dehydration.

"After curfew, I heard Ziegler leave his tent. I followed, my knife in my pants," Wheeler continued. "I figured on rescuin' someone that night, savin' some poor sod from him, seein' as that boy was hell-bent on killin' a Yank. He'd lusted for blood since the war started, but he'd had lots of schoolin' and was given a desk job. That made him mad too. He hadn't been able to take a shot at a single GI."

It was easy to get caught up in Wheeler's narrative, to see Ziegler creeping out in the darkness. The guards, who'd never been threatened by one of their prisoners, relaxed at their posts. Perhaps they played cards or dozed off or stared at the moon as they smoked cigarette after cigarette, their hushed voices rising with the smoke into the night air. "Did you fight him?"

Wheeler nodded. "Aye, but I was no good. He sucker punched me in the gut, grabbed my knife, and stuck it in the guard's back before I could catch my breath. I rolled the man on his side to see if I could help him, and that's when another pair of guards approached on their rounds. I knew they saw my face and that they'd find my knife. When all was said and done, I was still a Kraut. I was the enemy. Didn't matter that I loved everythin' about this country. Didn't matter how pretty my paintings were. Didn't matter that *she* was waitin' on me, waitin' for the war to be over . . ."

"You had to run," Olivia said soothingly.

His face clouding with grief, Wheeler nodded. "I wanted to go straight to Evie, just to tell her I'd be back for her and that I didn't do what they were gonna say I did, but I didn't know where she lived." He stared at the water, the hopelessness of that night replaying across his features. "I had a general idea, but there wasn't time to roam around the streets lookin' for her window."

"Did you know where Ziegler was headed?"

"No. If I'd known, I'd have gone after him, dragged him back by his hair. He was a snake and a coward and all twisted inside." Wheeler gestured to the west. "I made my way to the mountains. Took clothes hangin' out to dry and pinched scraps from farms. I hated myself for it too. I'd always been good with my hands and I found work at a mill, fixin' gears and wheels and such."

Olivia looked at him. "And you became Wheeler Ames. Wheeler by trade and Ames as a show of respect to the murdered guard?"

He sat back in surprise. "That's what his buddies called him. See, one of the non-English-speakin' prisoners couldn't get the *J* out, and after that, Ames just stuck. I never wanted to forget the man, so I used that name for my own. By that time, I could pass as a local and I never did talk much anyhow. Folks thought I had gone soft in the head durin' the war and they were only half wrong. Havin' to leave Evie . . . havin' her wake up to hear I was a murderer and a liar . . . a runaway . . ." He trailed off.

"You never tried to contact her?"

Anguish pulled the corners of Wheeler's mouth down. "I sent her letters in the beginning, but she didn't answer. I reckoned she'd washed her hands of me, that she thought I was a killer. I even found her house when I thought it was safe to come back, but she and her family were gone." He shook his head mournfully. "I let her go. Or tried to. I've been with other women, but I never loved any woman but her." His eyes flashed, anger chasing away the regret. "And when I heard Ziegler's boy talkin' about her, whisperin' to that ex-wife of his and her lump of a boyfriend, I knew I was gonna end him. It's a scary thing, girlie, to realize you've got that inside you. And I'm not real sorry either, 'Livia. Only about hurtin' folks like you. But I don't have much life left in me anyhow. If folks think bad of me, I won't hear about it for long and I don't have to read the papers in jail."

"You sound almost relieved that you'll be locked up," Olivia said gently.

Wheeler reached over and placed a weathered hand over hers. "I'm tired, my girl. I'm old and there are places achin' inside that I thought were all scarred over. I just wanna sit down for a spell, read a few books, and die in my sleep. Don't care where that happens. Jail's as good a place as any other."

Olivia tried to imagine her aged friend lying quietly on a cot, reading a novel as his cell neighbors adorned themselves with homemade tattoos or wrote entreating letters to a family member or, if they were lucky, to a lover.

"Do you wanna know it all?" Wheeler asked, and Olivia knew that he hoped she'd say no.

"I do," she answered without pause. "We've all been involved, my friends and I, in some way or another. I need to know."

Wheeler hesitated. "I hate to have you look at me with different eyes, but it's too late to fret about that now." He took a long drink of sun tea, and Olivia was aware that she had never heard Wheeler speak as much as he had for the past few minutes. The effort was draining him, the paper-thin wrinkles beneath his eyes drooped lower on his cheek and his breath was slightly labored.

"I didn't have a plan," he began slowly. "Just spent the whole night imaginin' how Plumley had killed Evie. They didn't whisper about that part, he and that Cora woman, and I only heard as much as I did because she thought he wasn't gonna pay up anymore. She started hollerin' at him when I was in the kitchen diggin' around for more coffee filters, but I heard. I heard her mention Evie and what Plumley did to her with her own pillow. I nearly went blind with hate. It crippled me, or I would have killed the man then and there."

"Cora Vickers," Olivia said. "She and Boyd came to Oyster Bay to collect Cora's scheduled payment. Plumley had to pay or she'd sell the story of what he'd done to Evelyn to the highest bidder."

"I don't know the ins and outs, but Plumley was stallin',

tellin' her to be patient. Guess he'd been burnin' through his book money real quick—seems he was a gambler and not a very good one—and had to wait for some check to come in. That's when his ex said Evie's name, and I felt like Ziegler had sucker punched me all over again." He put his glass down, hard, and strung his fingers together. "The next mornin', I grabbed Plumley's favorite bagel and drove over to the big house he was rentin' near yours." He frowned. "I never thought you'd find him, 'Livia. If there's somethin' I really regret, that's it."

Olivia touched him on the arm. "Go on."

Wheeler nodded. "He was in his robe with a cup of coffee in his hand when I rang the bell. He was surprised to see me, but he asked me in. I sat across from him at the table and told him my real name. I told him how Evelyn White had been the shinin' star, the brightest memory of my life and how a day didn't go by that I didn't think of her."

"Wow."

"I asked him if what that Cora woman said was true. For a second he thought about lyin', but he knew I'd already seen the answer in his eyes."

It was impossible for Olivia to imagine how Nick's confession had impacted Wheeler, and she listened in astonishment as her old friend continued to talk about the moments leading up to Nick Plumley's death.

"He told me how she'd read his book and nearly lost her mind. She was that upset. He promised that he'd just wanted to get her to hush up, and that before he even knew it, he'd killed her." Wheeler's hands curled into fists. "He acted sorry while I was starin' him down, but then he managed to finish most of his breakfast. What kind of man can do that?"

Turning her gaze to the horizon, where smudges of gray clouds hung low in the sky, Olivia thought about Wheeler's question. "A man who could no longer separate fact from fiction. I think Plumley had come to believe his own version of the truth. It allowed him to survive, to act normal."

Wheeler didn't acknowledge Olivia's reply. "Seein' him eat with the same hands he'd used to snuff the life outta my Evie . . . I felt myself growin' cold all over, deep into my bones. Every part of me was cold. I thought I'd surely see my own breath . . . I had the gloves I use for handlin' food in my pocket and I put them on. Then I unrolled a painting I'd done when I was in prison. It was nothin' special. Just a bunch of guys smokin' and playin' cards, but I told Plumley he needed to wear gloves if he wanted to touch it."

"And he put them on?"

Wheeler said nothing. The answer was obvious. "Then I walked behind him while he was porin' over the painting, slid the belt off his robe, and paid him in kind for what he'd done to my sweet, darlin' girl."

After a moment, he placed his hands on his chest. "I know I don't look strong, but I've worked every day of my life. It was over quick enough, but it felt like I was watchin' myself from far away. I barely remember doin' it. Then I saw the book . . ."

"You stopped to read the scene in *The Barbed Wire Flower*, the one that had upset Evelyn so much, the one depicting you as the villain," Olivia finished for him. When he still didn't say anything, she said, "It brought back all you'd lost."

But Wheeler had retreated somewhere within himself, and Olivia didn't try to draw him out. Her time was almost up and she wanted to say something comforting and poignant before Rawlings arrived, but when she most wanted to have the right words at her power, they zipped off like dragonflies.

"Evelyn always believed in your innocence," she spoke into the silence. "I visited her old friend Mabel in a nursing home. She told us that Evie never doubted you."

A light surfaced in Wheeler's eyes. "We showed her the painting Evelyn hid inside her house," Olivia continued. "Do you remember it?"

Wheeler smiled. "It was her favorite. She'd never seen snow, so I made her snow. She wanted me to paint a place in the woods, a place we'd build someday up in the mountains. Every time we had an art lesson, she'd ask me what a snowflake felt like. If they were really as different as stars. I promised her a million snowfalls as soon as the war was over." He sighed heavily, decades of sorrow in his breath.

"It's a beautiful piece," Olivia said softly. "People all over the country admire your work. Your paintings are worth tens of thousands of dollars."

At this, Wheeler released a dry laugh. "There's a sucker born every minute. I've got a pile of them in the bedroom. Besides fishing, it's how I pass the time. You can have the lot, 'Livia. I won't be takin' them with me."

Olivia heard the rumble of a car engine and knew that her hour was up. She needed to tell Wheeler that Evelyn had given birth to a child, his child, but she was still taking in everything he'd told her. She was overwhelmed by stories and images, by the past and the frightening future that would become the present the moment Chief Rawlings knocked on Wheeler's door.

Wheeler stood up and made his way to the bedroom.

He walked over to a large pine storage chest and lifted the lid. Removing a stack of unframed watercolors tucked between two pieces of cardboard, he untied the twine securing the package and fanned out a half dozen paintings on the top of the pile, Olivia observing him in mute awe.

There were scenes of men working at a paper mill, men and women harvesting peanuts, fishermen at the docks, shopkeepers sweeping their sidewalks, and a baker kneading dough. Olivia's favorite was a landscape featuring an elderly couple strolling hand in hand on a white beach. They were just smudges of peach skin and gray hair, disappearing into a large blur of blue sea and sky, but she couldn't take her eyes from them.

"Take it," Wheeler said tiredly. "Take 'em all."

Olivia stared unblinkingly at the watercolor couple, walking shoulder to stooped shoulder, two people who'd loved a lifetime together and knew how to take the time to enjoy a moment of peace and beauty.

She could not condone what Wheeler had done. Even in the name of revenge, even after what he'd suffered, she could not support his act of violence. Yet, his crime did not blot out the other things she knew about him, the other ways she knew him—all the years they'd shared snippets of gossip, laughter, or quiet conversation. He was still the man who supported a Little League team each year, who donated the day's leftover bagels and pastries to the food bank, who supported local artists by hanging their work on the café's walls. He'd always spoiled Haviland and treated Olivia like a daughter.

He was her friend. He was worthy of forgiveness.

To show Wheeler that nothing would stop her from caring about him, she took the painting. "Thank you."

Car doors slammed at the top of the driveway.

Olivia's heart beat faster at the sound. "Even though I'd be honored to take them all, I'm happy to have just one. There is someone else you might want to give the rest of these to, someone you've never met."

Wheeler wasn't listening. He'd raised his head at the sounds coming from outside and squared his shoulders. Without looking at Olivia, he headed into the kitchen, where he stood in front of the window and peered out toward the driveway.

"That's a good fellow, our chief, and a fine artist to boot. You could do worse, girlie."

Rawlings had parked at the top of the long drive and was now making his way with slow deliberation down the unpaved road, a giant of a man by his side.

"Who's the big guy?" Wheeler asked.

Exhaling, Olivia put her arm around the old man's back. "His name is Raymond Hatcher. He was raised by Agnes Hatcher, James's widow, but I believe he's your son. Yours and Evelyn's."

Wheeler's eyes fixed on Raymond, his face filling with wonder. Olivia could see it spread over his features, glowing like a full moon over the ocean. His mouth worked, but no sound came out. There was nothing but the radiance of this new discovery. It flowed out of his eyes, smoothing his wrinkles until he seemed young again. A young soldier. A young lover.

"We did have the one night together, but I never thought . . ." Wheeler whispered in awe. He refused to blink, drinking in every inch of the approaching figure. A smile began to form on his lips, and the closer Raymond drew, the bigger the smile became. "I'll be damned! Look at that boy. Evie, he's such a fine, strappin' man."

Olivia cast him a sidelong glance. Was he confusing her with his lost love, or was he speaking to Evelyn's ghost?

She moved away from him, opening the door and wordlessly inviting Rawlings inside.

Raymond waited on the stoop while the chief explained the charges and read the Miranda. His tone was soft and calm and held no judgment. Not for the first time, Olivia was grateful for his professional poise, his kind heart.

Wheeler ignored him completely. He didn't acknowledge his presence at all. He passed him by, his eyes locked on Raymond's. They were shining with joy. It was what every child hopes to see on their parent's face, and despite Raymond Hatcher's sixty-odd years, he reacted as any little boy would. He opened his huge arms and enfolded his father into them, holding him tenderly and murmuring his happiness through muffled sobs.

Rawlings and Olivia retreated deeper into the kitchen to give the men some privacy. They sat at the table and waited.

"Does Ray know?" she whispered.

"He knows everything about Heinrich Kamler. That he didn't kill James Hatcher and that he's his father. I showed him the records. I also told him about Wheeler Ames. And that while he was innocent of one murder, he was guilty of another."

Having seen the embrace between father and son, Olivia could tell that Ray Hatcher was prepared to accept these truths, if only to have a few minutes with a man he'd longed to meet all of his life.

Olivia reached under the polished laminate and searched for Rawlings' hand. He clutched hers in return, and they sat in silence, seeing the echoes of the last weeks' anguish and worry and wonder reflected in each other's eyes.

Listening to the soft murmurs being exchanged between Ray and Wheeler, Olivia wanted nothing more than to put her head on the chief's solid shoulder. She wanted to tell him that she was in love with him, but this was not their moment. Their time would come.

Easing her hand free, she placed her Heinrich Kamler watercolor on the table and smiled at the chief. Rawlings stared at the couple on the beach for a full minute and then brushed her cheek with his fingertips. He understood what she was silently conveying. The kiss of his fingers on her flesh was a clear message of "I'm in love with you too."

Several evenings later, Olivia and Haviland pulled in front of the Salters' house. A blue "Welcome Baby" balloon bounced from the mailbox, and Caitlyn was on the front lawn creating enormous, magical-looking bubbles by running across the grass with a hoop filled with a film of soapy water.

As Olivia watched, enthralled, a Chinese dragon of a bubble rippled from Caitlyn's hoop, wriggling and glistening with oil-slick rainbows in the fading light until it popped to the sound of the little girl's laughter.

This was why Olivia had come. She needed to be with this family, *her* family, to see them revolving around one another like a group of planets in orbit. She needed the noise and the joking and the certainty that Anders was truly okay.

Kim squealed upon seeing her, gushing thanks over

the nursery and hugging her repeatedly. Olivia left Haviland outside to snap at bubbles and tiptoed down the hall after Kim.

"He's asleep, but I want you to see how happy he is in the room his auntie made for him."

Olivia waited as Kim eased the door open and then stepped back. "Take your time. I love to watch him sleep. It makes me feel like all is right with the world."

Anders was on his back. The curtains were closed but the lamp was lit and the scattering of stars on his ceiling bathed his face with an angelic glow. He had filled out since Olivia had last seen him, and she marveled at his plump cheeks and chubby wrists, delighting in the rise and fall of his sturdy chest and the strands of silky hair covering his head.

He sighed and then smiled in his sleep. This was followed by a nearly inaudible coo. Olivia's breath caught.

As she stood wondering what Anders dreamed of, she felt someone coming into the room, Caitlyn crossed the carpet to Olivia's side without a sound and took her hand. Gazing up at her with compassion, she whispered, "They fixed his heart, Aunt Olivia. He's all better now. Everything's gonna be okay."

Olivia couldn't believe that such a young child had seen that she was in need of comfort. She knelt down and tucked a strand of loose hair behind Caitlyn's ear, her heart overflowing. "Thank you, honey. I really wanted someone to say those exact words to me."

And then Olivia held her niece close, trying her hardest to believe the little girl's promise.

Chapter 18

Love is the flower of life, and blossoms
unexpectedly and without law, and must
be plucked where it is found.
—D. H. LAWRENCE

It would take Oyster Bay a long time to recover from the shock.

From the outside, everything looked the same. The shops and beaches were filled with tanned tourists, and the rental homes and hotels were booked right through the first weekend of September. The locals smiled and appeared to be as merry and carefree as always, preserving the utopian image of their seaside town.

But in the privacy of bars like Fish Nets, the less glamorous hair salons, and on the fishing boats, people whispered about what had happened. They talked and wondered and argued over Wheeler's crime and then tied on their aprons or rolled up their sleeves and got back to work.

The Bayside Book Writers took a hiatus. Only Laurel was able to put pen to paper following Wheeler's arrest. Reluctantly, she wrote the article unveiling the identity of Nick Plumley's killer. It was her finest piece to date.

The front page spread was read by wide-eyed townsfolk and fascinated tourists, the latter flocking to Bagels 'n' Beans so they could later brag to neighbors and coworkers that they'd bought a bagel or a cappuccino from the killer's café.

Wheeler's employees, with a little guidance from Olivia, were struggling to keep the place running smoothly until Ray Hatcher decided what would become of it. The café belonged to him now, as Wheeler had legally transferred all of his worldly possessions to his son the morning after his arrest.

Ray, who'd spoken to Olivia shortly after a DNA test confirmed that Wheeler was his father, didn't seem interested in the windfall. He quit his job, moved into Wheeler's house, and spent his free time visiting his father in jail and avoiding the press. Rumor had it that he had enrolled in an introductory painting class at the community college and, come September, would see whether or not he'd inherited any of Heinrich Kamler's artistic talent.

As for Wheeler, he'd known that he would never return to Oyster Bay following his arrest. After confessing to murder and admitting that he was once a prisoner of war, he faced federal and state charges and was sure to spend the remainder of his life in prison. Before he was sentenced, he'd written Olivia a letter asking her to help Ray sell his paintings.

"If they're worth anything, you'll know how to get the most money for them on behalf of my boy," he'd written. "And don't let Ray spend a dime on lawyers. Being with him every day has been a gift I probably don't deserve. For the first time since I left my tent that night to follow Ziegler, I feel alive. I hear the deputy call my name and I know my son is waiting for me down the hall. He's got Evie's eyes."

Olivia had folded the letter in half and put it down on her desk blotter. Covering it with her palm, she made several phone calls regarding the paintings. Then, after sharing her opinion with Ray, she contacted Shala Knowles.

"We have one hundred and twenty-five Heinrich Kamler originals to lend your museum," she'd told the thunderstruck curator. "You may have them for a total of ninety days and then they're to be sold. Yours will be the only comprehensive exhibit of Kamler's work. Can you drop everything and set up a space for the first of next month?"

Shala eventually found her tongue and assured Olivia that she and her staff would work tirelessly to mount the finest possible exhibit.

"Then I'll bring the paintings to you tomorrow morning," Olivia said. "But I have one condition."

"Yes?" Shala asked, her voice still quavering with excitement.

"I'm sure you've read about the criminal charges brought against Mr. Kamler, but his son and I would like his art, and not the newspaper headlines, to speak for his life. I must personally approve any biographical information you plan to print in museum brochures or advertisements regarding the exhibit. Mr. Kamler's son has graciously agreed to put off the sale of these paintings at my request. I told him that I owed both you and the museum a favor."

Shala made a sound of protest at the other end. "I was just doing my job, Ms. Limoges."

"But with a rare blend of sincerity and passion,"

Olivia said before her voice became steely. "However, if I read a single line mentioning Kamler's connection to the death of author Nick Plumley or a World War Two prison guard from Camp New Bern, I will storm into your museum and rip his paintings right off the wall." She let her threat hang between them for a moment. "Do I have your word that you'll show me any material you mean to print on Kamler?"

The curator hesitated. Olivia knew she was asking this woman to deliberately ignore the sensational details of the artist's life, details that would lure hundreds of new visitors to the museum. "Do you mind if I ask why you're so keen on protecting Kamler?"

"He's been living in my town for over forty years, but I knew him under a different name," Olivia explained. "In fact, he's a friend. A close one."

Shala absorbed this unbelievable revelation in silence and then said, "In that case, I promise to respect your wishes, and I can't tell you how grateful I am that you're giving us this opportunity."

Olivia's final call was to an auction gallery in Hillsborough, the same town where Mabel, Evelyn's girlhood friend, passed her days in an assisted-living facility. The auction company had an excellent track record with art sales, and Olivia planned to bring Mabel to the preview so she could pick out a painting—a painting that Olivia would later purchase for her.

As for Olivia's Kamler original watercolor, it hung from the narrow wall of her bedroom, directly in the middle of a pair of large windows facing the ocean. It was one of the first things Olivia saw just before falling asleep and again when she woke.

While early-morning sunrays fell into her room, she

would stare at the old couple walking along the sand. Her eyes always found them first and then drifted to the water beyond her window. The picture elicited a contradictory mixture of sadness and hope, but Olivia loved it all the same.

When she drove to Wheeler's house the next day, it was jarring to be met at the front door by Ray. He seemed a little embarrassed to invite her inside a home that had belonged to his father for so many years, but Olivia was pleased to know that Ray was living there. He and the house were well suited. Each was weathered and worn but sturdy enough to bear the most ferocious storm. They were survivors, just as Wheeler was.

Together, Ray and Olivia collected the bundle of paintings and carried them to the Range Rover. Ray stroked Haviland's fur, his gaze fixed on the harbor, and in that moment, Olivia felt as if Wheeler were right there with them. "Did you keep any of the paintings?"

He nodded. "Yeah. I liked the ones of the peanut farms and paper mills. And I kept two of the bakery pictures. That's how my dad ended up with the bagel shop, you know. It used to be the town bakery." Ray led Olivia and Haviland into the bedroom and showed her a watercolor featuring shelves of pastries, breads, and cakes. "He worked in the back, baking bread and pies and cakes, for almost twenty years. He loved the job and was real good at it. He and the baker grew close, and when the man died, he left the place to my dad. I think that's so cool."

"Me too," Olivia agreed. "What will you do with the bagel shop?"

Ray shook his head. "I dunno. I gave one of the full-time guys a raise and told him to manage it for now.

I can't worry about that place. I only have so much time left with my dad."

Having lived a lifetime without knowing the names of his biological parents, Raymond Hatcher wasn't going to waste a second serving bagels and coffee to tourists when he could be with Wheeler instead.

Olivia thought back on the scant number of hours she'd had with her own father before he died. She smiled at Ray. "You've given him what he's wanted his entire life."

"What's that?" Ray asked, flustered by the compliment.

Opening the passenger door for Haviland, Olivia watched the poodle hop inside and then turned back to Ray. "A family and a home. In you, he's found both of those things."

A few weeks later, the Bayside Book Writers donned suits and cocktail dresses and drove to Raleigh to celebrate the opening of the largest exhibit of Heinrich Kamler work ever assembled.

The museum's illuminated gallery was packed with people. Carrying champagne glasses, they murmured to one another in discreet excitement as they studied the paintings. Laurel, who planned to interview several art connoisseurs for her next article, had actually brought Steve to the gala. The couple appeared rather stiff with each other, but Olivia noticed that Steve was serving as his wife's photographer and seemed to be enjoying the role. He'd show her the images he'd captured while she scribbled quotes down in a notebook.

"We're seeing a marriage counselor," Laurel told Olivia when Steve left the room to sample the array of heavy hors d'oeuvres in the lobby. The two women stood shoulder to shoulder in front of the painting that had started it all; the snow scene of the cabin in the woods.

"I'm glad to see you together tonight," Olivia said, and surprisingly, she meant it. She pointed at the cabin on the hill. "Maybe you and Steve could find a place like that and hide away for a few days."

Laurel nodded. "That's not a bad idea. One of my friends has a cabin in Boone. I bet she'd let me borrow it for a long weekend." Her blue eyes grew watery, and she spoke so quietly that Olivia barely heard her. "I wonder what it's like, to know a love that powerful."

Olivia gave her friend's hand a brief squeeze.

"During our interview, Wheeler told me about the art lessons he gave Evelyn. They were chaperoned at first, but after a few months, the guards gave them more and more space. It was as if the whole camp wanted to believe that the two of them could make it together, despite the odds." Laurel dabbed at her eyes with a tissue. "Everyone shared in their story, everyone wanted to play a part in the fantasy. I guess a world at war has no magic left."

"No. Their world was filled with propaganda and rations and uniformed men at the front door, holding telegrams," Olivia said softly. "But Heinrich and Evelyn were the antithesis of all that—they were young and full of laughter and as bright as the stars."

Catching a tear with the tip of her finger, Laurel sighed. "It was the hardest article I've ever had to write. It was nearly impossible to remain objective."

"You did an amazing job," Olivia said. "What did Steve think of the job offers you got from papers in Raleigh and Charlotte?"

Laurel smiled. "He asked me if I wanted to leave Oyster Bay, especially after all that's happened to our town, but I told him that I loved every inch of it. Even the ugly parts. We're not going anywhere." She winked at Olivia. "In fact, the retired schoolteacher I hired to watch the twins started work this week. The boys are crazy about her."

"Who's crazy?" Harris inquired, joining the women in front of the winter scene.

Millay materialized seconds later, a vision of jade green silk, and took the arm Harris offered. He looked every inch the southern gentleman in a tux with a white jacket, and Olivia gazed at him fondly. Having been with him when he'd been shot, having pressed her shirt against his wound, she would forever feel protective of Harris Williams.

"Harris! You could be the next James Bond!" Laurel exclaimed. "Very debonair."

Dipping his chin in recognition of the compliment, Harris produced a rose from the inside of his jacket and presented it to Millay. She rolled her eyes and pretended to be embarrassed but accepted the flower. Snapping off the stem, she put the rose behind her ear, a splash of red against the canvas of her black hair. Olivia did not miss the smile in Millay's eyes as she shot a quick look at Harris.

The entire party turned their attention back to the Kamler snow scene until Millay crossed her arms over her chest and frowned. "Does anyone want to tell me what happened to Plumley's sequel?"

When Olivia didn't answer, Harris scowled at Millay. "You don't have to talk about those things tonight,

Olivia. We're here to enjoy the art and some champagne and each other's company, remember?"

"It's all right, Harris. I know that it can be difficult to move forward without having a complete picture." Olivia waved her friends over to the next painting—a scene of a lone fisherman in a small skiff. Though his line was in the water, the man's upper body was slightly hunched over, giving the impression that he'd gone to sleep, lulled by the gentle waves and the soft sunlight.

"This isn't something you can publish, Laurel," Olivia began and pointed at the fisherman. "Wheeler gathered all of Nick's materials—his notebooks, laptop, thumb drives, and so on and stuffed them into a garbage bag. Later, he dumped the whole collection into the ocean."

Harris rubbed his chin and stared at Olivia, perplexed. "Come on, Nick must have had backup drives in his Beaufort house."

Olivia shook her head. "It's been searched."

"What about a remote storage unit? His laptop was a Mac. He *must* have had off-site back up!" Harris was growing more and more flustered by what he clearly viewed as carelessness on the writer's part.

"All I know is that Plumley's agent has called Rawlings a dozen times, pleading with him to turn Wheeler's house inside out in search of the tiniest remnant of the manuscript," Olivia said. "And the police did look, but there was nothing there. Ray gave them free range in both the house and the bagel shop. That story is now at the bottom of the sea."

Millay shrugged. "Maybe that's the best place for it. Creates some empty shelf space for some new writers

to fill. Here's to us getting back to work next week."
She raised her glass, and the four friends toasted one
another. "Where is Rawlings, anyway? I haven't seen
him for ages."

"I haven't either," Olivia answered. "And he must
really need a break. I called to see if he wanted a ride
to tonight, but he told me he wasn't up for a public event
just yet. I think he's bone weary."

The writers fell silent, listening to the hum of the
polished crowd as they strolled around the gallery.
Steve appeared and slid an arm around Laurel's waist,
easing her away to view the photography exhibit in the
next hall. Millay and Harris moved off as well, drifting
toward an outdoor courtyard flooded with moonlight
and the heady scent of Carolina jasmine.

Olivia glanced at her watch. It was still quite early,
but she decided to leave. Shala had graciously agreed to
let Haviland nap in her office and, at Olivia's request,
had emptied out the freezer in the staff room for the
evening. Olivia retrieved both the poodle and the cooler
she'd been storing in the freezer and left the museum.

She did not drive home to Oyster Bay but sped down
the quiet highway, her air-conditioning blasting cold
air onto the cooler on the floor of the passenger seat.
Knowing that its contents were at risk of melting before
she reached Beaufort, Olivia drove well over the speed
limit, the black asphalt slipping beneath her tires as
Haviland dozed in the backseat.

Luckily, the cemetery wasn't gated and a caretaker
had given Olivia excellent directions on how to find
Evelyn White's grave. Holding a battery-powered flashlight in one hand and the cooler in the other, Olivia

knelt down on the grass before an unremarkable marble marker.

"This is from your Henry," she whispered into the still air and removed the cooler lid. Inside were the gallon-sized plastic bags of snow she and Michel had made using dry ice in The Boot Top's kitchen the day before.

Now, with Haviland watching at a safe distance, his head cocked to the side in curiosity, Olivia opened the first bag and carefully sprinkled the chilled flakes over Evelyn's grave.

"This is snow, Evelyn," Olivia said. "He promised that one day, he'd give you snow. Here it is."

The thin coating of pure white twinkled in the light of the moon, shimmering briefly before the thirsty ground began to absorb it.

Olivia dusted the gravestone and grass with all that she had left inside the cooler. She only paused for a moment to look at the magical glint of the white crystals, but their beauty was not for her. They were Evelyn's gift, so Olivia turned away before she could see them melt.

She never looked back. All she wanted was to return to Oyster Bay feeling as she did at this moment. Her heart was full of hope, of promise. It was as if some of the pain and grief of the past month had been washed clean by another woman's dreams of snow.

It was nearly midnight when Olivia parked the Range Rover in front of the chief's house. This was what Jeannie, Sawyer's sister, had meant by doing something big to show him how she felt. For her to come here, to the house Rawlings and his wife had shared, took every ounce of courage Olivia possessed.

She had no idea what would be inside. Photographs of the Rawlings' life together, her favorite chair facing his in front of the fireplace, a collection of porcelain tea cups, a bureau covered by an array of perfume jars. Her monogram on the guest towels. Her portrait on the mantel.

None of that mattered. *He* was inside. *He* was what mattered.

Olivia rang the bell and then backed off the stoop. She wanted Rawlings to see her aglow in her floor-length silver dress. She wanted him to wonder if a moonbeam had transformed into a woman, the woman who'd come to claim him.

He opened the door wearing a T-shirt and shorts, sleep lingering in his eyes. The flickering light from a television screen danced behind him.

"Olivia? What are you . . . ?" The rest of the question died on his lips. He only had to look at her for the answer.

He took a step forward, his hand outstretched. "Come in," he whispered, his voice thick with longing.

She smiled, reveling in the yearning that propelled her into his arms.

And then his mouth was on hers, warm and wet, his hands sliding up the skin of her bare back. Deftly, he peeled off the straps of her gown before she had even crossed the threshold. She dug her fingertips into his hair and pressed her hips against him, surrendering to her desire.

Just before Rawlings closed the door against the night, Haviland shot inside and went off to explore.

Olivia barely noticed. Every cell in her body was tuned in to Rawlings. She knew nothing except for his breath in her ear, the feel of his lips on her neck, his wide, rough hands cupping her breasts.

He carried her like a bride into the bedroom and laid her down, easing off her heels and running his fingers up her smooth calves. She sat up only to pull off his shirt and then tugged him downward by the arms, inviting him to crush her under his weight.

They made love as if they'd known each other for decades. To Olivia, the feel of Sawyer Rawlings' body, his smell, even the sound of his groans, was intrinsically familiar.

The world beyond the bedroom slid away. Olivia felt as if she were drowning in heat, enveloped in a happiness far deeper than mere physical pleasure.

Sometime before dawn, with Rawlings sleeping soundly beside her, one of her hands captured in his own, she remained awake, drowsily studying his face.

Olivia felt as though she had entered the woods of Heinrich Kamler's painting. She had crossed the ice-crusted stream and maneuvered through the bare trees and the shadows on the snow. She'd seen the smoke curling from the chimney and the light radiating from the window and had climbed the gentle slope leading to the cabin. To this man. To love.

It had been a long and lonely journey.

But at last, Olivia Limoges was home.

AUTHOR'S NOTE

The Last Word sprang to life after I ran across an article about World War II POW camps in North Carolina. Stunned to learn that Germans, Italians, Poles, Czechs, Dutchmen, Austrians, and men from several other nations had been held prisoner in camps throughout the Tar Heel State, I began to research the subject in earnest.

From New Bern to Butner to Greensboro, North Carolina became home to thousands of POWs, including Nazis. What I found amazing is how quickly some of these men, foreigners to our land, adopted the American way of life. I was also awed by how well they were treated. Not only did these men work the vacant jobs at area farms and mills, but they also attended baseball games, went to the movies, and even dined out at local restaurants. And yet these camps were so secretive that the average North Carolinian had no idea that the men harvesting their peanut crops, for example, were prisoners of war.

As mentioned in *The Last Word*, many POWs were taught the principles of capitalism and democracy and were encouraged to produce their own wares with which they could barter with the guards or townsfolk. One of my primary sources was a book called *Nazi POWs in the Tar Heel State* by Dr. Robert D. Billinger Jr. While reading this book I came across a photograph of a German POW painting a landscape. It was from this single image that the central mystery of *The Last Word* was born.

Some of the dates and details have been altered in the name of good storytelling, but most of the Bayside Book Writers' discoveries about the POW camp in New Bern could have taken place.

Turn the page for a preview of Ellery Adams's
next Books by the Bay Mystery...

Written in Stone

Coming soon from Berkley Prime Crime!

He would have passed a pleasant life of it,
in despite of the Devil and all his works, if
his path had not been crossed by a being
that causes more perplexity to mortal man
than ghosts, goblins, and the whole race
of witches put together, and that was—a
woman.

—WASHINGTON IRVING

"There's a witch in Oyster Bay," Dixie, the roller-skating dwarf and diner proprietor, announced. She set a breakfast strata made of eggs, tomato, basil, and mozzarella on the table and slid a plate of bacon onto the floor.

Immediately, the black nose belonging to the standard poodle sleeping on the booth's vinyl cushion began to quiver. Flashing Dixie a brief look of gratitude, Captain Haviland lowered his paws to the checkered tiles and began to eat his breakfast with the delicacy and restraint of an English aristrocrat.

Olivia Limoges, oak barrel heiress, restaurateur, and aspiring author, reached for the pepper shaker and gave her eggs a quick dusting. "A witch? Does she lure small children into her house with candy bars and then lock them inside cages until they're plump enough to eat?"

Dixie put a hand on her hip and scowled, her false eyelashes leaving thin stripes of electric blue mascara on the skin above her lids. "I'm not pullin' your leg. Folks have talked about her for years. The stories have gotten wilder and wilder because only a handful of people have actually been brave or stupid enough to pay her a visit."

Watching as Dixie topped off her coffee, Olivia cocked her head to the side and asked, "Where does this supposed witch live?"

"In the swamp," Dixie said distastefully. "Word is you can only reach her house by boat, and she's not shy about greetin' unwelcome visitors with a few shotgun blasts."

Olivia, who owned a rifle and was an excellent shot thanks to regular visits to the shooting range, approved. "Perhaps she values her privacy. People always talk about those who don't abide by societal norms. I know plenty of locals who believe there's something wrong with me because Haviland is my constant companion. They disapprove of my refusal to attend every street fair, regatta, shop opening, and ribbon-cutting ceremony. When I don't buy a dozen boxes of stale Girl Scout cookies or chemically laced Boy Scout popcorn every time I leave the Stop 'n' Shop, the troop parents fold their arms and shake their heads at me." She paused to glance out the large picture window at the end of her booth. "Things were getting better, Dixie. I felt anchored here again, like a boat fastened to its moorings. For so long I was drifting, and that finally stopped. But after the events of the past few months, I feel like my tether is frayed . . ."

Dixie heard the pain in her friend's voice. "None of that was your fault, 'Livia. You're givin' yourself a bit too much credit, don't you think?" Dixie turned, slapped the coffee carafe on the counter, and faced Olivia again. "Chief Rawlings arrived at the same conclusion before you did."

A flush of pink spread across Olivia's cheeks. She hurriedly cut into her strata with the edge of her fork and filled her mouth with a bite of warm eggs, fresh tomatoes, and melted cheese.

"I see what you're doin'," Dixie said, shaking her pointer finger. "Stuffin' your face so you don't have to tell me what's goin' on between you and Sawyer Rawlings. The whole town knows you're an item, so don't bother denyin' it. One of the chief's neighbors saw you doin' the walk of shame. *She* said Haviland spent the night too. Must be serious."

Olivia bristled. "There wasn't the slightest trace of shame on my part, but I'm not foolish enough to discuss intimate details with the biggest gossip in all of Oyster Bay. Meaning you." The barb was softened by a smile, which was quickly hidden behind the rim of Olivia's coffee cup. "Get back to the witch. That's a far more interesting topic."

"No, it is not, but I'll play along. Hold on." Dixie skated over to the *Cats* booth and slapped a check on the table. She spent a moment chitchatting with an elderly couple clad in matching lighthouse T-shirts and was undoubtedly explaining for the millionth time why she'd decorated the diner using Andrew Lloyd Webber paraphernalia.

Next, she pivoted and moved on to the *Phantom of the Opera* table. A jowly man in his late fifties dug around in the pocket of his madras shorts in search of his wallet. Ignoring Dixie's question as to whether he enjoyed his food, he tossed bills on top of the check in dismissive little flicks of the wrist. His breakfast partner, a skeletally thin blonde in her early thirties clad in a miniskirt and a white tank top stretched taut over a pair of cartoonishly large implants, jabbed at the porcelain phantom mask with a long, curving fingernail.

From where she sat enjoying her meal, Olivia watched Dixie straighten to her full height. After donning her skates and teasing her hair a vertical inch into the air, she was barely five feet tall, but what Dixie lacked in stature she made up for in fearlessness.

"Y'all have a nice day," she said tightly, her farewell clearly meant as a command.

The top-heavy blonde grabbed her takeout coffee cup and shimmied across the vinyl seat, granting the diners in the opposite booths a clear view of her leopard-print panties.

"Hurry up, babe." The man in madras shorts began to walk away without waiting for his companion. He popped a toothpick in his mouth with one hand and jiggled a set of keys with the other. Using his elbow to push open the door, he let it go without bothering to see if his lady friend was behind him. She wasn't. The door slammed in her face, and she jumped back with a little shriek. Jutting her lower lip into a collagen-enhanced pout, she followed her man out of the diner.

"High-caliber clientele," Olivia teased Dixie after she'd cleared the couple's table.

Dixie wasn't happy. "Cheap bastard. Doctors are the worst tippers."

"How did you know he's a physician?"

"The caduceus on his key ring." Dixie pointed out the window. "And the vanity plate on his I-am-not-well-hung-mobile."

Olivia had been too absorbed rereading the latest chapter of her novel to notice the atomic-orange Corvette parked outside Grumpy's Diner. She peered at the showy convertible as the man settled into his seat and revved the engine. The vanity plate read NIPTUCK.

"Having seen the missus, perhaps the plate should say 'I Inflate You,' " Olivia said. "You could use the number eight and the letter *U* to save space."

"Lady Watermelons is *not* the missus," Dixie corrected. "I saw a picture of the missus and the doc's three kids when he opened his wallet. Such a cliché. Why do they come here anyway? Why not go to Vegas or Cancun?"

Olivia shrugged. "He wants to show off his car. See?"

The object of their derision was donning sunglasses as the Corvette's soft top folded back. The doctor glanced around, making sure he'd captured the interest of a few passersby before turning on the radio. The plate-glass window above Olivia's booth began to vibrate as the Corvette's speakers pounded out a thundering bass.

Dixie shook her head in disgust. "Pathetic." And then her eyes narrowed angrily. "She'd better not do what I think she's going to do."

Olivia looked at the blonde, who'd pulled back her arm and was preparing to throw her takeout cup into a trash can on the sidewalk. At the same moment she launched the cup, the doc flicked his used toothpick into the street, put the sports car in drive, and launched out of the parking spot. The cup missed the rim of the receptacle by several feet and bounced off a lamppost, splashing coffee onto a parked car, the newspaper box, and the bare legs of a teenage girl. The girl shouted, her face registering pain and surprise.

Dixie swore through gritted teeth as the orange Corvette raced out of view.

"Maybe the witch can put a curse on those two cretins," Olivia suggested, sharing Dixie's indignation over the couple's behavior. It was bad enough that they'd both blatantly littered, but to drive on after splattering a young woman's legs with hot coffee bordered on criminal conduct.

Collecting Haviland's empty plate, Dixie put a hand on the black curls of his head and sighed. "I wish all humans had your manners, Captain. But the spell thing isn't a bad idea either. We just need to hop a boat, cross the harbor, head up a creek borderin' the Croatan National Forest 'til it ends, and hike a trail for a few miles."

"She's hardly Oyster Bay's witch then," Olivia noted.

"Born and bred," Dixie retorted. "Anyway, what kind of mystique would she have if she lived in a beachfront condo? A shack in the swamp is way better for business."

This statement peeked Olivia's interest. "What kind of business?"

Delighted to have her friend on the hook, Dixie was just about to answer when Grumpy rang the order bell in the kitchen. The breakfast rush was nearly over, but the family of four in the *Evita* booth was casting expectant glances at Dixie. When she skated over with a tray laden with stacks of buttermilk pancakes, sizzling sausage patties, cinnamon-laced French toast, and an omelet the size of a beret, their eyes grew round with appreciation.

"That should hold 'em for five minutes," she said, coming to an abrupt stop at Olivia's booth, her silver tutu billowing as she applied the brakes. "Back to the witch. Her name is Munin, and one of my cousins went to see her over the weekend." Dixie pulled a stray thread from her left tube sock and lowered her voice. "He and his woman want a baby real bad, but it's just not happenin'. They've both been checked out and there's nothin' wrong, medically speakin'. Been goin' on five years since they started tryin'. Munin is kind of their last hope."

Olivia dabbed her lips with a paper napkin. "And can they expect a healthy set of triplets nine months from now?"

"I reckon not," Dixie replied. "See, Munin doesn't take cash or checks. You have to bring her somethin' that's real precious to you to get her help. If the witch doesn't think what you brought is special enough, she won't lift a finger for you."

"What does she do with the objects?"

Dixie shrugged. "Who knows?"

Impatient to return to her manuscript, Olivia offered to tell Laurel about Munin. "The big shot of the *Oyster Bay Gazette* staff might not cover the story herself, but maybe one of the Features writers would be interested."

With a scowl, Dixie picked up Olivia's empty plate. "I'm not tellin' you about the witch so that you can turn her into a Disneyland attraction. I'd rather have my teeth pulled than visit her remote hideaway, let alone spread word about the woman. I'm only tellin' you about her because she sent a message back with my cousin."

"For you?"

"No." Dixie piled Olivia's silverware and crumpled napkins on top of the dirty plate. "For you."

Bomb dropped, Dixie skated off to the kitchen with

her tray. She then tarried at the two remaining tables, filling water cups, delivering a fresh syrup jug, fetching extra napkins, and exchanging small talk.

Haviland stood up, yawned, and stretched, indicating he'd had enough of the diner for one day.

"Just a few more minutes, Captain," Olivia promised him. "Let me strangle the resident dwarf, and then we'll be on our way."

As though sensing her friend's ire, Dixie lazily coasted back over to the window booth. "Ah, so now you're chompin' at the bit to hear about our witch. Well, I won't keep you in suspense another second." She grinned wryly. "Munin asked my cousin if he knew you. He said everybody knows who you are, but only a couple of folks know you well. The jackass mentioned my name and told Munin that you and I were friends. So the message came to me."

Olivia felt a constriction in her gut. She sensed that once Dixie relayed the message, her life would be altered yet again. Perhaps not greatly, but she didn't welcome any more change.

In the last year alone, she'd opened a second restaurant, reunited with a father she'd believed dead only to watch him die, discovered the existence of a half brother, and fallen for Oyster Bay's chief of police. Olivia Limoges was a woman who liked to be in control of her own future, and as of late, she'd been unable to exert much influence over her fate.

She turned toward the window, observing locals and tourists going about their business unburdened by the press of circumstance. "What does the witch want from me?"

Dixie's grin faded, replaced by a look of solemn concern. Because she was adept at concealing her feelings, it was easy to forget that Olivia had been put through the wringer over the past few months. Dixie spoke to her friend very gently. "Munin wants you to come to her. Says she's got somethin' of your mama's to show you. Apparently, she's been waitin' for the right time to send for you, and now the time's come."

Olivia was unprepared for this. "That's ridiculous. Why would my mother, a librarian and do-gooder, have given something to a woman known as the local witch? And I use that term loosely."

"Maybe you shouldn't," Dixie warned. "If your mama handed over somethin' she treasured, then she was lookin' for help outside the normal realm. She obviously had a problem that couldn't be fixed by the folks she knew. The question is, did she get what she needed from Munin?"

The tightening sensation in Olivia's chest increased. It was difficult for her to picture her gentle and beautiful mother, the quiet and kind librarian, traipsing through a barely discernible track in the swamp in search of answers.

"I am *not* going to respond to this woman's summons," Olivia announced. "It's probably a scam, though more creative than most, I admit."

The family of four ambled out the door, waving at Dixie before leaving. Her mouth formed a smile, but her ale-brown eyes were troubled. "Munin said you wouldn't agree at first. That was part of the message. I was supposed to wait for you to refuse and then tell you the rest. I wonder how she knew . . ."

Her impatience morphing into full-blown annoyance, Olivia growled, "Oh, please! What's the magic word then? What's going to convince me to hire a boat and douse myself in mosquito repellant so I can waste an entire day finding some crazy hag?"

Dixie gestured at the hollow in Olivia's throat. Resting there was a golden starfish pendant attached to a delicate gold chain. Olivia's mother had given it to her only child shortly before her tragic death. Since reclaiming the necklace from the dollhouse in her childhood room, Olivia wore it every day. She touched it during rare moments of uncertainty or distress. It was her talisman.

Knowing that she was pointing at a sacred object, Dixie swallowed hard and then continued. "Munin said she has your mama's starfish, and if you want to know why, you'll have to come. And soon."

Olivia reached her hand out for Haviland, and he obediently moved closer. Her fingers sank into his soft curls, and her tilting world steadied itself. "This is a hell of a way to start my day," she grumbled, overpaid Dixie for breakfast, and strode out into the sunshine, one hand gripping her laptop case, the other curled protectively around the gold starfish on her neck.

ABOUT THE AUTHOR

Ellery Adams grew up on a beach near the Long Island Sound. Having spent her adult life in a series of landlocked towns, she cherishes her memories of open water, violent storms, and the smell of the sea. Ms. Adams has held many jobs, including caterer, retail clerk, car salesperson, teacher, tutor, and tech writer, all the while penning poems, children's books, and novels. She now writes full time from her home in Virginia. For more information, please visit www.elleryadamsmysteries.com.

ELLERY ADAMS

🐌

Wordplay becomes foul play . . .

A Deadly Cliché

A BOOKS BY THE BAY MYSTERY

While walking her poodle, Olivia Limoges discovers a dead body buried in the sand. Could it be connected to the bizarre burglaries plaguing Oyster Bay, North Carolina? The Bayside Book Writers prick up their ears and pick up their pens to get the story . . .

The thieves have a distinct MO. At every crime scene, they set up odd tableaus: a stick of butter with a knife through it, dolls with silver spoons in their mouths, a deck of cards with a missing queen. Olivia realizes each setup represents a cliché.

Who better to decode the cliché clues than the Bayside Book Writers group, especially since their newest member is Police Chief Rawlings? As the investigation proceeds, Olivia is surprised to find herself falling for the widowed policeman. But an even greater surprise is in store. Her father—lost at sea thirty years ago—may still be alive . . .